TRUST
in me

TRUST
in me

A NOVEL

Jennifer L. Armentrout
WRITING AS J. LYNN

WILLIAM MORROW IMPULSE
An Imprint of HarperCollinsPublishers

Excerpt from *Be With Me* copyright © 2014 by Jennifer L. Armentrout.

EPub Edition NOVEMBER 2013 ISBN: 9780062304643
Print Edition ISBN: 9780062304827

10 9 8 7 6 5 4

This is for all the fans of Cam and his cookies,
who wanted more of our egg-boiling lover boy. Enjoy.

TRUST
in me

One

Jase Winstead was a cruel motherfucker.

Going to Ass-tronomy 101 was the last thing I wanted to be doing at nine in the damn morning, especially since all the class did was remind me of the first time I entered Professor Drage's class and why I'd made a hasty, unplanned exit my freshman year. And I really didn't need Jase's taunting text messages about why scheduling classes before noon was unhealthy.

Considering I was going on—oh, I don't know, two hours of sleep—and I could still taste the tequila and other things I really didn't want to even think about from last night, I was currently a walking poster child for how not to have a healthy and happy first day of fall classes.

I watched the door to astronomy swing shut and then glanced back down at my phone. Jase's text mocked me.

Skip. I have beer. X-Box. FIFA '13

Well, shit. That was hella tempting. Ollie had trashed

our Xbox the weekend before, during a brutal showdown of Call of Duty.

I was a few minutes late for class.

Astronomy, or soccer on the Box? Not really a tough call.

Mind made up, I pivoted around and started to respond back to Jase when the double doors flung open like a tornado had ripped through the stairwell. My head jerked up just in time to see something *small* and something *red* come barreling straight at me.

There was no stopping the collision.

A little body smacked right into me and bounced back, arms flailing like a drowning victim. The bag, which looked like it weighed more than the owner, toppled her over.

Reacting out of instinct, I shot forward, dropping my own bag and wrapping my arm around her waist, but the backpack went in one direction, the contents in the other. She was still reeling, like one of those inflatable pop bags. I tightened my hold, stilling her before she did some serious damage to herself. She jerked upright. Deep auburn hair flew forward, snapping me in the face. The scent of berries and something musky and good filled me.

Holy shit, Strawberry Shortcake just ran me over.

I chuckled and slipped my cell into my pocket, about to let her go, but the girl locked up. Every muscle seemed to go rigid. As tiny as she was, barely reaching my shoulders, she seemed to suddenly get smaller, shrinking into herself. Was she hurt?

And did she somehow mistake Shepherd for a nearby middle school?

"Whoa," I said. "You okay, sweetheart?"

No response for about a half minute, and I started to get real concerned. Then she dragged in a deep breath, causing her chest to rise flush against mine. I froze at the feel of her curves. Definitely not a middle schooler, unless they were developing in ways they hadn't when I was there. And, if so, I was fucking envious of those boys.

Okay, now I felt like I needed a shower, because even that disturbed me.

Was I still drunk from last night? I was going to go with a yes.

"Hey," I tried again, voice lower. "Are you okay?" When there was still no response, I pressed two fingers under her chin. Her skin was soft and too cool. Wondering if it was possible for a person to pass out and remain standing, I gently lifted her head, my mouth opening to ask her again, but words died somewhere between my brain and my mouth.

I blinked, because like a total dumbass, I thought that would change what I was seeing. Not that I wanted to change what I was seeing, but *damn*. . .

What guy didn't have a soft spot for a redhead?

Pretty was too weak of a word to describe her. Her eyes were large and the color of warm whiskey. Freckles dotted the bridge of her small nose and her cheeks were well defined. Lips were a sweet cherry color and wide for her face, full and plump. The kind of lips that belonged to the kind of mouth that could and would bring a man—

"Let. Go. Of. Me."

The hardness of her voice, laced with barely controlled

panic, caused me to immediately drop her arm and take a healthy step back.

She swayed a little at the loss of support, and I almost reached for her again, but I valued my balls. One day I'd like to have a kid or some shit, and I had a feeling if I touched her again, that would not be in my future.

Pushing strands of thick hair out of her face, she cautiously stepped away from her bag. Thick lashes specked with red lifted, and, for a moment, neither of us moved and then her gaze moved over my face and then down. Chick was blatantly checking me out.

Perhaps my balls weren't in danger.

A pretty pink flush spread across her cheeks. "I'm sorry. I was in a hurry to get to class. I'm late and . . ."

I grinned as I knelt down, gathering up the spilled items. How one girl could have so many damn pens was beyond me. Blue. Purple. Black. Red. Orange. What the fuck? Who wrote with an orange pen?

She joined me, grabbing the rest of her pens as her head tilted in a way that a wall of coppery hair shielded her face. "You don't have to help me."

"It's no problem." I picked up a slip of paper that turned out to be her schedule. Quick glance at the classes confirmed she was a freshman. "Astronomy 101? I'm heading that way, too."

Jase and beer and FIFA '13 were going to have to wait.

"You're late." She was still hiding behind her hair. "I really am sorry."

Picking up her last notebook, I shoved it into the bag and stood. I handed it back to her, willing her to look up. I don't know why, call me a mama's boy, but I liked my girls smiling and not appearing like they were on the verge of tears. "It's okay. I'm used to having girls throw themselves at me." Her chin lifted up just the slightest, and my grin spread. "Trying to jump on my back is new, though. Kind of liked it."

Her head jerked up and all that hair slid back. "I wasn't trying to jump on your back or throw myself at you."

"You weren't?" My phone vibrated in my pocket. I ignored it. "Well, that's a shame. If so, it would have made this the best first day of class in history."

She studied me as she clutched her bag to her chest, and my gaze dropped to the piece of paper I held. "Avery Morgansten?"

"How do you know my name?" she snapped.

What a touchy little thing. "It's on your schedule."

"Oh." She tucked her hair back and a slight tremor rocked her hand as she took the schedule.

When I was little, my mom said I had a soft spot for the underdog. Wounded pigeons. Three-legged dogs. Skinny pigs. My sister was the same way. We had a sixth sense when it came to rooting them out, and I may not have known jack about this chick, but she was obviously new to this school, obviously uncomfortable, obviously having a shitty start to her day, and I felt bad for her.

"My name is Cameron Hamilton," I told her. "But everyone calls me Cam."

Her lips moved like she was repeating my name, and I sort of liked how that looked. "Thank you again, Cam."

Bending down, I picked up my bag and slung it over

my shoulder. Knocking my hair out of my face, I smiled the kind of smile that usually got me what I wanted. "Well, let's make our grand entrance."

I'd made it to the door to astronomy when I realized she hadn't moved. Glancing over my shoulder, I frowned as she started to back away. "You're going in the wrong direction, sweetheart."

"I can't," she croaked out.

"Can't what?" I faced her.

Avery's eyes met mine for a second and then she spun around and ran. Bag thumping off her hip, hair flying like a cape. The chick ran, actually freaking ran. My mouth dropped open.

What in the hell had just happened?

The door opened behind me, and a deep, slightly accented voice called out. "Mr. Hamilton, are you joining us today?"

Shit. I closed my eyes.

"Or are you planning to stand in the hallway the remaining time?" Professor Drage asked.

Sighing, I turned around. "Joining the class, clearly."

"Clearly," the professor repeated, holding a stack of stapled papers. "Syllabus."

I took one and then, on second thought, I took another. Just in case Avery Morgansten showed her face again.

Jase leaned against the back of my truck, one hand shoved through his brown hair, holding it off his glistening forehead. Several strands stuck straight up between his fingers. "It's as hot as balls."

For late August, it was sweltering. Not even the shade provided by the large oaks surrounding the back parking lot across from White Hall provided any relief. I was dreading opening the door to the sweatbox.

"Truest thing you've ever spoken." Ollie squinted up at the trees. "It's so hot the only answer is to get naked."

My gaze went to him. "You're already as naked as you need to be, dude."

Ollie glanced down at himself and grinned. No shirt. Shorts hanging low. Flip-flops. Nothing else. "You know damn well I could get more naked."

Unfortunately that was true. We'd shared a three-bedroom apartment in University Heights for the last three years. Within a week of living together, Ollie had said screw it to modesty. I'd seen the guy's junk more times then I cared to even think about. He was graduating in the spring, as I should've been, and I was going to miss the idiot.

"Ticket." Jase nodded at my windshield.

I sighed, looking over. A cream-colored slip of paper was neatly placed under my wiper. The parking lot was reserved for staff, but with the lack of parking around these parts, I helped myself to whatever spot I could find. "I'll add it to my collection."

"Which is massive." Ollie pulled a band off his wrist and tugged his shoulder-length blond hair into a ponytail. "So, party tonight at our place?"

My brows shot up. "Huh?"

Jase grinned as he folded his arms across his chest.

"It's a back-to-school party." Ollie stretched, cracking his back as he yawned. "Just a little get-together."

"Oh God."

Jase's grin spread, and I wanted to knock it off his face. The last time Ollie had had a 'little get-together' it had been standing room only in our apartment. Cops might have been involved.

"Order some pizza. I need to get—" Ollie stopped mid-sentence and turned toward a curvy brunette walking past. In a blink of an eye, he ditched us and was dropping an arm around the girl's shoulders. "Hey, girl, hey."

The brunette giggled, wrapping an arm around Ollie's waist.

I turned, raising my hands. "What?"

"Lost cause." Jase rolled his eyes. "That fucker has eyes in the back of his head when it comes to girls."

"Very true."

"How he gets laid on a regular basis is beyond me."

"It's the greatest mystery in life." I loped around the front of my truck, grabbed the ticket, and then opened the driver's door. Heat blew into my face. "Damn."

Jase angled his body toward me. "What happened with you today? You didn't respond to my text. Thought the FIFA hooked you in."

"Aw, did you miss me?" I tugged off my shirt, rolled it up, and tossed it into the truck.

"Maybe I did."

Laughing, I grabbed my cap off the seat and shoved it on, shielding my eyes. "I didn't know we were dating."

"My feelings are hurt now."

"I'll buy you a beer next time we're out."

"That works. I'm easy."

I grinned. "Don't I know."

Jase laughed as he turned, hanging his arms over the side of the truck bed. The easygoing smile faded as he slipped a pair of sunglasses on. I knew that look. Nothing good came from it. Very few people knew just how shitty life could get for Jase. It was easy for everyone to assume otherwise, with how Jase was the go-to guy for fixing other people's crap, including mine.

I turned the air on and shut the door, then joined him at the side of the truck. The metal was hot against the skin of my underarms as I leaned in, stretching my calves. "What's up?"

One dark eyebrow rose above the rim of his glasses. "You heading to the gym or something?"

"That's what I was thinking." I switched my legs, working out the kink. "You wanna go with me?"

"Nah," he said. "I've got to swing by the farm. Check on a few things."

"How's Jack?"

A wide smile broke out across Jase's face, causing a young professor walking past the truck to trip in her heels. "He's great," he said, his tone light like it was always was when he talked about his brother. "Told me yesterday that when he grows up, he wants to be Chuck Norris."

I laughed. "Can't go wrong with that."

"Nope." He looked over, peering at me above his shades. "How you doing?"

"Good." I pushed back, smacking my hands off the rail. "Why you ask?"

Jase raised a shoulder. "Just checking in."

Some days that comment pissed me off. Other days it did nothing. Luckily for Jase, it was one of those days when the shit just rolled off my back. "I'm not about to end up in a corner, whispering 'forever' anytime soon. It's all cool."

"Good to hear." Jase grinned as he backed off, his head turning toward where the young teacher had disappeared. "Party at your place, right?"

"Why not?" I headed to the driver's side. "Half the campus will be there I'm sure."

"True." Jase pivoted around. "See you later."

I climbed into the cool interior and headed out of the parking lot. My lazy ass needed to get to the gym on West Campus, but my ass also wanted to get to the couch for a nap.

Turning left at the stop sign, I passed the duplexes on the right as a football flew out one of the doors, smacking one of the guys in the back of the head. Laughing, I reached over for the—

Something *red* caught my attention.

My eyes were heat-seeking missiles, searching out the source, and hot damn. My gaze narrowed. Was that Shortcake?

A tree obscured my view for a second and then she reappeared, the sun reflecting off the wide bracelet circling her wrist.

Hells yeah, it was.

I didn't even think twice about what I did next. Grinning, I slid the cap around backward and hung a sharp right, blocking the road.

Avery jumped back onto the curb, her big eyes going round. As I hit the button to the passenger window, rolling it down, her mouth dropped open.

I grinned, happy to see that Shortcake had made it through her first day alive. "Avery Morgansten, we meet again."

She glanced around her, like she thought I might be talking to someone else. "Cameron Hamilton . . . hi."

I leaned forward, dropping an arm over the steering wheel. She looked damn cute standing there, fidgeting with her bracelet. "We have to stop meeting like this."

Biting down on that plump lower lip, her gaze dropped, zeroing in on my tattoo as she shifted her weight from foot to foot.

Shortcake was definitely what I would categorize as awkward. Maybe it came from having a younger sister, because the need to make her feel comfortable rode me hard, but it seemed like fighting a losing battle.

"You running into me, me almost running over you?" I elaborated. "It's like we're a catastrophe waiting to happen."

Silence.

Try this one more time. "Where are you heading?"

"My car," she said, proving to me that she could speak.

"I'm about to run out of time. She shifted her weight again. "So . . ."

"Well, hop in, sweetheart. I can give you a ride."

She stared at me like I asked her to get in the back of my kidnapper van. "No. It's okay. I'm right up the hill. No need at all."

"It's no problem." Never had met a female so damn resistant to common courtesy. "It's the least I can do after almost running you over."

"Thank you, but—"

"Yo! Cam!" Kevin came out of fucking nowhere, jogging past Avery. "What you up to, man?"

Oddly irritated, I kept my gaze on Shortcake and resisted the urge to nudge the dude out of the way with my truck. "Nothing, Kevin, just trying to have a conversation."

Avery raised her hand, wiggled her fingers, and bolted around Kevin and my truck. My gaze followed her as Kevin went on and on about some shit I didn't give a flying fuck about.

"Shit," I muttered, sitting back in the seat.

Avery ran *again*.

And I had the craziest urge to give chase.

Two

Shit got real at our parties the second Ollie had Raphael out of his habitat. Every single fucking time. Standing in the middle of the living room, I watched him, shaking my head.

"Why?" Jase asked, tipping the bottle of his beer back.

I snickered. "Don't you think if I knew why, I'd find a way to stop him?"

"I think it's cute," said a soft, feminine voice.

Jase and I turned toward the couch. No one sat quite the way Stephanie Keith did. One long, shapely tanned leg hooked over the knee of the other in the perfect picture of modesty. But the goddamn denim skirt of hers was as modest as Ollie after taking a shower. If I moved my head *just* a fraction of inch to the right and tipped my chin down, which I had about three minutes ago, I could see the curve of her ass cheek.

Steph was a thong girl.

Or a no-panties girl depending on her mood, and it was looking like she might be in the mood. Steph leaned forward slightly, crossing slender arms under her breasts, giving me and anyone else who happened to be looking— quick check told me Jase was—a nice view of her tits. And they were nice. I'd seen them up close and personal quite a few times. Those baby-blue eyes of hers promised a happy ending and they were fixed on mine.

Surprisingly, there was absolutely no shrinking of my nylon shorts in the crotch area, which was a damn waste of tits and ass.

Half of Jase's frat would give their left nut to be on the receiving end of Stephanie's attention. There was a time I gave my right one, back when I couldn't even keep track of who was who, but that felt like ages ago, back when the idea of staying with one girl made me want to chew off my own arm. Now?

Well, shit, I didn't know what I wanted now. Hadn't for a while, which probably explained why I wasn't scooping Steph up, taking her back to my bedroom, and dropping pants.

Steph was a good girl, but the time of giving up my right nut had long since passed.

Averting my gaze to where Ollie was dancing in front of the TV, holding the squirming Raphael in the air, I took a drink of my beer. "He's molesting my tortoise."

She laughed as she stood. "I don't think that's what he's doing." One arm wrapped around mine and she put her chin on my shoulder. A sheet of inky black hair slipped over the bare skin of my chest. "But I wouldn't mind being molested."

Over the music, I heard the oven timer go off. Gently disentangling myself, I shot Jase a look. An unsympathetic grin crossed his face. Bastard. "Be right back."

Dodging guys, I trotted into the kitchen before Steph could respond. The girl wasn't going to be that disappointed with my lack of interest. I'd bet ten bucks she'd moved on to Jase or someone else by the time I got back in.

I sat the beer down on the counter and opened the oven door, inhaling the aroma of freshly baked chocolate-chip cookies. And not that premade crap. This shit was from scratch.

And they would be banging.

Setting the sheet aside, I flipped off the oven and scooped up a cookie. So hot, the dough sunk in, squeezing the tiny chips of chocolate onto the chunks of walnut. I broke the cookie in half and popped it into my mouth.

"Fuck," I groaned.

Burned like holy fucking hell, but it was worth it. Washing it down with my beer, I stepped out of the kitchen just in time to see Ollie heading toward the front door. With Raphael.

"Oh, come the hell on." I put my beer down.

"Be free, little green buddy," he coaxed, kissing Raphael's shell. "Be free."

"Bring Raphael back!" I yelled, laughing as Ollie drunk-karate-kicked the front door the rest of the way open. "You fucktard!"

Ollie put Raphael down and gently nudged his shell. "Free."

Grabbing his arm, I spun him around and pushed him back into the apartment. Laughing, Ollie grabbed Steph's friend and lifted her over his shoulder. A riot of squeals broke out.

I scooped up the tortoise. "Sorry, Raphael. My friends are complete, fucking . . ." A strange tingle broke out across my neck. I looked to my left and then my right, seeing Avery standing in a doorway, her brown eyes wide. "Assholes. What the . . . ?"

I hadn't drunk nearly enough to be hallucinating, but I couldn't wrap my head around the fact that Shortcake was standing in my apartment building. The apartment had been empty whenever I'd been around over the summer, but someone, obviously, could've moved in.

And based on the way she was dressed, someone she was very *familiar* with. The cotton shorts were short, ending at the thigh, and my gaze got hung up on her legs. They were long, not too skinny and perfectly shaped. Who would've thought Shortcake would be rocking a pair of legs like that? Blood shot straight to my groin. The long-sleeve shirt she wore covered everything, but it was thin.

Hell yeah, it was *thin*.

Her breasts were soft swells under the shirt, fuller than they had felt pressed against my chest earlier, and those tips . . .

Her cheeks flushed several shades of pink. "Hey . . ."

I blinked and when she didn't disappear and neither

did my sudden, raging hard-on, I assumed she was real. "Avery Morgansten? This is becoming a habit."

"Yeah," she said. "It is."

"Do you live here or are you visiting . . . ?" Raphael started squirming.

She cleared her throat, watching the tortoise. "I . . . I live here."

"No shit?" Holy crap. I made my way around the railing to the stairwell and toward her door. I didn't miss how her eyes went to my abs. I liked. So did my cock. "You really live here?"

"Yes. I really live here."

"This is . . . I don't even know." I laughed, somewhat dumbstruck. "Really crazy."

"Why?" Confusion marked her pretty face, crinkling the skin between the delicate brows.

"I live here."

Her mouth dropped open. "You're joking, right?"

"No. I've been living here for a while—like a couple of years with my roommate. You know, the fucktard who put poor Raphael outside."

"Hey!" Ollie yelled. "I have a name. It's *Señor* Fucktard!"

I laughed. "Anyway, did you move in over the weekend?"

She nodded.

"Makes sense. I was back home, visiting the fam." I cradled Raphael against my chest before he wiggled his way to a broken shell. "Well, hell . . ."

Avery tipped her head back to meet my gaze. For a moment, she held mine with her own soulful gaze, before turning her attention to Raphael. Her eyes . . . they reminded me of something. "That's . . . um, your tortoise?"

"Yeah." I lifted him up. "Raphael, meet Avery."

She bit down on her lip and gave Raphael a wave, and a grin split my lips. Shortcake got pointers for that. "That's a very interesting pet."

"And those are very interesting shorts. What are they?" I took another long look at those legs. I couldn't help myself. "Pizza slices?"

"They're ice cream cones."

"Huh. I like them." I lifted my gaze, taking my time. "A lot."

She finally let go of her death grip on the door and crossed her arms over her chest. Her eyes narrowed when I grinned. "Thanks. That means a lot to me."

"It should. They have my seal of approval." I watched the flush continue to stain her cheeks. "I need to get Raphael back in his little habitat before he pees on my hand, which he's bound to do, and that sucks."

Her lips twitched into a small grin. "I can imagine."

Did Shortcake just grin? It had to be a first. I wondered what she looked like when she actually *smiled*. "So, you should come over. The guys are about to leave, but I'm sure they'll be around for a little longer. You can meet them." I leaned in, lowering my voice. "They're no way as interesting as I am, but they're not bad."

Avery's gaze flickered over my shoulder. Indecision crawled over her face. *Come on, Shortcake, come out and play.* She shook her head. "Thanks, but I was heading to bed."

Disappointment pricked at my skin. "This early?"

"It has to be after midnight."

I grinned. "That's still early."

"Maybe to you."

"Are you sure?" I was about to pull out the big guns. "I have cookies."

"Cookies?" Two brows rose.

"Yeah, and I made them. I'm quite the baker."

"You baked cookies?"

The way she asked that was like I'd just admitted to baking a homemade bomb in my kitchen. "I bake a lot of things, and I'm sure you're dying to know all about those things. But tonight, it was chocolate-and-walnut cookies. They are the shit if I do say so myself."

Her lips twitched again. "As great as that sounds, I'm going to have to pass."

"Maybe later then?"

"Maybe." She stepped back, reaching for the door. "Well, it's good seeing you again, Cameron."

"Cam," I corrected. "And hey, we didn't almost run each other over. Look at us, changing up the pattern."

"That's a good thing." She took a deep breath. "You should get back before Raphael pees on your hand."

"Would be worth it."

Confusion marked her features. "Why?"

I sure as hell wasn't going to explain it. "If you change your mind, I'll be up for a while."

"I'm not going to. Good night, Cam."

Ouch. Damn. Shortcake just dismissed my ass. For some reason, that made me smile. Maybe because I couldn't remember the last time a girl outright sent me away. Interesting. Here I thought I was incredibly charming.

I took a step back as Raphael poked his head out of his shell. "See you tomorrow."

"Tomorrow?"

"Astronomy class? Or are you skipping again?"

"No," she sighed, flushing, and I couldn't help but wonder how far that flush traveled south. The likelihood of me finding out seemed very slim. "I'll be there."

"Great." I forced myself to back away, because I was pretty sure I could stand there for an hour just to mess with her. "Good night, Avery."

Shortcake ducked behind the door like Raphael was about to pee on her head. I chuckled when I heard the lock click in place. I don't know how long I stood there while Raphael's little legs flailed, staring at the closed door.

"What are you doing, Cam?"

I turned at the sound of Steph's voice. She stood in the doorway, head tilted against the frame, smiling and the picture of willingness. Unlike the girl on the other side of the door I stood in front of.

"I don't know," I said, heading back to my apartment. I really didn't have a friggin' clue.

Three

I'd never been a morning person, but today, I was up at the butt crack of dawn, having only slept a few hours. While Ollie was still passed out on the couch, facedown, one arm flung toward the floor, I boiled four eggs, ate them, and scooped up some cookies for the road.

Ollie still hadn't moved when I slammed the door shut behind me.

I arrived on campus, weirdly early for probably the first time in my life, and headed into the Robert Byrd Building. Once inside the astronomy class, my gaze immediately started scanning the room.

If I were Shortcake, where would I sit? Probably in the back of the class.

I searched out a familiar bowed head. In the dimly lit classroom, her hair wasn't as red as it was in the sunlight. Why I even noticed that was beyond me. And why I headed straight for her went straight over my head.

In middle school, I had a crush on this girl in my class. She was a lot like Shortcake—tiny, rarely spoke, nervous as one of those small dogs that shook all the time. But when she smiled, the fucking sun seemed to rise. She never gave me the time of day, but like a goober, I looked forward to seeing her every day. Turned out in high school, she liked girls and not boys, which probably explained why she had absolutely no interest in me.

Sliding my hand up the strap of my book bag, I could easily admit it would be hella disappointing if that were the case with Shortcake.

I strolled up on Avery, and she had no idea I was even there. Shoulders rolled forward, right hand toying with the bracelet on her left wrist. She was staring straight ahead, the taut expression on her face telling me that she might be physically present, but she wasn't in this room.

Was Shortcake ever relaxed? Didn't seem that way.

I glanced up at the front of the class, where a few people I knew were sitting. That's where I should go. Instead, I eased my way down the row of seats. Shortcake still hadn't registered I was there.

"Morning, sweetheart," I said, deciding against sitting down first.

Shortcake jerked like a startled cat, twisting in the seat. Her jaw dropped as her eyes made contact with me. She said nothing as I slid into the seat next to her and settled back.

"You look a little rough this morning," I commented.

Her lips pursed. "Thanks."

"You're welcome. Glad to see you make it to class this

time." I scooted down, kicking my feet up on the seat in front of me. "Though, I kind of missed the whole running-into-each-other thing. Provided a lot of excitement."

"I don't miss that." She started digging around in her bag, pulling out a pristine notebook. I couldn't remember the last time I bought a new notebook for class. I believed in recycling them. "That was really embarrassing."

"It shouldn't have been."

"Easy for you to say. You're the one who got plowed. I was doing the plowing."

My mouth dropped open as a laugh caught in my throat, but then my brain took the word "plowing" to the gutter, and I had to spread my thighs a little to get comfortable. There were so many things I could do with that comment. They all rushed to the tip of my tongue. Some would burn the ears off of strippers, but one look at Shortcake told me that would not go over well.

Her face was as red as the cover of the notebook she was currently staring at. The chick . . . damn, she was so awkward—endearingly awkward. I wondered if she was homeschooled through high school.

While her awkwardness was damn cute and entertaining, I searched for something way off topic to say. "Raphael is doing great, by the way."

A small grin appeared on those pretty lips. "That's good to hear. Did he pee on your hand?"

"No, but it was a close call. Brought you something."

"Turtle pee?"

I laughed, amused by her quickness as I pulled out the syllabus, spying the cookies I'd brought with me. "Sorry to let you down, but no. It's a syllabus. I know. Thrilling shit right here, but figured since you didn't come to class on Monday, you'd need one, so I got it from the professor."

"Thank you. That was really thoughtful."

"Well, prepare yourself. I am all kinds of thoughtful this week. I brought you something else."

She started chewing on the edge of her pen as I pulled out the napkin. "Cookie for you. Cookie for me."

Slowly lowering the pen, she shook her head. "You didn't have to do that."

I didn't bring her a gold ring. "It's just a cookie, sweetheart."

Her head shook again as she stared at me. You'd think I was handing her crack or something. Sighing, I covered one of the cookies with the napkin and unceremoniously dropped the cookie on top of her notebook. "I know they say you shouldn't take candy from strangers, but it's a cookie and not candy and technically, I'm not a stranger."

She stared at me.

Watching her from under my lashes, I took a bite of the other cookie and closed my eyes. I tipped my head back as the chocolate-covered walnuts danced over my taste buds. I moaned, knowing exactly what I was doing. My cookies were damn good, so the next sound I made wasn't an overexaggeration.

"Is it really that good?" she asked.

"Oh, yeah, this is the shit. I told you that last night. Be better if I had some milk." I took another bite. "Mmm, milk."

In the following silence, I opened one eye and fought

a grin. She was watching me, lips slightly parted. "It's the combination of walnut and chocolate. You mix that together and it's like an explosion of sex in your mouth, but not as messy. The only thing better would be those teeny tiny Reese's cups. When the dough is warm, you plop those suckers in. . . . Anyway, you just need to try it. Take a small bite."

Her gaze dropped to the cookie in her lap and she let out a low breath. Picking up a cookie, she took a bite.

I couldn't stop watching her. "Good? Right?"

She nodded.

"Well, I have a whole ton of them at home. Just saying . . ." My gaze was riveted on her. Who knew watching a girl eat a cookie could be so interesting? As she wiped her slender fingers off, I moved without thinking.

The warmth of my knee brushing hers traveled up my leg as I twisted in the seat, reached over, and took the napkin from her. "Crumb."

"What?"

With my empty hand, I smoothed my thumb along her bottom lip. A jolt of *something* zinged up my arm and went straight to my cock. She stilled, her chest rising sharply and eyes widening. My hand lingered longer than it should have, but not as long as I wanted. Her lip was soft under my finger, her chin smooth against my palm. I forced myself to pull away.

There hadn't been a damn crumb on her lip. I was a liar. But I wanted to touch her.

"Got it." I smiled.

She looked flustered. Not upset, but unnerved. I tried

to feel some level of guilt for touching her but couldn't. I wasn't sure what that said about me.

But then Professor Drage finally entered the front of the classroom. Drage was an odd fella. The green polyester suit was a staple. When I took this class the first time around, he used to mix up his wardrobe with an orange one. The checkered Vans and bow tie hadn't changed in years.

I shifted in the seat, glancing over at Shortcake. The look on her face was priceless. I chuckled. "Professor Drage is a very . . . unique man."

"I can see," she murmured.

Professor Drage launched into a lecture. I wasn't sure what it was about. Honestly, I wasn't paying attention. Most of this stuff I already knew and hearing the shit again reminded me of my freshman year, something I didn't like to dwell on.

One night had completely fucked up the path of my life.

Pushing that out of my head, I started sketching. Before I knew it, I'd drawn Big Foot and class was coming to an end in typical Drage fashion.

He started passing out star maps. "I know today is only Wednesday, but here is your first assignment for the weekend. Skies are supposed to be clear as a baby's bottom on Saturday."

"Clear as a baby's bottom?" Avery muttered.

I chuckled.

"I want you to find the Corona Borealis in the sky— the actual, real, honest-to-goodness night sky," Professor

Drage explained. "You won't need a telescope. Use your eyes or glasses or contacts or whatever. You can view it either Friday or Saturday night, but the weather is looking sketchy on Friday, so choose wisely."

"Wait," someone from up front said. "How do you use this map?"

I handed Shortcake a map and the grid sheets.

Professor Drage stopped and pinned the kid with a look that asked are you stupid. "You look at it."

The student huffed. "I get that, but do we hold it up to the sky or something?"

"Sure. You could do that. Or you could just look at each of the constellations, see what they look like and then use your own eyes and brains to find it in the sky." Drage paused. "Or use Google. I want all of you to start to get familiar with stargazing . . ." I faded out during half of what he was saying, coming back in toward the end. "So get with your partner and pick out a time. The grid will be turned back in to me on Monday. That's all for the day. Good luck and may the force of the universe be with you today."

"Partner?" Avery frantically looked around the class-room. "When did we pick partners?"

"On Monday," I explained, shoving the notebook into my backpack. "You weren't here."

Shortcake looked like she was about to pass out as she leaned forward in her seat. "Avery?"

She took several deep breaths, like she was staving off a panic attack.

I arched a brow. "Avery."

Her gaze darted to the door Drage had disappeared through. Her knuckles were bleached white from how tight she was holding her notebook.

"*Avery.*"

"What?" she snapped, whipping her gaze on me.

"We're partners."

A deep crevice formed between her brows. "Huh?"

"We. Are. Partners." I sighed. "Apparently, Drage had the class pick their partners right at the beginning of class on Monday. I walked in afterward and at the end he told me to partner with anyone who joined the class on Wednesday or I'd be partner-less. And since I don't like the idea of being partner-less, you and I are partners."

She stared at me like I had just spoken Latin. "We have a choice to do this on our own?"

"Yeah, but who wants to go out staring at the sky at night by themselves?" Standing, I hefted my bag over my shoulder and started down the row. "Anyway, I know a perfect place we can do our assignment. Has to be Saturday, because I have plans Friday."

Sucking, annoying as fuck plans on Friday.

"Wait." She rushed after me. "I do."

"You have plans on Saturday?" Hold up. What could she be doing on a Saturday night? I couldn't skip out on Friday, but . . . "Well, I might—"

"No. I don't have plans on Saturday, but we don't have to be partners. I can do this by myself."

I stopped in front of the doors, unsure if I had heard her right. "Why would you want to do all the assignments—

and if you look at his class outline, there are a lot—all by yourself?"

She took a step back. "Well, I don't really want to, but you don't have to be my partner. I mean, you don't owe me or anything."

"I don't get what you're saying." I honestly, seriously, a hundred percent, did not get what she was saying.

"What I'm saying is that . . ." She stopped, brows knitting into the deep V again. "Why are you being so nice to me?"

My mouth formed around the words "what the fuck." "Is that a serious question?"

Shortcake ducked her gaze. "Yes."

I stared at her and waited for her to say she was joking, but she didn't. A knot formed in my chest, coming out of nowhere. Suddenly it was painfully obvious to me, and I mean *painfully*. Shortcake wasn't just awkward, she was obviously on the friendless side of things, and I don't know why that affected me. It shouldn't have. I barely knew the girl and guiding her into conversation was as easy as disarming a bomb with your teeth, but it did bother me.

Underdog syndrome strikes again.

I took a deep breath. "All right, I guess I'm just a nice guy. And you're obviously new—a freshman. You seemed to be a little out of it on Monday and then you ran off, wouldn't even come into class and I—"

"I don't want your pity." She sucked in a shrill sound.

I scowled at the insinuation. "You don't have my pity,

Avery. I'm just saying you seemed out of it on Monday and I figured we'd just be partners."

Doubt crossed her features.

"I can see that you don't believe me. Maybe it was the cookie? Well, you refused to taste my cookies last night and honestly, I was going to eat the other cookie, but you looked so tired and sad sitting there, I figured you needed the cookie more than I did."

Which might have been a lie. There was a good chance that I had brought two cookies because Shortcake might make an appearance. Then again, I may be reading too much into it.

She was watching me like I was a puzzle, and honestly, I wasn't *that* complicated.

"And you're pretty," I added.

She blinked "What?"

Trying and failing to hide my amusement, I turned and opened the door, guiding her into the hallway. "Do not tell me you don't know you're pretty. If so, I'm about to lose all faith in mankind. You don't want to be responsible for that."

"I know I'm pretty—I mean, that's not what I meant." She paused, groaning. "I don't think I'm ugly. That's what—"

"Good. Now we've cleared that up." I tugged on her bag, guiding her to the stairs. "Watch the door. It can be tricky."

"What does the whole pretty comment have to do with anything?"

"You asked why I'm so nice to you. It's mutually beneficial."

Shortcake came to a complete stop behind me. "You're nice to me because you think I'm pretty?"

"And because you have brown eyes. I'm a sucker for big old brown eyes." I laughed. "I'm a shallow, shallow boy. Hey, it helps that you're pretty. It brings out the nice guy in me. Makes me want to share my cookies with you."

"So if I was ugly, you wouldn't be nice to me?"

Spinning around, I faced her. "I'd still be nice to you if you were ugly."

"Okay."

I grinned as I tipped my chin down, bringing our mouths close. "I just wouldn't offer you any cookies."

She folded her arms. "I'm beginning to think 'cookie' is a code word for something else."

"Maybe it is." I tugged on her bag again as I went down a step. "And just think about it. If 'cookie' is a code word, whatever it symbolizes, it's been in your mouth, sweetheart."

For a moment, she stared at me and then she laughed. The sound was untried and hoarse, as if she didn't laugh often, and that caused that weird knot in my chest to throb. "You are really . . ."

"Amazing? Awesome?" I wanted to hear her laugh again. "Astonishing?"

"I was going to go with bizarre."

"Well, hell, if I had feelings that might actually hurt."

She grinned, and that meant we were close to a smile again. "I guess it's a good thing that you don't have feelings then, huh?"

"Guess so." I hopped onto the landing. "You better hurry or you're going to be late to your next class."

Her eyes widened, and I laughed, stepping out the way so Shortcake didn't run me over as she darted down the steps. "Damn, if only you moved that fast for my cookies, I'd be a happy guy."

"Shut up!"

"Hey!" I came around to the top of the next flight of stairs. "Don't you want to know what 'cookies' is a code word for?"

"No! Good God, no!"

I tipped back my head and laughed as the last strands of coppery hair disappeared from sight. I didn't know what it was about Avery Morgansten, but she was better than the quiet girl in middle school who turned out to like girls.

A lot better.

Four

There were moments in my life where I had no idea how I got where I was. Like what exactly had occurred to create the situation I was in?

Steph, wearing another skirt that barely covered her ass, slid a hand down my arm. She said something, whispered in my ear, but I really wasn't paying attention.

My gaze drifted from the TV to the hair band lying on my coffee table.

Oh, that's how this all got started.

A text from Steph claiming that she'd left something "super important" at my apartment from the night of the party. A rubber band. If I only had known that was what she was looking for, I would've walked my ass to the Rite Aid and bought her a whole package of them.

"Want me to get you a beer from the fridge?" she asked.

She really was the perfect woman. "No. I'm good."

I could feel her eyes on me as I lifted the glass of water

and took a drink. Beer. Me. Steph. No one else in the apartment. Not a good combination. Or maybe a good one depending on how you looked at it.

Cuddling up against my side, her full breasts pressed against my arm.

I so needed to look at this as a good thing instead of wondering how a couch that I could stretch out on suddenly felt too small.

"So, are you turning over a new leaf or something?" she asked, gaze fixed on the TV as she ran the tips of her nails up and down my arm. I was watching a boxing rerun and I doubted she was that interested. "Are you no longer drinking?"

I laughed under my breath. "Nah. Just not feeling it tonight."

"Oh." Steph's hand moved from my forearm to the center of my chest. "What are you feeling tonight?"

Loaded question, so I said nothing as a glove-covered fist slammed into a jaw. Steph perceived my silence the way she wanted, sliding her hand down the bare skin of my abs. Blood followed the tips of her fingers as they drifted below my navel, reaching the band on my shorts.

My body was into what was about to happen, thickening and swelling, straining up to meet her wandering fingers. And my body knew her fingers well, remembered exactly how skilled she was. But my head wasn't even in the same ballpark as my cock.

Tipping my head back against the couch, I exhaled slowly. There wasn't a damn thing wrong with what was happening. Her quick fingers skimmed over my limp hand, smoothing along my hip. The muscles jumped in response. So did something else.

I closed my eyes, inhaled deeply. My heart wasn't pounding. I was thinking about the meeting I'd have to attend Friday night. And I was thinking about Saturday night and stars when her hand curled around my cock, gripping me through the nylon shorts. A pulse shot straight up my spine as she moved her hand up.

Pleasure swirled low in my gut, and I knew if I let her continue, I would enjoy it. Already, it felt damn good. Always did, but I wouldn't return the act. Weeks ago, I would've, out of pure principal. Give. Take. But now I didn't care enough to do it and that wasn't right.

"Hey," I said, voice gruff as I gently grabbed her arm, pulling her hand away.

Her perfect lips formed a perfect O. "What?"

"I'm not feeling this." I brought her hand to my mouth and kissed her palm before placing it back on her thigh. My cock was already soft. "Okay?"

Surprise shuttled across her face, and a part of me was reeling in shock. Had I really just turned her down? I had.

Pink mottled her tan cheeks as she turned her gaze to the TV, and I, well, I felt like a dick. Shit. Sitting forward, I dropped my hands on my knees. "You want anything to eat?"

Mute, she shook her head no.

Double shit. "Look, Steph, it's not you, and I'm being serious about that. I'm just feeling weird tonight. All right?"

Steph glanced at me and slowly nodded. "Okay."

I let go of my breath in relief. Like I said before, Steph was a good girl and we had history. Things were just different now. She stayed for a little while longer and then she was ready to go. I got up to walk her out. At the door, she turned and stretched up, kissing my cheek.

I laughed. "What was that for?"

Steph shrugged as I closed the door behind us. "Are you going to the frat party?" she asked.

"Got plans," I told her.

She pouted prettily. "Can't you skip it Friday night?"

Reaching over, I tugged on a strand of soft, black hair. "You know I can't, sweetheart. Maybe next time."

"You suck." But she smiled as she hip bumped me.

"That I do."

We headed toward her car and when she caught her heel on a patch of loose gravel, I caught her arm, steadying her. "You haven't been drinking tonight?" I asked, eyes narrowing. "Right?"

Moonlight sliced over her face as she tipped her head back and let out a throaty laugh. "No." She smacked my chest. "And what if I did? Are you going to let me spend the night?"

"I'd put your little ass in my truck and drive you back to your dorm."

Her eyes rolled. "That sounds like a lot of fun."

We stopped behind her sedan and I pulled her in for a quick hug. "Text me when you get back to your dorm."

She laughed again, pulling back. "Seriously?"

I shot her a look. "You know I'm serious. It's late. A lot of people fucking suck in the world, so text me."

"And if I don't?"

My eyes narrowed. "You will."

"Okay. I will." Steph laughed as she backed toward the driver's door. "See you later, Cam."

Stepping back, I watched her pull out of the parking spot before I turned and headed back. Halfway across the parking lot, I looked up toward Shortcake's apartment. There were no lights on, and I bet she was already tucked away in her bed. Did she wear long-sleeve shirts to bed? Or did she sleep naked?

An image of her naked, her coppery hair spread out around her like a halo, invaded my head.

My cock swelled to life once again.

"Dammit," I muttered.

It was going to be a long night.

Thursday morning was IHOP morning, or at least that was what Ollie had deemed it when he rolled out of bed and busted up into my room. Snatching my cap off the arm of the couch, I saw Steph's rubber band on the coffee table and rolled my eyes.

Super important.

Ollie was already outside and I as approached the door, I caught the scent of rain in the air. As soon as I closed the door behind me, I realized he wasn't alone.

"Avery," Ollie said. "Cam told me your name."

Mental note to self: punt kick Ollie in the balls later.

There was a pause and then, "Oh. So . . . um, you're heading to—"

"Yo douchebag, you left the door open!" I smacked the cap on, rounding the stairs. Below, I got an eyeful of how Avery's blue jeans hugged her ass. Nice. "Hey, what are you doing with my girl?"

Ollie grinned up at me, but my attention was trained on Shortcake. The girl had to be wearing little or no makeup, because her face was . . . fresh. Natural. I liked it. Her gaze met mine and then flickered away.

"I was explaining to her how I go by two names," Ollie said.

"Oh yeah?" I caught up with them, dropping my arm over her shoulders. Her feet tripped up, and I tightened my arm, tucking her against my side. In the back of my head, I thought she fit perfectly. "Whoa, sweetheart, almost lost you there."

"Look at you." Ollie hopped down the stairs like a frog. "Got the girl tripping all over her feet."

I laughed, keeping an arm around her as I slid the cap backward. "I can't help it. It's my magnetic charm."

"Or it could be your smell." Ollie grinned. "I'm not sure I heard a shower this morning."

I gasped. "Do I smell bad, Avery?"

"You smell great," she said, and then a red flush quickened across her cheeks. "I mean, you don't smell bad."

Instinct told me she meant something completely different. "Heading to class?"

Shortcake didn't say anything as we walked down the stairs, but her face was pinched as if she was in deep thought about something.

"Avery?"

She squirmed away, and my eyes narrowed as she hurried off. "Yeah, I'm heading to art. What about you guys?"

Catching up with her on the third floor, I'd be damned if she got away that easily. "We're going out to breakfast. You should skip and join us."

She tightened her grip on her bag. "I think I've done enough skipping this week."

"I'm skipping," Ollie announced, "but Cam doesn't have a class until this afternoon, so he's a good boy."

"And you're a bad boy?" she asked.

He grinned at Shortcake, the kind of smile I'd seen him give countless girls. "Oh, I'm a bad, bad boy."

My skin prickled as I shot Ollie a look. "Yeah, as in bad at spelling, math, English, cleaning up after yourself, talking to people, and I could go on."

"But I'm good at the things that count," Ollie replied.

"And what are those things?" I asked as we stepped out under clouds fat with rain. It was going to be one of those days.

Ollie faced us, walking backward. A red truck started to back up, but he kept going, forcing the truck to grind to a halt. I shook my head. He held up a tanned hand and started ticking off his fingers. "Drinking, *socializing*, snowboarding, and soccer—remember that sport, Cam? Soccer?"

I stared at him. "Yeah, I remember it, asshole."

Ollie, probably having no idea what he'd just done, spun around and headed for my truck. A muscle started to tick in my jaw. I shoved my hands in my jeans as I glanced at Shortcake. "See you around, Avery."

Leaving her, I joined Ollie by my truck. Instead of hitting the unlock button to all the doors, I only did mine and climbed in, slamming the door shut behind me.

"Hello," came Ollie's muffled voice.

Ignoring him, I turned on the truck. A big, fat raindrop hit the windshield, and I smiled, looking up at the sky.

"Hey!"

Slowly, I raised my hand, giving him the finger.

Ollie jumped when the sky opened up in a torrential downpour, howling like a wounded animal. Only when his hair was plastered to his skull did I unlock his door.

He climbed in, shivering. "What the fuck, man?"

"You deserved it." I shifted into reverse, backing out. One look at Ollie's creased forehead told me he was racking his brain for what he did. I sighed. "You really need to lay off the pot."

"If I've heard that once, I've heard that a million times, but Mary Jane loves me, and she's the only girl I love."

Smoothing my hand over the baseball cap, I shook my head. "Fucking hippie."

Ollie shook his head like a wet dog, spraying the interior with droplets of chilly water. He must've knocked something loose in his brain, because he fell back against the seat. "Shit, man. I wasn't thinking."

I coughed out a laugh as I pulled out of the parking lot, a car behind Shortcake. "That's a huge surprise."

Ollie stared ahead, the normal smile he wore gone. "I forget sometimes, you know? It seems like forever ago."

Shit, I wished I could forget, especially now, as I watched Shortcake's car hang a left, heading toward campus.

He glanced at me. "I'm sorry, man. Truly. I know how much soccer meant to you."

I nodded absently as I turned right, heading for the bypass that would take us into Charles Town. Soccer had been my life since the moment Dad enrolled me in the local peewee league, and over years, I'd honed my skills as a striker, the middle scoring position. I was damn good, too, and it was no secret that when I registered for Shepherd and made their soccer team three years ago, I had no plans on staying here. I was biding my time before I could score a tryout with D.C. United. Soccer was how I met Jase and Ollie. Soccer had been my sanity.

But the only thing I was doing with soccer now was coaching a summer rec league program as *community service*. There would be no more soccer. At least for the foreseeable future, and one act of anger had ensured that.

Most people my age spent Friday night drinking and hanging out with friends. I spent *my* Friday night sitting in a circle—yes, a fucking circle—listening to people's problems. Some of the guys in the group weren't bad. Like Henry. He got drunk one night and got into a fight at a bar. He wasn't a psychopath. Neither was Aaron, who apparently had some road-rage problems. A couple of the other guys, and that one chick with the pasty-white makeup and heavy black eyeliner, I wasn't so sure about. They were kind of scary.

Screwed-up thing was that I wasn't the youngest person here. Not by far.

I only had . . . *ten more* motherfucking months of this.

I could do this. Seriously. I could easily do this.

"Cameron?" Dr. Bale cleared his throat, and I wanted to punch myself in the throat. "Is there anything you would like to share tonight?"

This was the part I couldn't do. The talking-about-me shit with a whole bunch of strangers staring at me. I looked up, and a sympathetic look crossed Henry's face before looking away.

"No," I said. "Not really."

Goth chick—who apparently had a penchant for knives—threw herself back in her seat, crossing her arms covered in black ink. "He *never* shares anything."

I pressed my lips together to keep from getting stabbed.

"That is true." Dr. Bale adjusted his wire-frame glasses. "You barely contribute to the group, Cameron."

Shrugging, I sat back and slid the baseball cap down lower. "I'm just taking it all in."

Henry jumped in, thankfully, diverting the attention, and I floated under the radar until the end of the session, but when I got up to leave, Dr. Bale summoned me.

Great.

As everyone filed out of the room, I dropped back in the metal folding chair and leaned forward, resting my elbows on my knees. "What's up?

Dr. Bale leaned over, picking out a folder from the plastic bin beside him. "I wanted to make sure you were getting something out of these meetings, Cameron."

Uh. No. No, I was not. "I am."

He eyed me as he hooked his leg over a knee as he

leaned back in his chair. "You've barely spoken about the event."

"There's really nothing to say."

"There's a lot to say." He smiled, pausing, and the skin around his eyes crinkled. "I know talking in front of people is hard in the beginning, but you have things in common with them."

I stiffened. "I'm not sure I have a lot in common with them."

"Are you sure about that?"

Sighing, I averted my gaze to the white walls. Posters lined them. Ones that spoke of talking, instead of throwing punches.

"Are you taking this seriously, Cameron?"

"Yes." I forced my gaze not to search out the only clock in the room, behind me.

"Good. I'd hate for you to not take this wonderful opportunity and use it to benefit your life."

I kept my expression blank.

"Do you realize how lucky you are, Cameron?" Dr. Bale asked when I said nothing. "What happened to that boy could have put you in jail for a very long time."

"I know," I said, meaning it. God knows I knew how lucky I was. And for the longest time I believed my ass should've been rotting in jail. I would've been if it hadn't been for my father's pull in the criminal courts and my otherwise spotless record. "I'm a really laid-back guy, Dr. Bale. What happened—"

"The beating you inflicted on that boy would beg to differ." His gaze flicked down to my file. "Severe head contusions. Broken jaw, nose, and *eye* socket, along with several broken ribs." He looked up, meeting my stare. That doesn't sound like something a 'laid-back guy' would do, now does it?"

My stomach soured, but I didn't look away. "I'm not proud of what I did. Looking back, I know there were plenty of other things I could've done."

"But?"

But I didn't have an "anger" or a "rage" problem. And as fucked up as it sounded, I still wasn't sure I regretted what I had done. The fucker had been beating on *my sister*, and well, I had lost my shit.

And truth be told, if I had to do the situation all over again, I wasn't sure I'd handle it any differently. You hurt my sister, you're fucking with me. It was as simple as that.

Five

*W*hen it came to my little Shortcake, patience paid off.

At first, the trip out to Antietam National Battlefield to do our astronomy assignment had started off as painful as my weekly anger-management classes were. She sat in my truck like I lured her in there with the offer of free puppies, tugging on the sleeves of her sweater and sitting as straight as a board. Her nervousness increased as we headed down Bloody Lane, picking a spot that would give us a clear view of the sky and . . . cornfields.

I learned she was a bit of a history nerd, which was cool, because those brown eyes lit up when she started talking about the battlefield. And I also learned she was in one hell of a hurry to get this done and over with.

Never in my life did I doubt my ability to attract a girl like I did with Avery. She acted like spending time with me was tantamount to sitting in music appreciation class for two semesters in a row. As cocky as this sounds,

I knew I could walk onto that campus and get a date with the nearest available girl. Probably even a girl who wasn't available, but with Avery, it was like trying to hit on a nun. And not a naughty nun.

"How long do you think this will take?" she asked.

"Why?" I paused as something occurred to me. Maybe my charm wasn't failing me. Holy shit, how had I not thought about this before? "You got a hot date tonight?"

She laughed dryly. "Uh, no."

Part of me was happy to hear this. The other part was thoroughly confused. "You sound like that's an insane idea. That no one would go out on a Saturday night for a date."

Shrugging, she dropped the piece of hair she'd been messing with. "I'm not dating anyone."

I walked on, tapping my hands off my thighs as the breeze stirred the cornstalks, causing them to rattle like dry bones. "So why the rush?" When there was no response, I glanced over my shoulder at her, grinning. "Are you worried that I've brought you out here for my own nefarious plans?"

Shortcake stopped, her face paling in a way that made her freckles punch out. "What?"

Whoa. I faced her, feeling the knot back in my chest and something else. Her reaction was too quick, too real. A bad taste filled my mouth. "Hey, Avery, I'm just joking. Seriously."

She stared at me and then averted her gaze, cheeks flushing. "I know. I'm just . . ."

"Jumpy?"

"Yeah, that."

I hoped—fuck, I prayed—that was all this was. Watching her fiddle with the bracelet on her left wrist, I couldn't let the train of thought go any further. Anger over the possibility of something fucked up in the most minor way happening to her was already pricking at my skin. I was sure I was overreacting. "Come on. It'll be dark soon."

I started walking, heading toward the tower, waving at two students from our class. Picking a spot on the hill overlooking the dirt lane, I pulled out a flashlight before I sat down. The grass was dry and in that stretch of silence, the hum of crickets was almost as loud as my pounding heart. I had no idea why my pulse was racing, but it felt like I'd run from the truck to here instead of walking.

Looking up, I found Shortcake hovering a few feet behind me. I patted the spot. "Join me? Pretty please? I'm lonely all by myself over here."

She sucked her lower lip in between her teeth, and the muscles in my stomach tensed. Finally, she moved forward and sat . . . three feet from me. My brows rose, but then . . . then our gazes collided, and I took a breath, but it didn't get really far. How many freckles did she have on the bridge of her nose? Nine. No. Nine and a half. One of them was faded. Her lips were parted, like she was waiting for a kiss.

The urge to kiss her hit me hard in the gut. Was it the first time? When I wiped the crumb from her lip, I had wanted to kiss her then, to taste those soft-looking lips. Any other girl I would've made a move, but not Shortcake.

And that's when the strangest damn thing happened.

I wanted to slow down. How I could slow down this nonexistent relationship was beyond me, but I don't know. My heart was still pounding.

Avery ducked her chin, studying her notebook as she cleared her throat.

Letting out a breath I didn't realize I was holding, I asked, "What constellation are we supposed to be mapping?"

"Um, the Corona Borealis, I think," she said, skimming the notes as I held the flashlight.

"Ah, the Northern Crown."

Her brows rose. "You knew that off the top of your head?"

I laughed at her dubious expression. "I might not take notes, but I do pay attention."

She wrinkled her nose. "I really don't understand how anyone sees shapes in the stars."

"Really?" I moved closer slowly and peeked over her shoulder. "The shapes are pretty obvious."

"Not to me. I mean, it's just a bunch of stars in the sky. You can probably see whatever you want to see."

"Look at the Borealis." I pointed at the map. "It's obviously a crown."

She laughed—a real laugh, and the knot tightened in my chest. "It does not look like a crown. It looks like an irregular half circle."

Grinning, I shook my head. "Look. You can see it now easily. That's a crown. Come on, see the seven stars."

"I see the seven stars, but I also see about a hundred others peeking out." She grabbed a pen. "I also see the cookie monster."

I laughed. "You're ridiculous."

As I watched her, her lips curved up in a smile as she posed her pen over the grid. It was clear she had no idea what latitude line to start at as she glanced up toward the Borealis. Finally, she connected two dots.

"You know where the name comes from?" I asked.

Shortcake shook her head, so I reached over and took the pen from her. In the process, my fingers brushed hers. A jolt zapped up my arm, and she pulled away immediately. "It represents the crown given from the god Dionysus to Ariadne," I told her. "When she married Bacchus, he placed her crown in the heavens in honor of their marriage."

She stared, brows furrowing. "Professor Drage didn't teach that in class."

"I know."

"Then how did you know that?"

"Why don't you know that?"

She tipped her head to the side, lips pursed.

"Okay. Maybe most people wouldn't know that off the top of their head." I twirled her pen. "I actually took part of this class as a freshman, but had to drop it."

Curiosity filled her brown eyes. "Really?"

I nodded.

"You're, what, a junior?"

"Yep." I paused, unsure of how much I should say. "I ended up having to take a year off, which put me behind."

She was quiet for a few moments "Why did you retake astronomy? Is it a part of your major?"

"No. I just like the class and Professor Drage." I turned

off the flashlight "I'm studying recreation and sport. Would like to get into sport rehabilitation."

"Oh. Did you . . ."

When she didn't finish her sentence, I looked over and followed her gaze. On the bench, the two from our astronomy class looked like they were about to practice making babies right then and there.

"Now that is an interesting form of stargazing," I said.

She watched them for a couple of more moments, her eyes wide like she was trying to figure out exactly what they were doing. Which was obvious. There was a lot of tongue involved.

I poked her with my pen.

"What?"

"Nothing. It's just that . . ." I had no idea how to say this. "You're watching them like . . . you've never seen a couple do that before."

"I am?"

I nodded. "So unless you were raised in a convent, I imagined you've been in a lap a time or two, right?"

"No, I haven't!" She cringed, focusing over the cornstalks. "I mean, I haven't been in a guy's lap."

A grin teased at my lips. "What about a girl's lap?"

Her mouth dropped open. "What? No!"

I smiled broadly, picturing her in a girl's lap and that wasn't a bad image. Made even better when I pictured her in my lap, though. "I was joking, Avery."

Her chin jutted out stubbornly. "I know, it's just that . . ."

"What?" I poked her arm with the pen again. "You what?"

"I've never been in a relationship."

Never? Never as in ever? No way.

Clutching her notebook, she glanced at me. "What? It's not a big deal."

I opened my mouth, said nothing. I blinked and then shook my head as I tipped my head back, staring at the sky. "You've never been in a relationship?"

"No."

"Nothing?"

"That's what no means."

I had no idea what to say. "How old are you?"

She rolled her eyes. "I'm nineteen."

"And you haven't been in a single relationship?"

"No. My parents . . . they were strict." She swallowed. "I mean, *really* strict."

"I can tell." I tapped the pen on the notebook, beyond curious, like obsessively curious as to how someone as pretty as Avery made it this far without ever being in a relationship "So have you gone on a date or anything?"

A deep sigh emanated from her. "I thought we were supposed to be mapping stars?"

"We are."

"No, we're not. All I have is a scribbly line and you have nothing."

"That *scribbly* line is between the Delta and Gamma." I leaned over, connecting the dots. "Here is the Theta and this is the Alpha—brightest star. See, we are halfway done."

She frowned, slowly shaking her head as she turned her gaze to the sky. While she was distracted, because I was done with the astronomy shit, I leaned in further, my shoulder pressing into hers as I finished the map, completing our homework assignment.

I turned my head. "Now we're done mapping stars . . ." Our faces were inches apart, and I heard the soft inhale of breath. She didn't move away, and my smile went up a notch. "See? That wasn't hard."

Avery's gaze dropped, and I knew she wasn't paying a damn bit of attention to what was coming out of my mouth even though she was staring at it. Not that I was complaining. She could stare at my mouth all she wanted.

Those thick lashes swept up and our gazes locked once more. A sudden, tangible pull spread out between us. Neither of us moved, and I wanted to. I wanted to pull her into my arms. Where the whole slowing down things went to I had no idea. She moved, visibly uncomfortable, and the good, decent part of me said to look away, to crack a joke and make her feel better, but I couldn't resist the lure of her eyes. In the darkness, they were like black pools.

I forced myself to say something. "You think you learned anything about the stars?"

There was no response, which was probably a good thing, because that was lame. So I went to what I really wanted to know. "Have you ever been on a date?"

Still no response.

My lips curved up. "Are you listening to me?"

Shortcake blinked like she was coming out of a daze. "Huh? Yes! Yes. Totally."

There was no mistaking she was feeling what I was

feeling. Not when she had stared at me that long. "Yeah . . . so, you haven't been on a date?"

"What?"

I chuckled. "You really haven't been listening to me at all. You've been too busy staring at me."

"I have not!"

"Yes, you were." I nudged her shoulder.

The expression she made was like she tasted something bad. "You are so beyond the acceptable level of arrogance."

"Arrogant? I'm just stating the truth." I tossed my notebook aside and leaned back on my arms, watching her. I couldn't resist teasing her. It was like finding a new hobby. "There's nothing wrong with staring at me. I like it."

She gaped at me. "I wasn't staring at you. Not really. I sort of . . . dazed out. That's how *thrilling* talking to you is."

"Everything about me is thrilling."

"About as thrilling as watching your tortoise cross a road."

"Uh-huh. Keep telling yourself that, sweetheart."

"Keep calling me sweetheart and you're going to be limping."

Ah, I liked that. "Oh, listen to you."

"Whatever."

"We should do it."

Her lips puckered. "Do what? Go home? I'm all about going home, like right now."

I smiled. "Go on a date."

Six

Shortcake stared at me like I'd just suggested that we strip naked and run through the cornstalks. She snapped her notebook closed and grabbed her bag. "I'm not sure I'm following this conversation."

"It's really not that complicated." I laughed at her hateful look. "We should go out on a date."

She stared at me a moment and then shoved her notebook into the bag with lethal force. "I don't understand."

Why wasn't I surprised that she didn't understand? Lying back, I stretched my arms above my head, feeling the bones pop. I watched her gaze sweep down the length of me, getting hung up on the skin exposed between my shirt and belt.

My smile spread. "Typically going on a date is when two people go out for the evening or sometimes during the day. Really, it can be any time of the day or night. It usually involves dinner. Sometimes a movie or a walk in the park. Though, I don't do walks in the park. Maybe on a beach, but since there aren't any—"

"I know what a date is." She jumped to her feet, eyes like chips of black ice in the darkness.

"You said you didn't understand. So I'm explaining what a date means."

Her lips twitched as she crossed her arms. "That's not the part I don't understand and you know that."

"I was just making sure we were on the same page."

"We're not."

Grinning shamelessly, I lowered my arms, but didn't tug down my shirt. "So now that we both know what a date entails, we should go out on one."

"Uh . . ."

I laughed as I sat up. The confusion on her face was adorable in a weird way. "That's not really a response, Avery."

"I . . ." Shaking her head, she took a step back. "Don't you have a girlfriend?"

Where in the hell did Shortcake get that idea? "A girlfriend? No."

"Then who was that brunette stumbling out of your apartment Wednesday night?" she demanded.

As her words sunk in, I smiled from ear to fucking ear. "Have you been watching me, Avery?"

"No. No!" Her face blanched. "What? I wasn't watching you. I do have a life."

I arched a brow. "Then how do you know about Stephanie?"

Shortcake shifted her weight. "That's her name?"

"Well, yes, she has a name and no, she's not my girl-friend. And she wasn't stumbling. Maybe shuffling."

She rolled her eyes.

"So how did you see her if you weren't watching me?" I crossed my ankles. "And I don't mind the idea of you watching me. Remember, I like that."

Her chest rose in a deep breath, and I could tell her patience was running thin. "I wasn't watching you. I couldn't sleep and I was staring out my living-room window. I just *happened* to see you walking her out to her car."

I didn't believe her. Hell to the no. Who just happens to be staring out the window at that time of night? As much as I'd love to tease her, it looked like she was about to punt kick my head, but I *was* a gambling sort of man. "Well, that makes sense. Not nearly as entertaining as you standing by your window hoping to catch a glimpse of me."

She stared at me.

I winked. "Steph's not my girlfriend by the way. We aren't like that."

Her hand went to the bracelet on her left wrist. "I'm not like that."

"Like what?"

Turning her stare to the many stars, she raised her hands. "I'm not like her."

"Do you know her?"

"I don't just hook up with guys for fun, okay? I don't see anything wrong with it. Totally not judging here, but that's not me. So I'm not interested. Sorry."

"Wait a sec. I'm confused. You're not judging her, but you've made the assumption that she's into random hookups? That she's my fuck buddy? Isn't that kind of making a rash judgment based on assumptions?"

Her forehead wrinkled. "You're right. I don't know if that's what you guys are about. Maybe you're just childhood buddies or something."

"We're not." I grinned. "We hook up every once in a while."

Shortcake's jaw hit the ground. "I was right! Then why did you accuse me of being judgmental?"

"I was just pointing it out." I couldn't stop teasing her. The array of emotions that crossed her face was fascinating to me. "And for the record, we didn't hook up Wednesday night. Not for the lack of trying on her part, but I wasn't feeling it."

"Whatever. This is a stupid conversation."

"I like this conversation."

She reached for the bag, but I was faster, grabbing her bag as I stood. A deep, annoyed sigh radiated from her. "Give it to me."

Ducking my chin, I said, "I'm trying to." I laid the strap over her shoulder, brushing the side of her neck with my fingers. It wasn't on purpose that time and when she jumped, so did my heart. Backing away, I picked up the flashlight. "See? I was just being a gentleman."

"I don't think you're a gentleman, but thank you."

Her words were an odd mix of sincerity and frustration, and she didn't say anything else as we started back with only the narrow swath of light from the flashlight.

"This place is kind of creepy at night, don't you think?"

She nodded as she looked over at the dark, looming

shadows of the monuments. "Well, I guess, if there's going to be any place in the world haunted, it would be a place like this."

"You believe in ghosts?"

Shortcake shrugged. "I don't know. Never seen one."

"Me neither."

One side of her lips curved up. "That's a good thing I suppose."

I stopped at the passenger side of the truck. "Milady."

"Thank you."

Since there was a little less frustration in her voice, I decided to test my luck. I leaned against the open door, watching the interior light caress the edges of her face. "So, what about it?"

"What about what?"

I tilted my head to the side. "Go out on a date with me."

She stiffened. "Why?"

"Why not?"

"That's not an answer." She grabbed the seatbelt, whipping it around her.

"What kind of question was that? How am I—hey, it's just a seat belt. Not that hard." I leaned over, taking the belt from her. As our hands brushed, she plastered herself against the seat. It was such a strange reaction that the tiny hairs on the back of my neck rose as I lifted my gaze. "Why shouldn't we go out on a date?"

Her hands balled into fists in her lap. I wanted to let go of the damn seat belt, take her hands in mine, and ease them out of the tight ball. "Because . . . because we don't know each other."

I smiled slightly as I moved my gaze up, centering on her mouth. "That's what a date is all about. Getting to know each other. Go out on a date with me."

"There's nothing to know about me," she whispered.

"I'm sure there is tons to know about you."

"There's not."

I leaned closer, inhaling her sweet scent. "Then we can spend the time with me talking."

"That sounds like fun."

"Oh, it will be more thrilling than watching Raphael cross a road."

"Ha." Amusement flashed in her dark eyes.

"Thought you'd like that."

Her gaze flickered to where her bag rested against her legs and then back to mine. "Can we go yet?"

"Can we go on a date?"

A sound of frustration came from her. "Good God, you don't give up."

"Nope."

Shortcake laughed, and I couldn't stop the smile from forming on my lips. I liked the sound of her laugh, when she really laughed. "I'm sure there are plenty of girls who want to go out on a date with you."

"There are."

"Wow. Modest aren't you?"

"Why should I be? And I want to go out on a date with you. Not them."

She shook her head slightly. "I don't understand why."

And I didn't understand why she didn't get it. "I can think of a few reasons. You're not like most girls." True.

"That interests me." And it really did. "You're awkward in this really . . . adorable way. You're smart. Want me to list more?"

"No. Not at all," she replied. "I don't want to go out on a date with you."

I didn't believe it. Call it intuition, experience, or plain old cockiness, I didn't believe her at all. "I figured you'd say that."

"Then why did you ask?"

I leaned back, grabbing the side of the door. "Because I wanted to."

"Oh. Well. Okay. Glad you got it out of your system."

What did she think this was? Hell, I didn't even know what this was. "I haven't gotten it out of my system."

Her shoulders slumped. "You haven't?"

"Nope." I smiled. "There's always tomorrow."

"What about tomorrow?"

"I'll ask you again."

She shook her head. "The answer will be the same."

"Maybe. Maybe not." I tapped the tip of her nose, grinning as she narrowed her eyes at me. "And maybe you'll say yes. I'm a patient guy, and hey, like you said, I don't give up easily."

"Great," she muttered, but there was a glimmer in her eyes, the same sheen that had been there when she was checking me out.

"Knew you'd see it that way." I tweaked the tip of her nose, and she smacked my hand away. "Don't worry. I know the truth."

"The truth about what?"

I moved back in case she swung again. "You want to say yes, but you're just not ready."

Shortcake looked like she actually did see a ghost.

"It's okay. I'm a lot to handle, but I can assure you, you'll have fun handling me." Before she could respond, I tapped her nose and then closed the door, grinning to myself as I loped around the front of the truck.

I watched Avery head into her apartment. She stopped halfway in, tucked the glossy copper strands behind her ear as she peeked over her shoulder at me.

A small, shy smile pulled at her lips as she waved good-bye and then slipped inside, quietly closing the door behind her.

Standing there a few more moments, like a creeper, I finally turned toward my door. As I reached for the knob, the door swung open.

Jase appeared, blocking the door. A curious look crossed his expression. "What are you doing standing in the hallway of your apartment building like a loser?"

"What are you doing in my apartment like a freak?"

He shrugged. "I was hanging out with Ollie, but he ran to Sheetz to get some nachos."

"Ah, a nachos night." Which meant Ollie would be up all night. I shifted my weight. "Are you going to let me in?"

"Well, since it is your place." He cocked his head to the side, casting half of his swarthy face into a shadow. "I guess so."

Jase stepped aside, allowing me to *squeeze* past him.

I went straight to the fridge, grabbed a beer and then dropped onto the couch. "You're not at the farm?"

He shook his head as he joined me, picking up a bottle from the coffee table. "No. Jack is with the grandparents."

"Ah . . ." That explained it. Jase was usually at his family farm on the weekends.

Jase glanced at me. "Sooo, you were out with the redhead?"

"Shortcake?"

His dark brows slipped out of the wave of hair and knitted. "Huh?"

"Avery's the redhead. And no. We were doing an astronomy assignment. We're partners."

"Oh." He took a swig of his beer and made a face. "Sooo," he said again, and I rolled my eyes. "Why were you staring at her apartment door?"

"How do you know?"

"I watched you through the peephole."

"Nice." I laughed, taking a drink. A couple of minutes passed and then I said, "I asked her out."

Jase didn't look that interested. "Okay."

"She turned me down."

His head swung toward me, his dove-gray eyes sparkling with interest. "What?"

"Yep." I fell back into the couch, grinning. "Turned me down flat."

Leaning onto the arm of the couch, Jase laughed so hard I think he hurt his stomach. "I like this girl."

"So do I," I said, sighing. "So do I."

Seven

Fresh banana-nut bread cooled on the counter, filling the apartment with its savory scent.

I glanced at the clock on the stove. Five till eight.

Shoving my hands through my damp hair, I gave up on the idea of actually sleeping. In the living room, Ollie was passed out on the floor snoring, and the last time I'd checked my bedroom, Jase was sprawled across the foot of my bed. And there was no way in hell any part of my skin or clothes were touching any part of Ollie's bed.

It wasn't so much that Jase and Ollie had kept me awake. At any point during the never-ending night, I could've locked myself in my bedroom, but my mind wouldn't shut down. Some of it had to do with the meeting on Friday and how Dr. Bale had laid everything out. I couldn't stop thinking about how Jase was going to make things work, because after Ollie had passed out and Jase was more drunk than an entire frat, he started talking, and well, I didn't know how to help him.

And I couldn't stop thinking about the girl a few doors down.

Shortcake had turned me down.

I grinned, thinking of how I was going to turn that no into a yes.

Pivoting around, I reached for the fridge and came to a stop. Was that it? The challenge? From the moment I met Avery, she was running from me, and females ran *toward* me.

But what I said to her last night about why I wanted to go out on a date was true. Avery did interest me. She wasn't like the girls I hung out with—the well put together, coy and flirtatious ones. Not that anything was wrong with them, but Avery was different. She made me laugh. Maybe not on purpose, but I loved watching her flush over the simplest things, and when she smiled?

Shortcake shone brighter than any chick I knew.

Perhaps it was all that, combined with the challenge. I really didn't know, and at that moment, as I opened the fridge and grabbed some eggs, I really didn't care.

I liked her.

And I wasn't sleeping anytime soon, so why should the object of my current restlessness be sleeping in on a Sunday morning?

The moment the idea sprung to mind, I didn't even think twice. Shortcake probably wasn't going to be happy with the plan, but no one—not even her—could resist my banana-nut bread.

Gathering up my items, I strolled toward the front door. There, I heard Ollie mumble, "No tomatoes. Extra bacon."

"What the?" I looked over my shoulder at him. He was still on his stomach, his check plastered to a throw pillow my mom had given me, dead to the world. "Freak," I muttered, slipping out of the apartment.

At Avery's door, I knocked softly at first, not wanting to wake the neighbors, but when a full minute passed and I hadn't heard footsteps, I knocked hard and kept knocking.

After what felt like an eternity of me banging on her door like the police and turning around to make sure I didn't have anyone seconds away from shooting my ass, I finally heard footsteps and then the door swung open.

"Is everything okay?" she asked in what was possibly the sexiest voice I'd ever heard.

I spun back to the door, getting an eyeful of a bedraggled Avery.

Coppery hair hung in loose tangles, flowing down her shoulders and grazing the golden skin of her arms. I didn't think I'd ever seen her in a short-sleeve shirt before. My gaze, all on its own, traveled sideways and stopped, devouring the way the thin shirt she wore stretched across the swell of her breasts. With a will I didn't know I possessed, I forced my eyes to her flushed face.

Suddenly unsure of what the hell I was doing, I offered a crooked smile and said to hell with it. "No, but it will be in about fifteen minutes."

"W-w-what?" She moved out of the way as I slipped past her. All the apartments were the same, so I knew where the kitchen was, but I did a quick scan of the living room. The furnishings looked new—the couch and dark end tables. A black moon chair sat beside a TV. No pictures hung on the walls. The moon chair was possibly the most personal thing in the room.

"Cam, what are you doing? It's eight in the morning."

"Thanks for the update on the time. It's one thing I've never been able to master: the telling of time."

She trailed after me, and I could feel her staring daggers in my back. "Why are you here?"

"Making breakfast."

"You can't do that in your own kitchen?"

"My kitchen isn't as exciting as yours." I placed the eggs and bread on the counter and faced her. Scrubbing her eyes, she looked so damn cute, and I wished I was wearing something more decent than sweats and a shirt I wasn't even sure was clean. "And Ollie is passed out on the living-room floor."

"On the floor?"

"Yep. Facedown, snoring and drooling a little. It's not an appetizing atmosphere."

Her lips twitched into a quick smile and then quickly disappeared. "Well, neither is my apartment."

I folded my arms as I leaned against the counter. "Oh, I don't know about that . . ." I let my gaze wander the exquisite length of hers. Her nipples were hard, pressing against her shirt, begging to be touched, licked, and kissed and God knows what else I would do to them. Lust slammed into my gut and I almost took a step toward her. "Your kitchen, right this second, is very appetizing."

She flushed. "I'm not going out with you, Cam."

"I didn't ask you at this moment, now did I?" I grinned. "But you will eventually."

"You're delusional."

"I'm determined."

"More like annoying," she retorted, brown eyes twinkling.

"Most would say amazing."

She rolled her eyes. "Only in your head."

"In many heads is what you meant." I turned to the stove. "I also brought banana-nut bread baked in my very own oven."

There was a pause. "I'm allergic to bananas."

I wheeled around. "Are you shitting me?"

"No. I'm not. I'm allergic to bananas."

"Man, that's a damn shame. You have no idea what you're missing out on. Bananas make the world a better place."

"I wouldn't know."

Well damn. Apparently she could resist my banana-nut bread. "Anything else you're allergic to?"

"Besides penicillin and guys who bust up into my apartment? No."

"Hardy-har-har." I turned and bent, opening the nearest cabinets. "How many weaker, less-assured guys have you slayed with that tongue of yours?"

"Apparently not enough." Her gasp was audible. "I'll be right back."

I had no idea what she was up to, but I doubted she'd leave the apartment. Humming under my breath, I found a pot to boil eggs in and filled it with water. Plopping it on the stove, I cranked up the heat. I could hear her back in her bedroom, her soft footfalls, heavier than I thought they'd be. A couple of moments went by and I turned to the doorway. It was quite possible that she would lock herself in her room.

Dammit.

"Hey! Are you hiding back there?" I yelled. "Because I will come back there and drag you out."

"Don't you dare come in here!" she shouted.

I laughed softly. As appealing as seeing firsthand what she was doing was, I didn't want to end up in the hospital for doing so. "Then hurry up. My eggs wait for no one."

By the time she returned, I found shredded cheese and had decided she was going to eat hers sunny side up. I didn't say anything even though I knew she was there, staring at me.

"Cam, why are you over here?" she finally asked.

"I already told you." I eased the eggs onto a plate and walked it over to the small table pressed up against the wall. "Do you want toast? Wait. Do you have bread? If not, I can—"

"No. I don't need toast." She watched me, eyes wide. "Don't you have anyone else to bother?"

"There are a shit ton of people that I could *reward* with my presence, but I chose you."

Her mouth moved, but there was no sound and then she spun around, hopping up on the chair, pulling her knees to her chest as she picked up a fork. "Thanks," she muttered.

I raised my brows. "I choose to believe that you mean that."

"I do!"

I turned back to the stove. "I doubt that for some reason."

There were several seconds of silence and then. "I do appreciate the eggs. I'm just surprised to see you here . . . at eight in the morning."

Waiting for my eggs to finish boiling, I found myself watching her. "Well, to be honest, I was planning to woo you with my banana-nut bread, but that shit ain't happening now. So all I have left are my delicious eggs."

"It is really good, but you're not wooing me."

"Oh, I'm wooing." I went to her fridge and found some OJ. Grabbing two glasses, I poured some sweetness and sat one in front of her. "It's just all about the stealth. You don't realize it yet."

She ducked her gaze to her plate. "Aren't you eating?"

"I am. I like boiled eggs." Sitting across from her, I rested my chin in my palm. Her hair fell forward, nearing hitting the plate. She kept batting the strands away. She was so fucking cute. "So, Avery Morgansten, I'm all yours."

Her lashes swept up. "I don't want you."

"Too bad. Tell me about yourself."

Shortcake pressed her lips into a thin line. "Do you do this often? Just walk into random girls' apartments and make eggs?"

"Well, you're not random, so technically no." Pushing up, I checked the eggs. "And I might be known to surprise lucky ladies every now and then."

Which wasn't exactly true. I mean, if I somehow found

myself in someone else's place and I was up, I'd make breakfast, but this? This was a first. But she didn't need to know that.

"Seriously? I mean, you do this normally?"

I glanced over my shoulder. "With friends, yes, and we're friends, aren't we, Avery?"

She studied me for a few moments and then placed her fork down. "Yeah, we're friends."

"Finally!" I shouted. "You've finally admitted that we are friends. It's only taken a week."

"We've only known each other for a week."

"Still took a week."

As I started devouring my eggs, she questioned me on how long it took for me to declare best-friend status. Sitting back at the table, I met her curious stare. "It usually takes me about five minutes before we've moved on to best-friend status."

A tiny smile appeared on her lips. "Then I guess I'm just the odd one."

"Maybe."

"I guess it's different for you."

"Hmm?" I peeled the last piece of shell off the egg.

"I bet you have girls hanging all over you. Dozens would probably kill to be in my spot and here I am, allergic to your bread."

I looked up. "Why? Because of my near godlike perfection?"

She laughed outright, and that goddamn knot was back in my chest. "I wouldn't go that far."

Shrugging, I chuckled. "I don't know. Don't really think about it."

"You don't think about it at all?"

"Nope." I popped the egg in my mouth and then wiped my hands on a napkin. "I only think about it when it matters."

Her gaze bounced off of mine as she toyed with her glass. "So you're a reformed player?"

"What makes you think that?"

"I heard you were quite the player in high school."

"Really? Who did you hear that from?"

"None of your business."

I took a deep breath. Her tongue was sharp as a blade. "With that mouth of yours, you don't have a lot of friends, do you?"

Shortcake flinched. "No. I wasn't really popular in high school."

Aw fuck, now I felt like a dick. I dropped my egg onto the plate. "Shit. I'm sorry. That was an asshole thing for me to say."

She shook her head.

I watched her as I picked up the egg and peeled it, unable to figure her out. "Hard to believe though that you weren't. You can be funny and nice when you're not insulting me and you're a pretty girl. Actually, you're really hot."

"Ah . . . thanks." She wiggled in her seat.

"I'm serious. You said your parents were strict. They didn't let you hang out in high school?" I popped the other egg in. Needed my protein. "I still can't imagine you not being popular in high school. You rock the trifecta—smart, funny, and hot."

"I wasn't. Okay?" Sitting the glass down, she started fiddling with the hem on her shorts. "I was like the very opposite of popular."

Unsure of what to think about that comment, I peeled the third egg. I'd seen her around campus with a girl I went to high school with and Jacob Massey. It wasn't like she was incapable of making friends. "I am sorry, Avery. That . . . that sucks. High school is a big deal."

"Yeah, it is. You had a lot of friends?"

I nodded. I had a busload of friends.

"Still talk to them?"

"Some of them. Ollie and I went to high school together, but he spent his first two years at WVU and transferred down here and I see a few around campus and back home."

She huddled in on herself, looking incredibly small. "Have any brothers or sisters?"

"A sister." I went for the final egg, smiling. "She's younger than me. Just turned eighteen. She graduates this year."

"You guys close?"

"Yeah, we're close." I liked that she was asking me questions, but talking about my sister made me think of other things. "She means a lot to me. How about you? A big brother I have to worry about visiting and kicking my ass for being here?"

One side of her lips curved up. "No. I'm an only child. Have a cousin who's older, but I doubt he'd do that."

"Ah, good." I finished off the last egg, leaned back and patted my stomach. "Where you from?" When she didn't answer, I decided I was so not letting this go. I wanted to *know* her. Exchange of information was necessary. "Okay. You obviously know where I'm from if you've heard of my extracurricular activities in high school, but I'll just confirm it. I'm from the Fort Hill area. Never heard of that? Well, most people haven't. It's near Morgantown. Why didn't I go to WVU? Everyone wants to know that. Just wanted to get away, but be somewhat close to my family. And yes, I was . . . very busy in high school."

"You're not anymore?"

"Depends on who you ask." I laughed. "Yeah, I don't know. When I was a freshman—those first couple of months, being around all the older girls? I probably put more effort into them than I did my classes."

She grinned. "But not now?"

I shook my head and went back to what I wanted to know. "So where are you from?"

Shortcake sighed. "I'm from Texas."

"Texas?" I leaned onto the table. "Really? You don't have an accent."

"I wasn't born in Texas. My family was originally from Ohio. We moved to Texas when I was eleven and I never picked up any accent."

"Texas to West Virginia? That's a hell of a difference."

Her eyes met mine for a fraction of a second and then she stood, picking up her plate and the bowl. "Well, I lived in the strip-mall-hell part of Texas, but besides that, it's kind of the same here."

"I should clean up." I started to stand. "I made the mess."

"No." She shot me a serious look. "You cooked. I clean."

Watching her take care of the dishes, I couldn't help but think how intimate this was—me cooking, her cleaning. While I may have cooked some breakfasts for girls before, it had been nothing like this.

And I really wasn't sure how to process that.

Turning to the bread, I peeled the foil back. "What made you choose here?"

She finished washing the little frying pan I'd brought over before answering the question. "I just wanted to get away, like you."

"Got to be hard though."

"No. It was incredibly easy to make the decision."

It was? I couldn't imagine moving that far away from my family. I was pretty sure my mom would hunt me down if I did. I broke the bread in half. "You are an enigma, Avery Morgansten."

She leaned against the counter. "Not really. More like you are."

"How so?"

She gestured at me and my half-eaten loaf of bread. "You just ate four hard-boiled eggs, you're eating half of a loaf, and you have abs that look like they belong on a Bowflex ad."

My smile was the size of an earthquake crater. "You've been checking me out, haven't you? In between your flaming insults? I feel like man candy."

She laughed, and the sound was soft and sweet. "Shut up."

"I'm a growing boy."

Her brows rose at that, and I laughed. In the following silence, I found myself telling her more than I told most girls I'd known for years. "My dad is a lawyer, runs his own firm back home. So he probably wanted me to go to law school."

She stayed by the counter. "Why didn't you?"

"Law is not my thing. Mom's a doctor—cardiologist— and before you ask, med school also wasn't my thing."

Her right hand went to that bracelet, a nervous habit I was beginning to realize. "And sports recreation is your thing?"

"Soccer is my thing. So if I can get on with a team, helping their players, then I'm happy." I paused, shifting my weight. "Or I'd love to coach, maybe high school or whatever."

Her gaze dipped to the floor as she crept forward. She reminded me of a scared animal that had been hurt before and was distrustful of those around her. The knot expanded in my chest and the horrible pricking sensation was back, telling me something I didn't want to hear.

"Why don't you play soccer?" she asked.

And that was a subject I didn't want to touch, but she was asking questions and there was no way I could shoot her down. "It's a long . . . complicated story, but it's not something I can do right now."

She was by the table, hovering near the chair. "What about later?"

"Later . . . later might work." And that was true. If I kept in shape, kept up with the game, who knew? It just wasn't something I allowed myself to think about a lot. "So you flying back to Texas for fall break or Thanksgiving?"

She snorted. "Probably not."

"Got other plans?"

Avery shrugged and then started asking me about soccer. Hours had passed and I was sure she was as knowledgeable about soccer as she ever would be. It was near noon when I stood. I didn't really want to leave, but I had sucked up all her morning.

Flipping the skillet in one hand and carrying the bread in the other, I stopped in front of her door. "So, Avery . . ."

She leaned against the couch. "So, Cam . . ."

"Whatcha you doing Tuesday night?"

"I don't know." Wariness settled in her brow. "Why?"

"How about you go out with me?"

"Cam," she sighed.

"That's not a no."

"No."

"Well, that's a no," I admitted.

"Yes, it is." She moved away from the couch, grabbing the door. "Thanks for the eggs."

I backed away, undaunted. "How about Wednesday night?"

"Good-bye, Cam."

Shortcake closed the door, but not before I saw her smile, and I knew it wouldn't be too much longer before she said yes.

Eight

Apparently I had seriously misjudged how long "much longer" really was.

Days had turned into weeks as summer finally slipped into the past and the leaves on all the oaks turned gold and red. The skies had started to grow darker each day a minute earlier, and the clouds that rolled in and the wind that came off the Potomac warned that winter was right around the corner.

I asked Avery out at least twice a week. Each time, she said no and each time, I became even more determined. At some point in the middle of astronomy, as she hastily took notes, and I sketched the Winchesters' Chevy Impala, I recognized that the whole challenge aspect of this *chase* was no longer really in the equation.

Glancing over at her as she watched Drage float from one side of the raised platform to the other in his acid-wash jeans, a fond smile split my lips.

The more time I spent around Avery, the more I wanted to be around her, and all we ever did was talk. Hanging out with a chick, just chilling without any physical fun, was uncharted territory for me. While I'd be down for more, lots more, I was *content* just being with her. And that was so new to me.

Each Sunday I showed up at her apartment with eggs and a different type of baked goods, learning pretty quickly that anything chocolate was a win with her. The second time I went over, she was as happy to see me as she had been the first time, but she quickly dropped the act. And it was an act, because the way her brown eyes warmed when she saw me told me what she wasn't willing to say vocally.

She was always wary, every single time we were together, but after a little while, she would begin to relax and that was when the real Avery poked her head out.

Professor Drage paused in his lecture and Shortcake stopped, twisting her right hand at the wrist like she was trying to work a kink out of it.

Dropping my pen in my lap, I didn't think about what I was doing. When it came to Shortcake, I rarely did think. Maybe that was a problem.

Shortcake gasped as I snatched the pen from between her fingers and placed it on her notebook. Her head swung sharply toward me, brows raised. "What are you doing?" she asked in a low voice.

"Nothing," I murmured, shifting toward her.

Avery's chest rose as I curved my hands around her right one. "You're doing something."

"Shh." I pressed my thumbs into her hand, gently running them up the side, over her pinky finger and between.

Her eyes widened as they darted from our hands to my face. "What . . . what are you doing?"

"What does it look like?" I whispered, moving my thumbs to her ring finger and then the middle, following the path of delicate bones. "Your hand looked like it was cramped. I'm doing my good deed of the day."

"But—"

"Shush it." My finger slipped into the fleshy part between her pointer and thumb, and Avery gasped. "You're going to get us in trouble."

A pink stain bled across her cheeks. "You're the one touching me."

"And you're the one making noise."

She snapped her mouth shut as I turned her hand over, working her palm. She took a deep breath and then eased back in the seat, her arm and body not so rigid. I watched her from under my lashes and when she sucked her bottom lip between her teeth, the action sent a jolt straight through me. My cock jumped, and I suddenly realized what I was doing wasn't a very good idea. Nothing more awkward than having a hard-on during class.

But her skin warmed under mine, smooth and soft as satin, and David Beckham could kick a soccer ball off the side of my head, and I wouldn't be able to stop.

My hands wandered up to her wrist, slipping under the sleeve of her light sweater. Her skin was even softer there, the thin blue vein forming a delicate line I wanted to trace with my lips and then my tongue.

God, I wanted to taste her skin. My jeans felt like they had shrunk about three sizes in the crotch. There was no mistaking that I was attracted to her, but sometimes, like right now, it was almost painful. I wondered if I could kiss her—if anyone would notice if I brought her hand to my lips? We were far enough in the back that Drage would have no clue what we were doing, even if I did kiss her . . . or slipped a hand between those pretty thighs.

But something . . . that fucking prickling sensation along the nape of my neck held me back. Having no idea where I developed this level of self-control, I made myself put her hand down and lean back before I did anything stupid. And right now, I was capable of a whole lot of stupid. Several seconds passed as I forced my breathing to slow and before I could look at her.

Shortcake was staring at me, her eyes a wealth of secrets. Our gazes locked and something infinite passed between us, a spark I swore I could almost see with my eyes.

God, I sounded like a vagina.

"Thank you," she said, a bit breathlessly as she picked up her pen.

Sliding down in my seat, I spread my thighs, hoping to ease the ache, but I imagined I'd be walking over to the Butcher Center with a major hard-on. "Avery?" I whispered.

"Cam?" she responded back, equally low.

"Go out with me."

Her throat worked on a swallow and her lips twitched into a small smile. "No."

Tipping my head against the back of the seat, I grinned.

On Wednesday, I was supposed to be in Principles of Sports Nutrition, along with Ollie and Jase, but I didn't feel like walking my ass all the way over to the Butcher Center. If I drove, I'd lose my parking spot and that would be a real bitch.

And I was outside of the Den, which coincidentally was around the time Avery ate lunch with her friends. Not that my presence had anything to do with Shortcake.

Oh, who the fuck was I kidding? I knew exactly why my lily-white ass was standing out in front of the Den. I started up the stairs when the doors to the bookstore opened.

"Cam!"

I started at the shrill cry, turning to see Susan and Sally. Or were they Molly and Mary? I had no idea. The two looked identical to me. One had platinum-blonde hair, the other light brown with platinum streaks. Both were tan. Both had rocking tight bodies, and I think I might have made out with one of them at some point.

Or both.

"Hey," I said, smiling. "What are you two up to?"

"Nothing," replied the *über*blonde. She bounced up the stairs, closely followed by her friend. It was then when I realized she *was* Susan, which meant the other had to be Sally. "I haven't seen you in forever."

"Like for-ever," Sally reiterated. "You haven't been at any of the parties recently."

That much was true. It had been weeks, if not months, since I'd attended any of the parties being thrown at the frats. I started back up the stairs. "I've been busy."

Susan pouted as she flicked her hair over her shoulder. "That's no fun. Everyone misses you."

I wondered who everyone was as I crossed the balcony and opened the blue-and-gold double doors, heading into the Den. "Have I been missing a lot of fun?"

"A lot." Susan somehow ended up in front of me, and we were stopped in front of the couches crowding the TV. She placed her hand on my chest as my gaze moved beyond her, flickering over the rows of tables. "I'm sure we could get you caught up, Sally and I."

"Is that so?" The top of a coppery head came into view, and I recognized the dark-skinned boy sitting across from her. The girls said something else, but I wasn't paying attention. Stepping back, I smiled at the girls. "Look, I've got to run. See you guys later."

I didn't wait for a response, slipping away and cutting in front of a group of people heading out into the autumn sun. A wide smile broke out across Jacob's face as he spotted me. He said something to Shortcake, and her shoulders tensed. I wasn't surprised. I expected this. Every time we got together, we had to start over. Even I was amazed by my patience when it came to her.

"Hey, Cameron!" Jacob said, awfully cheerful. "How's it going?"

"Hey, Jacob. Brittany." I took the seat next to Shortcake and nudged her arm. "Avery."

She murmured hello and then asked, "What are you up to?"

"Oh, you know, mischief and mayhem."

"That so reminds me of Harry Potter," Brit said, smiling faintly. "I need a reread."

All eyes turned on her.

Red bloomed across her cheeks as she ran her hand through her hair. I didn't know Brittany very well, but knew she had gone to my high school and seemed pretty cool. "What?" she said. "I'm not ashamed to admit that random things remind me of Harry Potter."

"That guy over there reminds me of Snape." I tipped my chin at the table behind us. "So I understand."

A thankful smile crossed Brittany's face.

"Anyway, what are you guys doing?" I shifted so that my leg pressed against Shortcake's. "Playing with M&M's and Skittles?"

"Yes, that and we're studying for our history midterm next week. We have to map out Europe," Jacob explained.

"Ouch." I knocked my leg into hers.

She returned the favor.

"But Avery, wonderful, Avery . . ." Jacob's grin spread as Shortcake's glare increased. "She's been helping us study."

"That she has." Brittany exchanged a look with Jacob, and my interest peaked.

Jacob leaned forward, resting his chin in his hand. "Before we started studying, I was telling Avery that she should wear the color green more often. It makes her sexy with that hair of hers."

"Do you like the color green on her, Cam?" Brit asked.

I hadn't noticed what she was wearing, but I turned to

her, my gaze slipping over the green sweater. "The color looks great on her, but she looks beautiful every day."

Shortcake flushed as she exhaled.

"Beautiful?" Brit sighed.

"Beautiful," I repeated, nudging her knee again. "So did you guys learn anything from studying?"

Shortcake said, "I think we got it."

"Because of you." Jacob shared another look with Brittany. "Avery came up with this song to help me remember where the countries were."

"Sing him your song." Brittany elbowed her, causing her to bounce into me.

"What song?" I asked.

She shook her head. "I am not singing that song again."

Jacob smiled. "It's the Croatia song."

The look on Avery's face could kill.

I laughed. "The Croatia song? What?"

"No," she said. "I am not singing again. That is so not my talent."

"What kind of talents do you have?" I asked, and she looked at me, her eyes impossibly large. "Avery?"

"Do tell," Jacob coaxed.

Brit jumped. "Talents are fun."

"They can be." I was thinking about all the talents I had that I was more than willing to share with her as I bent my head. There was only a mere inch or two between our mouths, and her soft sigh trilled through my blood. "Tell me what your talents are, sweetheart."

"Sweetheart," Jacob murmured, sighing.

"Dancing," she said. "I danced. I *used* to dance."

Curiosity poured into me. What were the chances? "What kind of dancing?"

"I don't know." She grabbed the package of Skittles, dumping them into her palm. "Ballet, jazz, tap, contemporary—that kind of stuff."

"No shit?" Jacob's brows shot up. "I did tap when I was like six, for about a month, and then decided I wanted to be a fireman or something like that. That shit was hard."

Brit snickered. "I tried dance and discovered I had no coordination or grace beyond shaking my ass. Were you any good at it?"

Shortcake shrugged, her gaze fastened to the pieces of candy. "I took classes for about ten years, did some competitions and a lot of recitals."

"Then you were good!" Brit exclaimed. "I bet you did all those crazy turns and tricks."

I couldn't believe it as I stared at her. She was a dancer. I never would've thought it, because all the dancers I knew were overflowing with confidence, but it explained the lean muscle I had spied in her legs, the kind of tone that never really went away.

"My sister did dance since she was around five," I told her, somewhat amazed. "Still does. I think she'd cut someone if they made her stop."

She finished off the Skittles, nodding. "Dancing can be addictive if you like it."

"Or are good at it," Brit interjected.

I bumped her shoulder with mine, drawing her attention.

For her to be dancing for that many years, I was surprised that she talked about it in the past tense. "Why'd you stop?"

A far-off look appeared in her stare, and I knew that where she was at that moment, it wasn't in the present. I'd seen that look creep over her a lot and I always wondered where she went in those moments.

Finally, she shrugged again as she went for the M&M's. "I guess I got tired of it. Does your sister do competitions?"

I didn't believe her. Not one bit. Dancing was in the blood, but I didn't press it. Not right now. "She's traveled all over and spent the summer at the Joffrey Ballet School on a scholarship."

"Holy shit!" Her mouth dropped. "She must be damn good."

Full of pride, I smiled. "She is."

Avery smiled up at me, but as the minutes ticked by, that smile faded as her gaze drifted to the empty pack of candy. She really didn't say anything after that, no matter how hard her friends and I tried to lull her into conversation. Something was up with her and I knew it had to do with where she went when she got quiet.

When she got up to leave, I said good-bye and followed her out into the cool breeze and bright sun. I was quiet as we headed up the hill, unsure of how to approach her. Although there was a lot I had discovered about Avery, there was still so much I didn't know. She kept her past and her thoughts close to her.

Someone yelled my name over by the Byrd Center, and I waved absently as we crossed the street.

We stopped by the empty benches in front of Knutti, and I took a deep breath. "Are you okay?"

Tipping her chin up, she squinted. "Yeah, I'm fine. Are you?"

Not feeling the smile on my face, I nodded. "We still on for tomorrow night?"

"Tomorrow night? Oh! The astronomy assignment. Yeah, it works for me."

"Good." I backed away, knowing I needed to get my ass to class. "See you then."

Shortcake turned and then pivoted back to me. "Cam?"

The knot pulsed in my chest. "Yeah?"

She fiddled with her bracelet as her gaze flicked away before settling back on me. "What were you doing in the Den? Don't you normally have class, like right now?"

I smiled as I held her gaze. "Yeah, I normally have class right now, but I wanted to see you."

Shock splashed over her face, and then I saw the smile light up her eyes before it even hit her lips. Feeling that knot do a funny, twisting thing, I pivoted around before I grabbed her and kissed her.

Because I was really close to doing that.

I made it across the street before a low whistle caught my attention. Looking toward the left, I saw Jase standing under a tree, cell phone in hand. Damn. He must've high-tailed his ass from West Campus.

"Skipping class without me?" he asked as I made my way over to him, his eyes obscured by the aviator shades he was wearing. Very few people could pull off those sunglasses without looking like a douche. I was not one of them.

I shrugged as my attention drifted beyond Jase's shoulder, across the street, catching one last glimpse of Shortcake disappearing through the doors of Knutti Hall.

Jase sighed. "You're obsessed."

"Huh?"

He nodded toward Knutti. "I don't think you've ever skipped a class to hang out with a girl before."

I frowned. "How do you know I skipped a class to hang out with Avery?"

His brows rose above the sunglasses. "I'm not stupid."

"That's up for debate."

Jase flipped me off. "Well, let's see. Class let out early, so I came over here just in time to see you walking along like a good little boy. I called your name. You *waved* at me and kept going—or staring at her."

My brows lifted as I wheeled around, heading for the doors. "That was you yelling my name?"

"Exactly," he said, sighing. He looked at me, and all I saw was my face in his sunglasses. "Has she agreed to go out with you yet?"

"Nope."

Jase shook his head. "Man, you are so fucked when it comes to this girl."

Nine

"Apple pie for you." I handed the small treat over to Avery and then dug the other one out of the McDonald's bag. "And apple pie for me."

Shortcake peeled open the box. "Do you think they use real apples?"

"God, I don't really want to know." I bit into the crust, groaning at the sweetness. "Ah, this shit is so good."

Her eyes settled on me. "I swear. Every time you eat something, you sound like you're about to have an orgasm." She flushed as she said that. "Or whatever."

"Well, now you know what I sound like when I come."

She wrinkled her nose as she picked a section of the crust off. "That is something I've been dying to know."

"Knew it."

Shortcake laughed and then popped the crust in her mouth. "You are terrible."

"I'm perfect." I fixed my gaze out the windshield. We

were sitting in the parking lot behind the science building. The dark blue of the sky was quickly turning to night, but the thick clouds rolling in looked ominous. "We should've probably picked a different night to do this."

She picked up the bag and scraped off all the sliced apples into it, leaving the bottom crust cleared.

"That's such a waste."

Her eyes were warm as she cast me a side look. "You want to dig them out of the bag and eat them? You sound like you have a couple more good groans left in you."

"Sweetheart, you haven't heard anything . . ." I paused, winking at her. "Yet."

She rolled her eyes. "More like never."

"Does the lady protest too much, methinks?"

"You dork." Shortcake laughed, and the sound was light. "It's 'the lady doth protest too much, methinks.' "

I reached over, brushing the thick strands of hair back from her shoulder. She didn't flinch away, which was huge progress. "The fact that you can correct that is further proof."

Another laugh bubbled up from her as she wiped her fingers cleaned. "Whatever. You ready?"

"Been ready, but you had to stop and get an apple pie."

"What?" She flipped in the seat toward me. "That was your idea."

I blinked innocently. "That is not how I recollect the past twenty minutes."

She pinned me with a dry look.

"You were all like 'I need an apple pie' and what could I do? I live to serve you."

Rolling up the bag, she tossed it at me, but I caught it. "Actually, it was you saying something like 'I need food in my belly.' "

I laughed. "That is not how I recall this little adventure."

She smacked my arm and as she pulled back, I caught her hand. Her lips parted as I lifted her hand, pressing a quick, completely 100-percent chaste kiss on the center of her palm. "Ready?"

Eyes wide, she pulled her hand back to her chest and nodded. As we climbed out of the truck and headed into the building, she was flushed. The pretty pink made me want to chase it with my lips, but then she slipped in front of me.

Not that I was complaining.

I watched the sweet sway of Avery's ass as she climbed the stairwell in front of me and by the time we reached the rooftop and were standing in front of the Philips telescope, I was throbbing between my legs.

This was getting ridiculous.

It had been *months* since I'd gotten off with anything except my hand, and I knew Jase would tell me to go screw someone else to just get off, but I couldn't even think of anyone else besides Avery.

Jase had been right yesterday.

I was so fucked when it came to her, and not in the way I wanted to be.

"Are you sure you know how to use this thing?" she asked, head tilted to the side.

Moving in front of her, I shot her a look. "What? You don't?"

"Nope."

"Weren't you paying attention in class when Drage went over this and the imaging cameras?"

She popped a hip out as she folded her arms. "You were drawing the cast of Duck Dynasty when he was going over that."

I laughed, pleased because that was exactly what I had been doing when Drage went over how to operate the telescope. Which meant Shortcake was paying a hell of a lot of attention to me. I adjusted the controls. "I was listening."

"Uh-huh." She shifted closer as the wind picked up, whirling across the roof, picking up strands of her hair and whipping it back from her face. Christ, she looked beautiful standing there. I shook my head, focusing on the telescope again, but it was hard—I was hard.

"You're actually a pretty good artist," she said.

"I know."

She made a sound that wasn't exactly friendly.

I shifted the lever. "I've used a telescope a time or two in my life."

"That's random."

"Okay. I used it when I had the class previously." I flashed her a quick grin, then checked the positioning of the scope. "Man, I don't know if we're going to be able to get anything before those clouds roll in."

"Well, you better hurry then."

"Bossy."

Shortcake grinned.

"Come over here and I'll show you how to use this." Giving her just enough space to get in, I bit the inside of my cheek as her hip brushed mine, coming fucking close to where I literally *ached*. "Are you going to pay attention?"

"Not really." She was still smiling.

"At least you're honest." I was into self-torture. That was the only excuse to why I leaned in, caging her with my arms. Her scent, that heavenly mixture of berries and musk, caused a lot of my body parts to twitch. I vaguely realized that she hadn't stiffened. That was good.

"This is a Philips ToUcam Pro II." I cleared my throat. "It hooks to the telescope. At these settings, you should be able to get a clear image of Saturn. Press this and it will capture an image."

"Okay." She tucked the sides of her hair back behind her ears. "I don't think we're supposed to be getting an image of Saturn."

"Huh." What the fuck was Saturn? All I could think about was how close we were, how I could feel the warmth rolling off her body. I didn't even know why were on the roof. "Hey."

She tipped her head back, causing the edges of her hair to glide over my cheek. My pulse pounded as I imagined that hair sliding over other parts of my body. "Hey what?"

"Go out with me."

"Shut up." A grin appeared as she leaned forward, peering into the telescope. Her body brushed mine again, and I bit back a groan. "I don't see anything."

My laugh sounded strangled. "That's because I haven't taken the lens cap off."

She elbowed me in the stomach, which made me laugh again. "Asshole."

I was pushing the boundaries tonight. Didn't even know why, but I couldn't stop myself as I reached for the lens, pressing against her back. She stilled then, and her soft inhale rattled through me. I waited for her to move away, because she could if she wanted to, but she didn't.

I glanced down at her and saw that her thick lashes fanned her cheeks. "What?"

"It would've been easier for you to just go to the side and do that," she said, her voice different, heavier.

"True." I bent so that my mouth was beside her ear. "But what fun would that be?"

Avery shivered, and my entire body tensed. "Go have fun by yourself."

She had no idea how often that was the case. "Well, that's really no fun." I paused, not moving. "Try it again."

Hesitating for a moment, she then leaned forward, pressing her eye to the telescope. A couple of seconds passed. "Wow."

"You see it?"

She straightened. "Yeah, that's pretty cool. I've never really seen a planet in real life. I mean, like taken the time to do so. It's pretty cool."

"I think so, too." I snatched a few strands of her hair, stopping them from hitting me in the eye. "What are we supposed to be looking at?"

"Sagittarius and then the Teapot asterism and its steam, whatever—"A nasty, cold raindrop splattered off her forehead and she jerked back against my chest. "Oh crap."

Shortcake squeaked as another drop came down and she whirled, her eyes meeting mine. We were about to get soaked to the bone. Swearing under my breath, I grabbed her hand, pulling her across the roof. We were almost to dry land when the sky ripped open and freezing rain drenched us.

"Oh my God," she shrieked. "It's so freaking cold!"

Laughing, I stopped and spun around, hauling her against my chest. There was a brief second when her wide eyes met mine as rain poured down on us. My smile was my only warning.

I wrapped an arm around her slim waist as I dipped, lifting her off her feet and tossing her over my shoulder. Her surprised squeal caused me to laugh, and this balloon-like pressure—it was the only way I could explain it—expanded in my chest and it felt good, like scoring a goal.

"You were running too slow!"

Her fingers dug into the back of my sweater. "Put me down, you son of a—"

"Hold on!" I clamped my arm over her hips and took off.

Slipping in the deep puddles, we almost ate cement as I slid across the roof. The words that were coming out of her mouth, directed at me, would've burned the ears off of soldiers.

I skidded to a stop and yanked open the door, bending down as we escaped the rain. Turning so she wasn't facing the wall, I grabbed her hips and lowered her down.

Sharp need punched right through me as her body slid down my front. My hands tightened on her hips and she tipped her head back. Her eyes darkened to a deep chocolate brown, and my brain clicked off as I somehow tugged her closer. I knew she had to feel my arousal, and considering we hadn't even kissed, something about that seemed wrong, but I couldn't let her go.

Her hands pressed against my chest, and I thought she was going to push me away, and swore to God right then and there, no matter how hard it would be, I would let her go if she did.

But she didn't.

Avery's hands flattened against my chest, above my pounding heart, and she had to have felt it.

My hand moved on its own accord, curving up her waist and then over her arm, to her throat and then her cheek. She gasped when my fingertips grazed her cheeks, catching the hair stuck to her temples. I tucked the strands back behind her ears, my hand lingering.

"You're soaked."

"So are you."

I smoothed my thumb over the slant of her cheek. "I guess we're going to have to try this another night."

"Yeah," she whispered as her eyes flickered shut and then swept back open.

"Maybe we should've checked the weather first." When she smiled, I shifted my hips in response. Her body shuddered in such a mind-blowing way and her lashes lowered. Her lips parted even further, and I didn't want to let her go. She felt too good this close.

Her chest rose in short, deep breaths as I lowered my head, wanting and needing to kiss her. Just once. That's all I wanted. My eyes started to drift closed.

Avery suddenly jerked back, pressing a hand between her breasts. "I think we . . . we should call it a night."

For a moment I couldn't move and then leaned back, tipping my head against the wall. It took a couple of moments before I could speak. "Yeah, we should."

The trip out of the building and back to the apartment wasn't easy. I was still strung tight as a bow. Nothing seemed to make the raw edge go away. I tried reciting the alphabet backwards, tried thinking about the old lady who lived in the building nearby, who sometimes walked her dog in a white nightgown. The sight was not pretty, but it still didn't work.

The rain was still coming down as we dashed across the parking lot and under the awning. I shook my head, spraying water everywhere. Avery stopped at the base of the stairwell leading up to our apartments, and I thought it was all the rain I'd just pelted her with. I opened my mouth to apologize, but she turned sideways, her face pale as she peered up at me.

A very different kind of ache sliced through my chest, stirring up that knot in there, at the stark confusion and fear in her eyes. Fear. I didn't get it. Had I done that to her? No. I couldn't believe that. Not the way she had reacted to me. I saw it in her eyes. She had wanted me to kiss her, probably even as badly as I wanted to kiss her, but she had pulled away because . . . I honestly didn't know.

I thrust my hand through my hair, pulling it off my forehead. "Go out with me."

"No," she whispered.

I grinned slightly, and her chest fell, her shoulders relaxed, as if she needed to hear this. "There's always tomorrow."

She followed me up the stairs. "Tomorrow's not going to change anything."

"We'll see."

"There's nothing to see. You're wasting your time."

"When it concerns you, it's never a waste of my time."

And that was the damn truth.

Ten

The Wednesday before fall break, I skipped nutrition again and searched Avery out, finding her where she always was during this class: in the Den with Brittany and Jacob. It was a good thing that I had. I discovered three important things.

Shortcake was talking about me to her friends, because they knew that I had been asking her out. Score for that.

And she also compared me to a serial killer.

Not that I was offended, but it wasn't every day that one found himself mentioned in the same sentence as Ted Bundy.

But her friends totally supported a date. I liked them.

"Anyway," Brittany was saying, her eyes glimmering with amusement as she stared at a blood-red, absolutely mortified Avery. "This is not about me and my vast knowledge of serial killers. I can wow you later about that. This is about you, Avery. This fine young gentleman, who is not a serial killer, is asking you out. You're single. You're young. You should say yes."

"Oh my God." She moaned, planting her hands against her face. "Is it time for all of you to go home yet?"

I laughed deeply. "Go out with me, Avery."

She turned to me, somewhat surprised-looking. "No."

"See?" I addressed Brittany and Jacob. "Keeps turning me down."

Jacob looked dumbfounded. "You're an idiot, Avery."

"Whatever." She stood, grabbing her bag. "I'm going to class."

"We love you!" Jacob shouted.

She muttered, "Uh-huh," but stopped to say good-bye. Fall break kicked off tomorrow and they were going home. I was still surprised that Avery was remaining behind. Traveling to Texas was a hell of trip for four days, but she could've gone home with one of them. Admittedly, I didn't like the idea of her being alone here.

I waited until she was done and then followed her across the Den. She arched a brow at me. "Following me?"

"Like a true serial killer," I replied.

"You know we weren't being serious, right? And I'm sorry about saying something to them about it. They just started pestering me about you and the next thing I know—"

"It's okay." I dropped my arm over her shoulders, steering her toward the cluster of trees outside of the building. It was chilly and she hunkered down, pressing closer, whether she realized it or not. "I don't care."

"You don't care?"

I shook my head. Maybe it should bother me that there was now an audience to my repeated rejection, but it just didn't. I glanced down at her and smiled. Her attention was focused on one of the blue vans that were always on campus.

"Uh-oh," I murmured.

"What?" She looked up at me.

I lowered my arm, catching a strand of hair blowing across her face and tucking it behind her ear. Ever since the night on the roof of Byrd, I took every freaking opportunity to touch her and she let me. "You're thinking."

"I am."

"About?"

"Nothing important." She smiled absently. It wasn't a huge smile, but she *was* smiling more. "You going home this weekend?"

"I am." I moved closer, gathering up her hair and separating it into two long sections. I smiled, thinking she looked cute like that. "I'm leaving tomorrow morning, bright and early. I'm not coming back until Sunday night. So, no eggs for you this week."

"Boo." Her face fell a little.

"Don't cry too much about it." I brushed the ends of her hair across her cheek and tried again with her doing something this weekend instead of being alone. "Are you going to take Brit up on her offer and go home with her?"

She shook her head no. "I'm just going to hang out here and get some reading done."

"Nerd."

"Jerk."

I smiled as I spread her hair over her shoulders. "You know what?"

"What?"

Taking a deep breath, I stepped back and shoved my hands into the pockets of my jeans. "You should go out with me tonight since I'll be gone all weekend."

She laughed. "I'm not going out with you."

"Then hang out with me."

Her brow puckered. "How's that any different from going out with you?"

"How is me asking you to hang out with me tonight any different than us hanging out on Sunday?"

The knit between her brows started to fade. "What do you want to do?"

I shrugged casually, but my heart was pounding like a drum. "Order some food in and watch a movie."

She shifted her weight, wary. "That sounds like a date."

"That's not a date with me, sweetheart." I laughed. "I'd take you out, like out in public. This is just two friends hanging out, watching a movie and eating food."

Her lips formed a tight line as she looked away. Several moments passed, and I steeled myself for yet another rejection. For some reason, if she said no to this, it would sting worse than the others. I didn't know why, but if I couldn't get her to do this, I was really going to have to reevaluate what the hell I was doing.

Shortcake sighed. "Yeah, sure. Come over."

Holy shit? She said yes? I had to force myself to play cool, because I was about to fist pump the sky or some shit. "Wow. Calm down before you get too excited."

"I am excited." She playfully shoved my shoulder. "When are you coming over?"

"How's seven?"

She smiled as she fiddled with her bracelet. "Works for me. See you then."

I let her get to the sidewalk before I stopped her. "Avery?"

"Yeah?" she replied, turning.

My lips curved up as a bolt of nervous energy rolled through me. "See you tonight."

"You're spending a lot of time with this girl."

"Whoa!" I stepped out of the shower, buck-ass naked, finding Ollie standing in the doorway of the bathroom. "What the hell, man?"

"What?" He shrugged. "Not like I haven't seen your junk before."

Shaking my head, I grabbed a towel and wrapped it around my hips. "What in the hell are you yapping about? And can it wait? Kind of have stuff to do." Namely dinner and movies to acquire.

Ollie followed me into my bedroom. "I was asking about Avery. You've been spending a lot of time with her."

I didn't respond as I pulled on a pair of jeans, buttoning them up and then dropping the towel.

"Free balling it tonight?" Ollie grinned as he smacked his hands on the upper frame of the door. "Planning on getting laid?"

I shot him a dark look as I turned and grabbed a shirt. "Don't you have anything better to do?"

He leaned forward, stretching out his arms. His hair fell forward, shielding most of his face. "Nope. Not at this moment."

"Great." I pulled the shirt on.

"Steve's having a party tonight. You going?"

"No."

"Of course not."

I arched a brow as I brushed him out the way, heading into the living room to find my sneakers. "If you're not surprised, why did you ask?"

Ollie shrugged. "You used to go to all the parties."

Sighing, I pulled my shoes on and straightened. That part was true. So was the fact that my face had been absent from all of them since late August. "I'll go to the Halloween one. I won't miss that."

"Uh-huh." Ollie plopped down on the couch.

I looked at him a moment, then shook my head as I grabbed some movies off the rack. Sometimes I wondered if Ollie even knew what he was talking about or doing.

"Cam?"

"Yeah?"

He tipped his head back and grinned. "I think it's pretty cool that you're spending time with Avery. I like her. She's nice."

"Thank you." The moment those words came out of my mouth, I had no idea why I said them. My cheeks heated when Ollie laughed. "Fuck you."

Ollie's laughter followed me out to the hall and down to my truck. Thank you? That didn't even make any sense. What the hell was I thanking him for? But as I headed down to the nearby Chinese restaurant and ordered Avery's favorite—shrimp stir-fry—I realized I felt thankful. Strangest damn thing, because all Shortcake had done was say yes to hanging out, but I knew she didn't allow people to get very close to her. This . . . this was a big step she was taking.

Avery was such a mystery to me; a paradox of innocence and allure—a mystery I was determined to solve.

Eleven

"Let's go with *Resident Evil*," Avery said as she stood in front of the counter, doling out the shrimp stir-fry. Her hair hung in loose waves all the way to the middle of her back. She was dressed low-key, in a pair of tight workout pants and a loose-fitting shirt that slipped over one shoulder, revealing a swath of smooth, golden skin and a thin strap.

The girl had no idea how good she looked like that and I resisted the urge to move closer to her. When I'd walked up on her in the kitchen earlier, she had reacted strangely, stiffening *and* paling.

"A girl after my own heart," I replied, picking up two DVDs and taking them into the living room. "Zombies for the win."

A sudden soft glow alerted me to her presence. "What do you want to drink?" she asked.

I glanced over my shoulder. "Do you have milk?"

Her nose wrinkled. "You want that with Chinese food?"

"Need my calcium."

She made a face and disappeared into the kitchen, returning with a glass of milk and a can of soda. "That's kind of gross, you know?" She sat, tucking her legs under her. "Weird combination."

"Have you ever tried it?" I sat, staring at the remote.

"No."

"Then how do you know it's gross?"

"I'll go with my assumption that it is." She picked up her plate, sending me a cheeky grin.

"Before the end of the year, I will have you trying milk and Chinese."

The look on her face said over her dead body, and I grinned. As *Resident Evil* kicked off, we dug into our dinner and spent more time discussing how women in a zombie apocalypse managed to look so attractive. As Alice faced down zombie Dobermans, I gathered up our plates and took them into the kitchen. While I was there, I grabbed another glass of milk and a can of root beer for her.

"Thank you," she said, smiling as I placed the soda on the coffee table.

I sat down closer to her. "I live to service you."

Shortcake grinned and we continued to poke at the movie and its sequel. At one point, her cell phone went off. My gaze flicked to the screen on the iPhone and saw UNKNOWN CALLER flash.

"Not going to answer?" I asked.

She quickly leaned forward, snatching the phone and turning off the ringer. Seemed a little strange, how stiff she was when she did it. "I think it's rude to answer the phone when you have company."

All we were doing was being overly critical about the movies. "I don't mind."

Shortcake sat back, nibbling on her thumbnail as she turned her attention to the TV. Come to think of it, I couldn't recall a time when I saw her on her phone—not before class or around the campus. Most girls had their phones glued to their hands or the side of their face. She said she wasn't popular in school and it was obvious she wasn't that close to her family, but . . .

Well, something was off about it all, but I didn't know what.

Minutes went by and she was still chewing away on her fingernail, something I hadn't see her do before now. I reached over, wrapping my fingers around her wrist.

Her chin jerked up and her gaze landed on my hand. "What?"

"You've been biting your nail for the last ten minutes." I lowered her arm to her thigh, but kept my hand around her wrist. The tips of my fingers touched. That was how small her wrist was. "What's up?"

"Nothing." She inhaled sharply. "I'm watching the movie."

"I don't think you're really seeing the movie." Our gazes met. "What's going on?"

She pulled her hand free, and I let go. Reluctantly. "Nothing is going on. Watch the movie."

"Uh-huh." I dropped the subject, knowing that pushing

Shortcake got me absolutely nowhere.

She grew quiet, and I checked out the time on the digital box below the DVD player. It was well after ten, and I expected her to kick my ass out any minute now, but when I shifted on the couch, throwing my right arm along the back, the entire left side of her body ended up against mine.

I froze and I believed my heart literally stopped as I waited for her to squirm away, keeping the mandatory two feet of personal space between us.

But she didn't.

Holy shit, she *didn't*.

I glanced down at the top of her head, forcing my breathing to remain steady. Over the next half hour, every cell in my body became aware of her weight, her warmth and her deep, even breaths.

My heart skipped a beat when her head came down on the spot just below my shoulder. Was she asleep? "Avery?"

When there was no answer, I determined that she had, in fact, fallen asleep on me. There was a swelling in my chest, bigger and tighter than the knot that seemed to form whenever I was around her. And the strangest damn thing happened as I stared down at her. Parts of my body hardened at her closeness, but my insides softened like butter left out in the sun.

You're so fucked when it comes to that girl.

Those words kept coming back to me, time and time again. Maybe I was fucked, but I wouldn't trade this moment for anything. Carefully, so that I didn't wake her, I brought my arm off the back of the couch and gently guided her down so that her head rested on my thigh.

And something not too far north enlarged. Perhaps that wasn't the smartest idea, because it was too tempting to have her this close, but this . . . well, it felt right in a way that it had never felt with any other girl.

My chest lurched as Shortcake snuggled in, folding her hands together under her chin. I watched her for a moment, soaking up the smooth line of her jaw, the curve of her cheek and those rosy lips.

Damn, I was fucked in all the right ways.

I tried to pay attention to the movie, but I hadn't even realized when it ended and the regular channel kicked back in. My eyes were on Avery once more. I wasn't even sure my attention had ever left her.

I thought it was cool in the room, so I pulled the brown and green patchwork quilt over the back of the couch and draped it over her body. The bare expanse of her shoulder snagged my attention. Her shirt had slipped down her right arm and there was nothing but that little strap.

The soft glow of her skin lured me in and I was absolutely powerless to resist it. Lowering my hand, my breath caught as I touched the elegant curve of her shoulder.

Avery murmured in her sleep and wiggled a bit, but she didn't wake up. It probably wasn't cool to keep touching her, but I dragged my fingertips down her arm, relishing in the feel of her. Stopping at the hem of her shirt, my fingers grazed her silky skin all the way up to her cheek.

I was glad she was asleep, because the thought of her knowing how badly my hands shook would probably have been embarrassing as hell. Boy, they were trembling too, like I'd never touched a girl before.

Avery . . . hell, she completely undid me.

Tipping my head back against the couch, I closed my eyes and swallowed hard as I rested my hand on the flare of her hip. I could probably count on two fingers how many times I spent the evening with a beautiful girl curled up against me and asleep, when I was just content to be there with her. Part of my brain was telling me there was a word for this, as crazy as that word sounded and felt, so I ignored that part.

"No," she murmured, and my eyes flew open. Her brow wrinkled, but she seemed to be asleep. "That's not why I'm here . . ."

I cocked my head to the side, straining to hear what else she said, but the only other word I could pick up was "sorry" before she settled back down.

My heart pounded as I turned those words over. They didn't make any sense and probably didn't mean anything, but a ball of unease formed in my gut.

Time passed, and I didn't sleep, not really. I was stuck in the weird in-between phase, half awake, half not there. But I knew the moment she woke up. Her body stiffened and she dragged in a deep breath. Several moments passed and she didn't move or speak. I would've cut off my thumb to know what she was thinking.

Shortcake slowly rolled onto her back, surprising me and leaving no time to react. My hand slipped from her hip and landed on her lower belly, fingers reaching the top of her pants. God knows I should've pulled my hand away, but I didn't.

My hand had a mind of its own and did something entirely on its own. My thumb moved in slow, idle circles just below her navel. I watched her under my lashes, nearly groaning when she sucked in her lower lip. Then my gaze flicked up and I could see the hardened tips of her breasts, pushing through the thin material. I was hard again. No surprise there.

I turned my head to the side, my lips tipping up on the corners as she drew in a deep breath. I clenched my jaw as she tipped her head back against my thigh, coming close to my erection.

"Cam."

I opened an eye. "Avery?"

"You're not asleep," she said, voice husky and unbelievably sexy.

"You were." I turned my head side to side. "And I was asleep." Total lie, but I doubted she'd be cool with knowing I sat here almost the entire time and watched her.

She wetted her lips, and dammit if I didn't want to swoop down and catch the tip of that tongue. "I'm sorry I fell asleep on you."

"I'm not."

Her cheeks flushed. "What time is it?"

"After midnight," I said, staring at her moist lips.

"You didn't even look at the clock."

"I just know these kinds of things."

"Really?" she whispered.

"Yes."

"That's a remarkable talent." Her hand curled into a loose fist on her leg. "What time are you leaving in the morning?"

"Are you going to miss me?"

She made a face, but her eyes glimmered up at me. "That's not why I was asking. I was just curious."

"I told my parents I'd be home by lunch." Using my other hand, I scooped a few strands of hair off her face and then I rested my hand on the top of her head.

"So I probably have to leave between eight and nine."

"That's early."

"It is." When her eyes drifted shut, I wanted to kiss her. "But the drive is easy."

"And you're not coming back until Sunday night?"

"Correct." I took a deep breath. "Are you sure you're not going to miss me?"

She smiled, but with anxiety. "It'll be like a vacation for me."

I laughed. "That was entirely mean."

"Wasn't it?"

"But I know you're lying."

"You do?"

"Yep." I moved my hand, gently touching her cheek. Her eyes snapped open, and I smiled down at her. "You're going to miss me, but you're not going to admit it."

Shortcake was silent as I trailed my fingers from her jaw to her chin, coming close to her bottom lip. "I'll miss you."

"Really?"

"Yeah."

Her eyes drifted closed as she relaxed against me once more. I continued to trace a path from her cheek to her lip, haunted by what she had said in her sleep. "You talk in your sleep."

Her eyes opened, and I swear she paled. "I do?"

I nodded.

"Are you messing with me? Because I swear to God, if you're messing with me, I'm going to hurt you."

That unease was back, and I wasn't sure why. "I'm not messing with you, sweetheart."

She sat up, twisting on the couch, facing me. "What did I say?"

"Nothing really."

"For real?" Her expression was so earnest and so serious I wished I hadn't said anything.

I leaned forward, scrubbing my hands down my face. "You were just murmuring stuff. I couldn't really make out what you were saying." I looked at her. "It was kind of cute."

She held my gaze, seeming to take what I said as word and then glanced at the clock. "Holy crap, you suck at your special ability at knowing the time."

I shrugged. I knew it was well past three in the morning. "I guess I should be going home."

She opened her mouth, closed it, and then tried again. "Be careful when you drive."

Standing, I stretched my back. "I will." And before she could freak on me, I bent down and kissed her on the forehead. "Good night, Avery."

Her eyes were closed, hands balled together in front of her chest. When she spoke, it sounded like she was whispering a prayer. "Good night, Cam."

I made it to the door before she sprung up like a tight coil, hands gripping the back of the couch. "Cam?"

My heart beat wildly as I stopped. "Yeah?"

She took a deep breath and that heartfelt expression was back. "I had a really good time tonight."

I smiled and was amazed to see her lips do the same. "I know." I opened the door, stopping on my way out as I turned to her. She was still there, kneeling on the couch, watching me. "I'll see you Monday."

"Okay."

I didn't want to leave. "Bright and early."

The smile reached her eyes, lightening them. "All right."

And for the first time in forever, I didn't want to go home. I wanted to stay here. I had to force myself out the door.

Twelve

$\mathcal{J}$ase shocked me with a text before I got out of town, asking if he could tag along. Him going home with me wasn't so much of a surprise, but I had thought with the four-day break, he'd be at the farm.

He was waiting for me at the house he stayed at when he wasn't home—a frat-run party central not too far from campus. I'd spent many a night, none recently, passed out in one of the many rooms in the large three-story home.

Climbing in, Jase clapped his hands together, rubbing them. "God, it's getting fucking cold."

"True." I slipped the gears into drive and whipped around in a mean U-turn. "You're not spending time . . . ?"

He ran a hand through his hair, causing it to flop all over the place. "Got an extra hat?"

"Just the one on my head. Want it?"

"No." Slinking down in the seat, he sighed as he shook

his hair out. "They decided to head up to Pennsylvania to see some cousins or something.

I stole a glance at him as I hit the main route, heading for the interstate. "And you didn't want to go?"

"Nah."

There was definitely something else behind it, because there was no way that Jase would pass up spending that kind of time with Jack, but if I knew anything about Jase, he talked about shit when he was damn well ready to do so.

Halfway into the drive, Jase passed out and only woke when I hooked a right onto the narrow lane leading up to my parents' home. Sunlight sliced through the thick trees, casting patches of shimmery light on the road. When we were kids, my sister and I played a mean game of hide-and-go-seek in these woods.

I followed the driveway around the back of the house, parking the truck next to the detached garage I'd help Dad put in during my, uh, extended stay.

The house was silent and toasty warm as we entered through the back patio. There was a faint smell of pumpkin in the air, and I grinned. Mom must've been baking. It was still early afternoon though, and neither of my parents or my sister would be home for a while.

Jase and I devoured the freshly baked pumpkin pie over a beer. There was a pensive, brooding look to his face and when he disappeared upstairs to the guest bedroom he typically stayed in; I let him be and headed to my old bedroom.

Mom kept it the way it was when I lived here, except neater. The same bed was butted up against the wall, in the middle of the room. Trophies lined the wall shelving that Dad had built. The TV on the dresser and the desk I rarely used hadn't collected even a speck of dust.

I smiled as I shuffled toward the bed, kicking off my sneakers. There was a time, after the incident with Teresa's *ex*-boyfriend, when I had hated these four walls. I'd loathed this house and this town and this state and myself.

Crashing on the bed, I stretched out and closed my eyes. Things were . . . different now, better. The only problem with coming home, it was impossible to not think about what happened in the house almost three years ago or Thanksgiving morning when Teresa finally told us the truth. The kind of rage that had slipped over me was something I'd never experienced before, but had only read about.

Murderous rage. It really did exist and it really was like tasting blood in your mouth. And that anger hadn't faded in the hours after learning the truth nor had it really dissipated when I found that living punk ass and returned the favor with my fists. Afterward, that anger had warped into something unmanageable and it had eaten away at me like a cancer.

To this day I wished I had done something different that night, but there still wasn't an ounce of regret in my veins. The judge, the lawyers, the community service and the weekly meetings had done nothing to change that, but when I thought about Avery, I wished I did feel that way. I doubted that she would want to be around me if she knew the truth.

Mom gave the best hugs.

There was a sheen to her eyes and she stepped back, clasping my shoulders. Still dressed in her white lab coat, she had come straight home after surgery. "I see you found the pie I left you."

"I had help."

Her smile spread. "Jase is here?"

I nodded as I leaned against the counter. "He's upstairs sleeping."

She smoothed back a few strands of hair that had escaped her twist. "Well, I'm sure a certain someone will be thrilled to see that you've brought him along with you."

My brows lifted and then I groaned. "Please tell me she is not still infatuated with Jase."

Mom laughed softly as she shrugged off her oversized sweater, draping it along the back of her chair. "I think 'infatuated' would be the wrong word to use."

Rolling my eyes, I groaned. When I'd been on home confinement, Jase had spent almost every free moment up here, pulling my head out of my ass. And Teresa had spent *every* spare second spying on us and stalking Jase.

Mom drifted over to the coffeemaker, pulling out the empty pot. "Jase is a really nice boy. I think—"

"Do not even think about going there," I warned, folding my arms. Jase was a good guy—a good guy, with a shit ton of baggage and a long list of broken hearts, who wouldn't come within ten feet of my little sister. "Where's Dad?" I asked, deftly changing the subject.

"He's still at the office, but he'll be home shortly." She

filled the pot with water. "I was thinking we all could do dinner at Joe's. I think both you and Jase like that place, and as long as it serves red meat—"

"Dad will be happy." I smiled, pushing off the counter. "That works for me."

"Want a cup?"

"Sure." I came up behind her and wrapped my arms around her shoulders, squeezing her. "Have I told you lately that you're the best mom ever?"

She laughed as she patted my arms. "I'm the only mom you got, boy."

"Still," I replied. "Best mom."

I let go as she shook her head and was in the process of heading upstairs to wake up Jase's lazy ass when Teresa came in the front door.

"Cam!" She let out a high-pitched squeal when she saw me in the foyer and dropped her book bag. The pint-sized terror took one step and *launched* herself at me.

Laughing, I caught her before she knocked me down. "Well, hello to you."

"When did you get here?" she asked once I sat her down.

"This morning."

She smacked my arm. "You should've texted me! I would've skipped my afternoon classes and come home early."

"I heard that!" yelled Mom from the kitchen.

Teresa rolled her eyes, and I laughed. Somewhere in the last two years or so, she'd grown up from a gangly child into a stunning young woman. And every time I saw her, I wanted to pull a paper sack over her head. Everywhere she went, guys looked, and they *really* looked.

She had inherited the dark hair and blue eyes from Dad, but she had Mom's delicate features. Her beauty and small frame were really misleading, because she had also developed mom's snappy, quick wit. When she and Mom got going, no one was safe.

"I'm going to skip dance tonight," she said, tugging the tie from her hair. It seemed to have grown overnight, falling well past her shoulders.

"You don't have to do that," I told her. "I'll be here all weekend."

"Yeah, but I never get to see you!" She pouted, giving me the look that probably got her a lot of things. "You're too busy and too cool to hang out with your sister anymore."

"Exactly," I said, grinning.

She smacked my arm *hard*. "Jerk."

Facing the stairs, I saw Jase come down before Teresa did. He was as quiet as a freaking ninja and he came to a stop at the bottom, his hair damp and clothing unwrinkled. He hadn't made a sound, but Teresa stiffened in front of me. Her eyes, so like mine, widened a fraction of an inch.

My gaze narrowed on her.

Teresa whipped around with the elegance of a dancer, and I cringed when she shrieked, "Jase!"

The pensive look that had been on Jase's face from the moment I picked him up vanished like a bad nightmare. He came down on the landing a second before my sister threw herself at the guy, greeting him in the same way she'd done with me. His eyes were only on her, and while I completely trusted Jase, even he wasn't immune to her.

I also didn't like it when he wrapped his arms around her, keeping them both from tumbling backward.

"Cam didn't tell me you were here!" she cried, clinging to him like a little monkey. "You're staying here the whole weekend, too?"

Jase smiled down at the top of Teresa's head—the head that was currently plastered against his chest. "Yeah, I'm here until Cam heads back."

I knew in that exact moment, Teresa would be bowing out on dance not only tonight, but also the rest of the weekend. I sighed.

Teresa said something that only Jase could hear and his smile spread in a way that had me taking deep, even breaths. Then he looked up, his gaze meeting mine. He shot me a helpless look, and I rolled my eyes, strolling forward.

"Okay." I grabbed her arms, physically lifting her away from Jase. "I think you can let him go now. He probably wants to breathe at some point."

Jase laughed as Teresa shot me a look that promised death and dismemberment and yanked her arms free. I stepped back, just in case she was going to try to hit me again. My sister had muscles.

"I think Mom wants to see you in the kitchen," I said, pushing her in that general direction.

A frowned pulled the corners of her lips down. "What for?"

"Probably something to do with all the classes you're planning to skip," I teased.

"You're skipping classes?" Jase asked, crossing his arms. "You shouldn't be doing that, Tess. It's your senior year.

Tess? Two what the fucks just happened. When had that nickname occurred? I knew the two of them had grown close, but *dayum*. And that piece of advice coming from Jase of all people?

A faint pink flush stained her cheeks. "I don't do it often."

My brows shot up.

Jase winked at me.

Finally, Teresa left us and I snuck Jase off to the basement. Dad had created one hell of a man cave down there. Pool tables, a bar, air hockey and TV the size of a wall.

Picking up a pool cue, Jase arched an eyebrow at me. "Who pissed in your Cheerios?"

"Teresa has a crush on you," I said, knowing I sounded like I'd tasted something bad.

Jase chuckled as he glanced at me. "Is that so?"

I shot him a look as I grabbed a stick.

"What?" He laughed again. "Are you surprised? It's my stunning charm and good looks. It's hard to resist."

"Well, she better resist."

Jase watched me as I racked the balls. "Dude, as hot as your sister is—sorry." He raised his hands as I straightened. "As *beautiful* as your sister is, that's your *sister*. I wouldn't even dream about what you're worried about."

I smiled tightly. "Good to hear."

"Do you really think I would? She's a kid."

"She just turned eighteen, Jase. She's not a kid anymore." I scowled as that little ditty sunk in. My stomach roiled. "Damn, she's really not a kid."

"She's still your sister," Jase said, pointing the pool stick at me. "And that's never going to change."

Go out with me.

Grinning, I put the phone on the table and waited for Avery's response. Across from me, my dad studied his cards. There was more gray peppered in his hair, but his face was still absent of wrinkles.

"Anytime now, old man." I sat back in the chair. "I'm not getting any younger."

"Isn't that the truth?" Dad looked up at me, eyes narrowed. "You cannot rush perfection."

Jase chuckled under his breath. Beside him, Teresa's head hung forward. She hadn't been able to get out of dance practice since it was Saturday and that had been an all-day event. She would've crashed by now, like Mom, who'd dozed off in the living room, but I knew why she was still up.

I glanced over at Jase, and he arched a brow at me as he took a swig of beer.

My phone vibrated. *Asking me over text is no different from in person.*

The grin spread into a full smile as I texted her back. *Thought I'd give it a try. What r u doing now? I'm beating my dad at poker.*

As Dad threw two cards forward, she responded with a *Getting ready for bed.*

Wish I was there. And then I sent, *Wait r u naked?*

No!!! came the immediate response.

I could almost picture her, face blood red and eyes wide, and I grinned. Even miles away, I couldn't resist teasing her. Hell, I couldn't stop thinking about her. It seemed odd to have not seen her on Friday and facing a Sunday without eggs just didn't seem right. We exchanged a couple of more texts and then I tossed my phone aside before Dad had a shit fit and threw it out the window.

In the next round, Jase bowed out and then Teresa quickly disappeared and the poker game fell apart after that.

"How's school?" Dad asked once we were alone.

Nursing my beer, I leaned back in the chair. "It's going good. Got a really easy semester."

He nodded as he picked at the label on his bottle. "And the meetings? You're going?"

I sat my bottle down. "Dad, you'd be the first to know if I wasn't going. And I talked to Dr. Bale about this weekend. He was cool with it."

"Just want to make sure." He sat back, hooking his knee over his other leg. If anyone saw my dad now in his flannel shirt and ripped jeans, they wouldn't believe he was a successful lawyer. "What about soccer? You give any more thought about next year?"

"Dad . . . I won't be able to join the team at Shepherd my senior year." I ran my hand through my hair and then dropped my arm. "And I'll be twenty-two by then."

"What about afterwards?" he asked, not ready to let it go.

My gaze settled over his shoulder, landing on the fridge. Photos of me scoring goals and Teresa dancing covered almost the entire door. "I don't know, Dad."

"Can't fail unless you try," he said, drinking deep.

My brows knitted. "Isn't that you can't succeed if you don't try?"

"Does it matter?" He flashed a grin. "Cam, you're a damn good player. Soccer is, or at least, *was* a passion. We have videos to send to coaches. And you know the coach at Shepherd would help you take new ones."

"I know." I sighed, shaking my head slowly. "And I keep up my workouts and practice with the guys when I can, but . . . I don't know. Maybe next year, when I'm about to graduate . . ."

"Uh-huh." His gaze was shrewd. "Cameron . . . Cameron . . ."

Yakking on about soccer was hard for me. Wasn't like a future playing was completely out of the question. That was why I kept up the training, but there was nothing I could do about right now.

"Is there a young lady in your life now?" he asked.

Perhaps I should've let him ask about soccer. "Dad . . ."

"What?" He smiled again and then finished off the beer. "I like to have the four-one-one on my son's life."

My head dropped back. "Four-one-one? Are you drunk?"

"I'm buzzing."

I laughed out loud. "Nice."

"You didn't answer my question."

Reaching for the bottle, I eyed my father and then laughed at myself, because I knew what the words that were forming on my tongue were before I spoke them. "There's . . . there's someone."

"Do tell." Interest sparked in his eyes.

I smiled as I took the last gulp from the bottle. "We're friends."

"Friends as in . . ."

"Oh, come on, Dad." I groaned, shaking my head.

"What?" He cocked his head to the side. "Like I don't know what you kids are doing. Like I didn't do the same thing when I was your age."

I might vomit. "We're not like that. Avery isn't like that."

"She has a name? Avery?"

Shit. I couldn't believe I even said her name. Was I buzzing? "We're friends, Dad. And she's a . . . she's . . ."

Dad's dark brows rose. "She's . . . ?"

Perfect. Beautiful. Smart. Funny. Prideful. Infuriating. The list could go on and on. "I've asked her out a couple of times." A "couple of times" was literally the understatement of the year. "She's turned me down each time."

"And you keep asking?"

I nodded.

"And you think she's going to say yes eventually?"

Smiling a little, I nodded again.

Dad leaned forward, crossing his arms on the round, oak table. "Did I ever tell you how many times your mother turned me down before she agreed to go out me? No? A lot of times."

"Really?" I hadn't known that.

Dad nodded. "I was a bit of a . . . rakehell in college.

Had a reputation." One side of his mouth tipped up, revealing a dimple in his left cheek. "Your mother didn't make it easy."

"So what changed it?"

He shrugged. "Ah, she was secretly in love with me from the beginning, but you know what? I had to chase her, and to be honest, if you don't have to chase a woman, she's probably not worth the effort. You get what I'm saying?"

Not really. There was a good chance my dad was more than just buzzing, but I nodded, and then he said something that sort of clicked in my head.

"Surprise," he said, winking. "Surprise the girl. Do something she's not expecting. *Always* do something good she's not expecting."

Surprise her? There were a lot of things I could do that would surprise Shortcake, but I doubted he meant any of those things. But as I said good night to Dad and started toward the stairs, I knew what to do.

And I wanted to do it.

I smiled as I took the steps two at a time. As I rounded the second floor, I caught sight of Teresa slipping into her bedroom. I opened my mouth to call out to her, but the door closed quietly before I could utter a word.

Okay.

Shaking my head, I continued on to the guest bedroom Jase was in—the green room. Or at least that's what Mom called it, because the walls were painted a deep olive green.

The door was cracked and I pushed it open. Jase sat at the foot of the bed, bent forward slightly, his arms resting on his thighs, hands over his face.

"Hey, man." I entered the room, concerned. Had something happened back home? "Are you okay?"

"Yeah. Yeah," he said, standing up and smoothing both hands through his hair. He walked over to where his duffel bag was and pulled out a pair of nylon shorts. "I'm just not feeling . . . well. Beer didn't settle right, you know? What's up?"

Hadn't he only drunk like two beers? I watched him toss the shorts on the bed, his back a tense, rigid line. "I was thinking about a change of plans."

"Oh, yeah?" He moved to the nightstand, dug out his cell and dropped it there. "What are you thinking?"

"I was thinking about leaving really early in the morning," I told him. "Probably close to five or so. Is that cool with you?"

His shoulders relaxed. "Yeah, man, that works perfectly. Just wake me up."

"Cool." I backed up and stopped at the door. "You sure you're okay?"

"Perfect," he replied, sitting down on the bed again. "See you in the morning."

As I shut the door behind me, I realized Jase hadn't looked me in the face the whole time I was in there.

It was a little before nine a.m. the following morning when I stopped in front of Avery's apartment and knocked. Hopefully my dad's advice of "surprising her" didn't equate to "freaking her out."

Doubt rose swiftly, like fire to a stick house, and I

turned around, about to dive-bomb into my apartment. But the door whipped open like she was trying to pull it off its hinges.

"Cam?"

Taking a deep breath, I faced her and smiled crookedly. I held up a grocery bag. "So, I woke up around four this morning and thought I could really eat some eggs. And eggs with you are so much better than eggs with my sister or my dad. Plus my mom made pumpkin bread. I know how you like pumpkin bread."

Eyes wide and lips parted, she slowly stepped aside, allowing me in. She wasn't freaking. That much was good. But she also wasn't saying anything. I carried the bag into the kitchen and placed it on the counter. Closing my eyes, I cursed under my breath. Maybe this wasn't the best idea. That ache was back in my chest, this time a different, piercing feeling.

I pivoted around, about to apologize when I hadn't apologized for any other time I'd busted up into her apartment, but she was in the kitchen, practically airborne. Coming at me the way Teresa had when she greeted me. The same way my sister had launched herself at Jase.

I caught her, wrapping my arms around her waist as I stumbled back, hitting the counter. Shock radiated through me, quickly followed by a wild warmth that lit up my veins.

My arms tightened around her as she pressed her cheek to my chest and held on just as strongly as I held her. I dropped my face to the top of her head, inhaling her scent and soaking her response in, holding her close to my heart.

Avery inhaled a shaky breath and said, "I missed you."

Thirteen

A cold snap hit our little speck of the world right before Halloween. Chilly air whipped through the campus, creating a sheer, frigid wind tunnel between the buildings.

Jase was staring at Ollie with a dumbfounded expression on his face. As cold as it was, Ollie was wearing shorts and sandals. At least he had a hoodie on, but I doubted he wore anything other than that. Or even felt the wind.

But Shortcake was a different story.

The four of us stood in between Whitehall and Knutti, waiting for the next class to begin. She was hunkered down in her sweater that was fitted to her slim waist and the flare of her hips.

"I'm doing it," Ollie said, grinning. "No one can stop me."

I sighed.

Shortcake brushed a strand of hair that had come loose

from the twist at the nape of her neck. "It will really look weird."

Jase nodded. "I have to agree."

"I don't care," Ollie announced. "I think it's perfect."

Wind whipped its way across the clearing, smacking into Shortcake. She pressed her lips into a tight line as a shiver worked its way through her. "I don't think I've ever seen someone put a leash on a tortoise."

"Doesn't mean it can't be done," Ollie replied, rocking back on his heels. "And I kind of like the idea of being the first."

Jase rolled his eyes as I shifted toward Shortcake, hoping to block some of the brutal burst of wind. "How are you even going to get a leash around Raphael?" Jase asked, sounding genuinely curious.

Another gust of wind rattled our bones, and Shortcake's lips started to tremble. I'd had enough of just standing here. From behind her, I wrapped an arm around her shoulders and hauled her back against my front. She stiffened and her breath came out in a harsh exhale. Jase and Ollie didn't notice because they were busying arguing over whether or not it was considered animal cruelty to tie a ball of yarn around Raphael's shell.

"Don't fight me," I said, voice low in her ear. "You're freezing cold. So am I. If you don't like it, then go inside."

Her back was stiff against my chest. "Why don't you go inside?"

"I will if you do."

She muttered something very unflattering under her breath, but she didn't pull away, and my grin spread, and as each second passed, her muscles relaxed. "This is probably the stupidest conversation I've ever heard," she said, watching Jase and Ollie.

"I have to agree." My body reacted when she leaned into me. There was no helping that. "The thing is, I'd bet a thousand bucks when I go home tonight, there will be a string around Raphael."

She giggled. "I want a picture of that."

"I'm sure I'll be able to do that for you." I closed my eyes, knowing that if Ollie or Jase happened to look over, I'd never live it down, but having her in my arms was too good of a thing to not risk.

"I hope he doesn't take him outside though," she said softly. "It's too cold for the little guy."

Surprised, I opened my eyes and tilted my head to the side. "How do you know that?"

She shrugged as she turned her head toward mine, putting her lips within kissing distance of mine. "Raphael is a Russian tortoise, right?" When I nodded, she bit down on her lower lip and almost groaned. "I was bored one night and looked them up. He has to be kept in a warm environment, right?"

"Right." For some weird reason, that pleased me to no end to know that she had looked that up. "I won't let Ollie take him outside."

Shortcake let out a little sigh. "I need to get to class."

"Me too."

"I don't want to."

I grinned. "We should skip."

"You're a bad influence."

"I'm the kind of influence you need." When she laughed at that, I felt lighter somehow. "So you're really going to go to the Halloween party?"

"Between you and Brittany, I don't see a way out of it." She started to pull away, but I tightened my grip. "I told you I was going to go. I will."

I wasn't sure I believed her. I had a feeling that come tomorrow night, she would make up some excuse for how she couldn't make it, so I wasn't holding my breath. Avery hadn't gone to a single party since she started college, even though I knew Brittany and Jacob had.

Sighing, I let go and stepped back. My class was over in Byrd. "You sure you don't want me to give you a ride tomorrow night?"

Ollie's head whipped around so fast you'd think I said nachos. "It would be a ride you'd never forget, Avery."

I shot him a dark look. "That's not what I meant."

Her cheeks were flushed, either from what Ollie had said or from the cold. "I know. And it's okay. I don't need a ride, but I'll be there."

I really didn't believe her.

There were a lot of angels and cats in high heels, so much so that I had a hell of a time not wanting to separate the girls into two groups: the fallen and the catty.

Brittany, Avery's friend, was in the group of the fallen, her white dress absolutely no protection against the chilly night. She was with Jacob, who looked remarkably like Bruno Mars, but I hadn't seen Avery.

Figured.

I'd spent a good part of the evening wondering if she'd really show and if she did, what she would wear. Would she be an angel? A cat? Really stupid, considering that I did have better things to dwell on.

Irritated, I roamed from one room to the next. The house was packed, standing room only, and people spilled out onto the front porch and the lawn. If the cops didn't show up at some point tonight, breaking up the party, I'd be amazed.

There was too much going on inside the house for me. Music thumped loudly, but not quite drowning out the shouts and laughter. Couples were in every corner, some who appeared to have forgotten who their boyfriend/girlfriend was. I used to love this scene, but now, it made my skin itchy.

I'd retreated outside to the garage with Jase, in the midst of a mean game of beer pong.

"You look thrilled to be here," Jase said, squinting an eye as he held the white ball, lining it up with the plastic cups.

"Not feeling it tonight."

"Uh-huh." Jase bounced the ball into a cup in the first row. The guys on the other side of the table groaned. "Is that because I haven't see *Shortcake* around?"

Why I had made the mistake of calling her that in front of Jase was beyond me. I didn't respond as the ball from the other side bounced right off the table.

Jase chuckled. "Amateurs." He turned to me. "But do you know who I do see? Steph. And she's been looking for you."

"So?"

"Just thought I'd share that knowledge with you." He tossed me the ball. "Let's kick some ass."

With nothing else better to do and wanting to get out of my own head, I joined the game. Jase had been right. The group across from us really were amateurs. Fifteen minutes into the game, our opponents were swaying like weeds in the wind.

"This is actually shameful," I muttered, eyeing one of them, who punched the end of the table to hold himself up, rattling the cups.

Jase grinned evilly. "They should've known better than to challenge me."

I laughed as I folded my arms, running a hand over my bare bicep. Jase bounced another perfect throw and the other side erupted in curses. Straightening, Jase raised his hands out to his sides and then he stopped, eyes widening.

He elbowed me and turned, voice low. "Well, look at who just wandered in here."

My brows lifted as I followed his gaze, looking past a group dancing. Air punched out of my lungs. I couldn't believe it. Unfolding my arms, I stared for a second, absolutely shocked.

Avery was here.

Standing next to Brittany and Jacob, she stood out and not because she wasn't in a costume. Her formfitting black turtleneck revealed a small section of her flat stomach. It was the first time I'd seen her stomach. Crazy. My mouth dried.

A big, old goofy-ass smile broke out across my face and I set my cup down. I didn't even say anything to Jase as I crossed the crowded garage. Jacob said something to her that caused her cheeks to flush and, a second later, I had her in my arms.

Lifting her up, I spun around as she clutched my shoulders. "Holy shit, I can't believe you're actually here."

Her warm brown eyes met mine. "I told you I was coming."

I set her down, but kept her tucked close. God, she looked gorgeous with her coppery hair falling in waves down her shoulders, curling around the swells of her breasts. "When did you get here?"

"I don't know. Not that long ago."

"Why didn't you come say hi?"

"You were busy and I didn't want to bother you."

She had been staring at my lips, which was entirely distracting up until those last words left her mouth. I bent my head, my lips brushing her ear as I spoke. I didn't miss the way she shivered. "You are *never* a bother to me."

When I lifted my head, our gazes collided and held. The hue of her eyes deepened, almost blending in with her pupils. There was a connection there between us. No mistaking the electricity shimmering in the tiny space between our lips. And when hers parted, I lowered my head, wholly intent on kissing her.

"Yo, Cam!" Jase yelled, obliterating the moment. "You're up."

I smiled tightly. "Don't go too far."

"Okay," she said, her hands slipping away.

Stalking back over to the table, I shot Jase a dirty look. "Perfect timing."

"What?" He watched me pick up the Ping Pong ball. "Did I interrupt Avery turning you down?"

"Funny." I bounced the ball, missing my target. Cursing, I picked up the cup. "Fuck you all."

Jase let out a loud laugh and said something, but my narrowed gaze found Avery. I could barely see her. Her friends flanked either side and a red cup had ended up in her hands. She really wasn't drinking and, for some reason, I was glad to see that. Their group grew and every so often, she disappeared from view, reappearing a few minutes later. Once this stupid game was over, it was her and me, and no interruptions. And, dammit, tonight she would tell me yes when I asked her out.

"Incoming," Jase warned.

I didn't realize what he was talking about at first, but arms went around me from behind. I knew immediately it wasn't Avery. I couldn't get that lucky.

"What are you dressed as?" Steph asked.

"Myself," I told her, turning around. She was dressed as if Little Red Riding Hood had wandered onto a porn set.

She smiled, twirling the edge of one of her pigtails. "That's not really a costume."

"We are too awesome to wear costumes," Jase said, eyeing Steph's friend.

I gently untangled Steph's arms. "You guys look hot."

"I know." Steph giggled. "Can we join?" she asked, nodding at the game.

Jase stepped aside, and I knew by the way he was paying attention to Steph's friend, he wouldn't be spending the night alone.

My attention immediately sought out Shortcake. I was surprised for a second time that night when I saw what she was doing.

She was dancing.

It shouldn't be such a big deal, but I had the suspicion that whatever caused her to stop dancing professionally hindered her from doing it at all.

God, she was . . . there were no words.

The song was fast, with a lot of beats, and her hips hit them all. Holding on to Brittany's hand, the two of them danced together. A smile pulled at my lips as Jacob joined them. Her head was tipped back, arms raised, and she was *laughing*.

In that moment, I realized I was seeing a very different side of Avery. One I'd never seen before, where she was lively and carefree, and fucking perfect.

"I'm going to marry that girl one day," I heard myself say.

Jase choked on his beer and bent over, dragging in deep breaths. "Holy shit."

I grinned.

But it immediately began to fade as some guy came up behind her, slapping his hands on her hips. Avery jumped a good half foot off the floor as she looked over her shoulder.

Tony. That was his name. A freshman who was just initiated into Jase's frat. He'd been a part of the first group we'd beaten at beer pong—the one who'd almost fallen face-first into the table. I didn't know him, but I didn't like him. And I sure as fuck didn't like what he was doing with his hips.

Avery twisted to the side and Tony was attached to her like a fucking octopus. He was obviously plastered and it was also obvious that Avery didn't want to dance with him. Every time she pulled away, he tugged her back.

Anger exploded in my gut like buckshot. I started forward, ignoring Jase when he called out to me. I was halfway across the garage when Tony slipped his hand across her stomach.

"Let me go!" she yelled.

The hair on the back of my neck rose at the real fear in her voice. I tripped—*fucking tripped*—and then I shot forward, plowing through those in the way. I didn't even see them.

Fury tasted like blood in my mouth as I grabbed ahold of Avery's arm, pulling her away. Her startled gasp was like thunder in my ears as I shoved Tony back. The fucker stumbled as he backpedaled, hitting the wall.

I was on him in a heartbeat.

Fourteen

I was going to break this motherfucker's face. It was as simple as that. He was touching her and it was obvious to anyone with a pea-sized brain that she hadn't wanted to be touched.

Shoving my hand into his chest, I slammed him back into the wall as my other hand curled into a fist. "What the fuck, man? Do you have a fucking hearing problem?"

"I'm sorry." Tony raised his hands, shaking. "We were just dancing. Didn't mean any shit by it."

"Cam," Avery cried out.

I shoved Tony back as he started to speak again, and Jase was suddenly at my back, grabbing ahold of me. He wrenched me away, and Tony staggered against the wall.

"You need to chill the fuck out," Jase said.

I tried to duck Jase's hold. "Let me the fuck go, Jase."

"Fuck no." He was in my face, hands on my chest. "You don't need this, remember? Getting into a fight is the last thing you fucking need right now. So back down."

My blood boiled with the need to put my fist through the guy's face, but Jase . . . dammit, Jase was right. I couldn't get into a fight. My probation would be revoked, and I couldn't put my family through that, or Avery.

Avery.

I spun around. A crowd had gathered between us and she stood with Brittany, her face pale and eyes glittering with unshed tears. I started toward her, but Jase blocked me.

"You need to calm down before you do anything."

Ollie appeared at my side, shoving a beer in my hand. "Jase speaks the truth, man. Avery will be fine, but you . . ." Serious for once in his life, he shook his head. "You need to chill out for a little while."

I let them push me toward the door and when I looked up, I couldn't find Avery in the crowd. She was gone.

Sitting on the edge of the bed Jase slept in whenever he stayed in this house, I pulled out my phone, sending Avery a quick text. Jase slammed the door, but I ignored it, waiting for a response. I shouldn't have let them drag me in here. Right now, Ollie was outside the door, playing guard. I should be with Avery, making sure she was okay.

"What the fuck got into you, man?"

I stared up at Jase. "She used to dance."

His brows shot up. "What the fuck?" he demanded again. "What in the fuck does that have to do with anything?"

Dropping my head into my hands, I shrugged. I had no idea what the hell that had to do with anything, but I had this feeling that dancing for Avery—for her to do that—was a big deal.

Jase cursed as he spun around and then pivoted right back at me. "What is going on with you, Cam? You don't get pissed off like this. You don't get bent out of shape over—"

"Don't you dare say over nothing." My chin jerked up, eyes narrowing on Jase as fury roared through me like an out of control freight train. I shot to my feet. "He was *touching* her, Jase. He was grabbing on her and—" I cut myself off before I said the words I didn't want to, the ones forming on my tongue.

"So?"

"Are you fucking serious?" I shot forward, but Jase didn't back down. He went toe to toe with me. "So? You okay with a guy—"

"Fuck no, I'm not, but Jesus H. Christ in a manger, Cam, he was some drunk idiot freshman and you and I have seen much worse go down than that." His eyes flashed an intense silver, a sure sign he was about to lose his shit. Good. So was I. Again. "And before you say you've intervened in those situations, too, I know. We both have, but you've never tried to take a guy's head off."

He had a point. What the fuck ever. "This is different."

"Because it's *her*?"

The way he said "her" made me want to put my fist through the wall. "You better be very careful, bro, when it comes to your next words."

His pupils flared wide as he held up his hands. "Look, Avery seems like a nice girl. She does, but the last time I checked, you two aren't seeing each other."

"So?" I threw the word back at him.

Jase looked like he now wanted to put *his* fist through *me.* "She's turned you down how many times? And you're acting like a pissed-off, possessive boyfriend, and the last thing you need is to get into a fight. Or need I remind you that if you do, you break your probation and you will in up in prison? Not jail, but—"

"You don't need to remind me." I turned, shoving my hands through my hair. "You don't understand."

He didn't immediately respond. "You're right. I don't understand how this girl is leading you around by your *dick.* Have you ever considered that's she playing you, for some fucked-up reason?"

I whirled on him, hands clenching into fists. If he hadn't been my closest friend, the one to pull my head out of my ass when I was on home confinement, I would've broken his jaw. I took several deep breaths before replying. "She's not like that, Jase. I know that's hard for you to believe. I get it. You've been screwed over in a way I can't even begin to fathom, but she is not like *that.*"

Shaking his head, Jase turned and leaned against the closed door. "That's what every guy says before they are royally fucked over."

"Avery is different," I told him, pulling out my cell again. No response. A ball of unease formed in my stomach. "You don't know her like I do. You don't know her at all."

He stared at me as he scrubbed a palm over his jaw. "I don't know you right now."

I didn't know how to respond to that.

"What is it about her?" he asked, sounding like he truly wanted to understand the attraction I could barely figure out. "She's not like any other girl you've gone out with. She's fucking awkward as hell and quiet. She's pretty, but—"

"She's fucking *beautiful*," I cut in, daring him to disagree.

He didn't. "Is she worth this?"

"Yes," I said, glancing at my phone again. Still nothing. "Yes, she is, and I need to make sure she's okay."

"Cam—"

"I'm leaving this room right this fucking second and you're not going to stop me." When Jase didn't move, I cursed under my breath and reminded myself that he was only doing this because he was my friend. "I'm not going to go beat the shit out of someone. I'm going to go find Avery. That's all I care about right now."

Jase looked away, a muscle flexing in his jaw and then he shook his head. "I'm sure she's okay, Cam."

"You don't . . ." I paused, rubbing a spot on my chest as the white walls in the room seemed to blur. My chest constricted. "You don't understand, Jase. I think . . . I think *something* happened to her before."

Comprehension settled across his face and then he stepped aside. "Aw, shit."

"Yeah," I muttered, feeling that horrible sensation along the nape of my neck. "Shit."

My heart was pounding as I stared down at Brittany. "You haven't seen her?"

"No." She shook her head, causing her angel wings to droop. "After you went inside with Jase and Ollie, she said she was stepping outside for fresh air, but she never came back in."

"Shit." I glanced down at my phone as I pressed her name on my phone again. Walking out to the driveway, I cursed again when there was no answer. I hadn't seen Tony inside or anywhere, but I doubted he would've gone after her. Jase was right. The guy was just a drunk idiot, but that didn't tell me where Avery was.

And I had looked everywhere.

Brittany trailed behind me. "She hasn't answered my calls or Jacob's. I don't even think she's here anymore." She paused, pushing her hair off her face. "I'm going to go to her—"

"No," I said, clenching my phone. "I'm going to go."

"But—"

"I'll let you know if I find her." I already started walking and then I was jogging to where my truck was parked near the cul-de-sac.

Slamming the door shut, I turned on the engine and gunned it down the residential street. Unease formed an icy ball in the pit of my stomach. The fear in her voice . . . she had been *terrified* when Tony grabbed her. The wigged-out feeling was back. As much as I wanted to deny it, to push it out of my thoughts, I couldn't any longer. Something had happened to her. What, to be exact, I wasn't sure.

I tried calling her on the way home, but as expected, there was no answer. My hands clenched the steering wheel until my knuckles bleached white. I pulled into the first parking spot I found at University Heights and raced across the parking lot. There was no point in checking for her car. In the darkness, it would be like looking for a needle in a pile of fucking needles.

My stomach was in knots when I reached our floor and rapped my knuckles on her door. If she didn't answer, I would kick this door in, and if she wasn't here, I would scour this damn county for her.

Then the door opened and Avery was standing there, eyes swollen and red, mascara and tears laying tracks on her cheeks.

But she was okay.

She was okay.

With my heart reaching my throat, I went inside and wrapped my arms around her, hauling her against my chest. Reaching up, I cradled her close, dropping my chin to the top of her bowed head.

I didn't trust myself to speak at first and when I did, my fingers curled around the strands of her hair. "Jesus Christ, why haven't you answered your damn phone?"

She didn't lift her head as she spoke. "I left my phone in the car, I think."

"Shit, Avery." I pulled back, cupping her cheeks. "I've been blowing up your phone—so have Jacob and Brittany."

"I'm sorry. I didn't—"

"You've been crying." Anger rose again. "You've been fucking crying."

"No, I haven't."

"Have you looked in the mirror?" When she shook her head, I closed the door behind me and then took her small hand. "Come on."

She swallowed hard, but let me tug her along. I took her into the bathroom and flipped on the light. She sucked in a sharp breath as she caught sight of her reflection. "Oh God . . ." Our gazes met in the mirror, and then she dropped her head into her hands. "Perfect—just perfect."

"It's not that bad, sweetheart." The knot in my chest ached as I gently pulled her hands away. "Sit down."

Avery sat on the closed toilet seat and stared down at her fingers. "What are you doing here?"

Grabbing a washcloth, I ran it under the tap and then knelt in front of her. Disbelief kept me from speaking at first. "What am I doing here? Is that a serious question?"

"Guess not." She hadn't lifted her gaze.

"Look at me. Dammit, Avery, look at me."

Her chin jerked up, eyes narrowed until only thin strips of dark brown showed. "Happy?"

My molars cracked as I grinded my jaw. "Why would I come here? You left a party without saying a word to anyone."

"I told—"

"You told Brittany you were getting some fresh air. That was three hours ago, Avery. They thought you were with me, but when they saw me later they knew you weren't. After what happened with that asshole, you scared them."

Her face fell. "I didn't mean to. I just left my phone in the car."

Silent, I swiped the washcloth under her cheeks, erasing the streaky makeup. "You didn't need to leave."

"I overreacted. The guy . . . he really hadn't done anything wrong. He just surprised me and I overreacted. I ruined the party."

"You didn't ruin the party. And that son of a bitch shouldn't have been grabbing you. Fuck. I heard you say 'let me go' and I know damn well he did, too. Maybe I shouldn't have reacted as . . . strongly as I did, but fuck it. He was grabbing you and I didn't like it."

Her shoulders slumped forward. "You didn't need to come here. You should be at the party having fun."

I honestly couldn't believe that she thought I should be at the party while she was here crying. She watched me, her features pinched with confusion. "We're friends, right?"

"Yes."

"This is what friends do. They check on each other. Brittany and Jacob would've been here, but I made them stay there."

"I need to get my phone and call—"

"I'll text Brittany. I got her number." I sat back, watching her. "The fact that you wouldn't expect anyone to check up on you is . . . I don't even know what it is."

Her mouth opened, then she shook her head and started to look away. I palmed her cheek, stopping her. Using my thumb, I chased away the last of the tears that had been there. Her damp lashes lifted, and I would give anything to take back every one of her tears that fell.

"Why were you crying?" I asked. "Wait. Did that fucker hurt you, because I will—"

"No! Not at all."

"Then why?" I held my breath as she turned her cheek into my palm. "Talk to me?"

"I don't know. I guess I was just being a girl."

My brows shot up "You sure that's all?"

"Yes," she whispered.

There was more, there had to be, but how did one ask a question like that? I didn't know. "You okay?"

Shortcake nodded.

I moved my hand down, brushing my thumb over her lip by accident, but when I did, she inhaled softly. Our eyes locked. The same feeling I had while we were at the party hit me in the chest. I wanted to kiss her. I wanted to make her forget Tony and the party and all those tears. But the first time I kissed her I didn't want her to taste her own tears.

Closing the space between us, I pressed my forehead to hers and let out a tired breath. "You drive me fucking insane sometimes."

"Sorry."

I pulled back, searching her face. "Don't run off like that again, okay? I was worried shitless when I couldn't find you and no one knew where you were."

Shortcake stared at me and then she scooted forward, pressing a kiss to my cheek, surprising the ever-loving shit out of me. My eyes widened as I leaned back, unable to look away from her. I started to say screw the not kissing part right now, but I stopped myself. "Avery?"

"Cam?"

With all seriousness, I held her gaze. "Go out on a date with me."

There was a tiny second of hesitation where her lips parted and two tiny pink spots bloomed on her cheeks, but then she spoke and at first I didn't think I heard her right, but I did.

"Yes," she said.

Fifteen

---

*W*hen Brittany cornered me outside of sports management the following Wednesday, I really had no idea what she wanted.

"Can we talk?" she asked, huddled down in her neon-pink hoodie. Short strands of blonde hair framed her face.

"Sure." I guided her over to one of the empty benches. "Is Avery okay?"

Her lips tipped up as she leaned forward. The faint smell of smoke lingered on her clothes. In her hand, she turned a lighter over. "She's as okay as Avery ever is."

I turned my head toward her, frowning slightly. "What does that mean?"

Her eyes fastened on mine. "Come on, Cam. As much as you hang out with Avery . . ." She trailed off, shaking her head as her lips pursed. "Anyway, she told me that she finally told you yes? That she'd go out with you?"

My frown faded, but I really had no idea where this

conversation was going. "Yes, she did. We're going out Saturday night." Or at least I believed so. "Unless she's changed her mind and is planning to bail on me."

Brittany shook her head. "No. I don't think she's going to bail."

"Think?"

She laughed. "Well, you never really know with her."

"That's true." I paused, turning toward her. "So, I doubt you wanted to confirm that she said yes."

"No." She took a deep breath as she sat back, twisting the blue lighter between her fingers. "I'm going to be straight with you, okay?"

"Okay."

She looked up, her bright eyes landing on mine, and I fought a grin at the seriousness in her expression. "Avery really does like you. I know she probably doesn't show it, but she does."

I relaxed. "I know she does."

She arched a brow. "But do you really like her?" Another class had let out and a rush of people filled the walkway, blocking the wind. "Because I know what you were like in high school and you could seriously have any girl here, but you want the one who's turned you down."

"So?" I folded my arms. "What does that have to do with anything?"

"Is it because she's a challenge to you?" she asked, not looking away. "Because if you're going out with her because she's not easy, I swear to God, I will cut you."

I burst into laughter. "Cut me?"

Her eyes narrowed. "I'm not joking."

Struggling to stop laughing, I nodded and hopefully plastered a serious look on my face. "I believe you."

"Good." She nodded. "But you didn't answer my question."

I bit the inside of my cheek. "I like her, Brittany. It has nothing to do with a challenge or any shit like that. And the way I was in school is obviously not the way I am now." I took a deep breath, letting it out slowly. "And I know she's . . . different."

Brittany nodded again and she didn't say anything to that. Part of me was glad that someone else had picked up on a few of Avery's behaviors, or she could've confided in her, but there was another part that was uneasy. I glanced at her. "Did she tell you anything?"

"About you?"

"No," I laughed. "Did she tell you . . . ?" Still, I had no idea how to ask the question. Luckily, Brittany got what I wasn't willing to say.

"It was the way she acted at the party, so I asked her the other day." Brittany stood, slipping the lighter into the pocket of her jeans. My stomach tightened as I waited. She gripped the strap on her bag. "She told me nothing happened to her."

Air stopped somewhere in my throat. "Do you believe her?"

She stepped back and then forward, lowering her voice. "She looked me straight in the eye and said nothing happened. I don't know what to believe. How about you?"

"I don't know, but you're her friend, she would've told you." I hoped that was the case. "Right?"

"I guess," she replied, smiling tightly. "I've got to run before I'm late to history. Yay."

"Hey." I stood.

Brittany turned. "What?"

"You're a good friend."

She smiled as she dug a cigarette out of her bag. "I know."

A certain edginess had me strung tight as I pulled the black sweater over my head and then went in search of my shoes. I couldn't remember the last time I was this nervous, but it made sense. How many weeks—hell months—did it take for me to get Shortcake to say yes? I had a reason to be nervous.

I slipped out of the apartment before Ollie could make an appearance. My heart was pounding way too fast and my head was full of too much to deal with whatever smart-ass comments that would come from him.

When I knocked on Shortcake's door, it opened almost immediately, and the nervousness turned into something completely different when I laid eyes on Avery.

The deep green blouse she wore mixed with the loveli-ness of her hair and complexion. Part of me couldn't even believe I noticed that and was about to start waxing poetic verses in my head. The ever-present bracelet was in place. My gaze traveled down the skintight jeans tucked into black boots and then back up, straying where the soft red waves curled over her breasts.

I cleared my throat. "You look . . . really, really great."

She ducked her chin as I stepped into her apartment. "Thank you. So do you."

Grinning, I leaned against the back of her couch. "You ready? Got a jacket?"

Shortcake spun around, practically darting back down the hall. She returned with a black coat and started for the door. I picked up her purse and handed it over.

"Thank you." Her cheeks flamed and then she breathlessly added, "Ready."

"Not quite yet." I stilled her, brushing the strands of hair back over her shoulders and then set about buttoning her jacket. "It's freezing outside."

Shortcake stared up at me as I continued up her coat, slipping the buttons into the holes. My knuckles grazed where her jacket swelled sweetly and she shuddered in a way that made me want to pull her close.

"Perfect," I murmured, forcing myself to lower my hands. "Now we're ready."

I held the door open and the moment we stepped out into the hall, Ollie burst out from our apartment, cell phone in one hand and a wiggling Raphael in the other.

What the . . . ?

"Smile!" Ollie snapped a picture. "It's like my two kids are going to prom."

Oh. My. God.

"Putting this in my scrapbook. Have fun!" Grinning, Ollie bounced back into the apartment, closing the door behind him.

Shortcake looked up at me. "Um . . ."

I laughed loudly. "Oh God, that was different."

"He doesn't normally do that?"

"No." I put my hand on her lower back. "Let's get out of here before he tries to go along with us."

She grinned. "With Raphael?"

"Raphael would be welcomed. Ollie, however, would not be." I grinned as we hit the steps. "The last thing I'd want is for you to be distracted on this date."

"Why me?" Avery blurted out, and then squeezed her eyes shut. "Okay. Don't answer that."

The small candle on the linen-covered table flickered in the space between us. We'd placed our orders with the waiter, and Avery had nervously bounced from one topic to the next as she nibbled on her bread.

What had provoked that question had been the truth. I had told her that she didn't have to worry about impressing me. And she had stared at me like I was a crackhead and had asked that question.

I couldn't even believe she had asked the question. Sometimes the woman absolutely dumbfounded me.

The waiter arrived with our food, deterring me for about two minutes. "I'm going to answer that question."

She cringed. "You don't have to."

I picked up my glass, eyeing her over the rim. "No, I think I do."

"I know it's a stupid question to ask, but you're gorgeous, Cam." Her fingers clenched the silverware. "You're nice and you're funny. You're smart. I've been turning you down for two months. You could go out with anyone, but you're here with me."

A grin pulled at my lips. "Yes, I am."

"With the girl who's never been out on a date before." She looked up, meeting my gaze. "It just doesn't seem real."

"Okay. I'm here with you because I want to be—because I like you. Ah—let me finish." The look of doubt that crossed her face was obvious. "I've already told you. You're different—in a good way, so get that look off your face."

She narrowed her eyes at me.

"And I'll admit, some of the times I asked you out, I knew you weren't going to say yes. And maybe while I wasn't always being serious when I did, I was always serious about wanting to take you out. You get that? And I like hanging out with you." I popped a piece of steak into my mouth. "And hey, I think I'm a pretty damn good catch for your first date."

"Oh my God." She laughed, crinkling the skin around her eyes. "I can't believe you just said you were a good catch."

I shrugged. "I am. Now eat your chicken before I do."

And she did.

More importantly, she finally relaxed enough to be enjoying herself. And wasn't that the whole point of a date? I liked to think so.

"So, what are you doing for Thanksgiving?" I asked. "Going back home to Texas?"

She made a face. "No."

"You're not going home?"

Shortcake finished off the last of her chicken. "I'm staying here. Are you going home?"

"I'm going home, not sure exactly when." I didn't like the idea of her being here alone. "You're seriously not going home at all? It's more than a week—nine days. You have time."

"My parents . . . are traveling, so I'm staying here." Her gaze flicked away. "Do your parents do the big Thanksgiving dinner?"

"Yeah," I said, distracted.

As the check arrived and we headed out into the chilly night air, I dropped an arm over her shoulder, tucking her close as we walked across the dark parking lot. She didn't resist, instead staying pressed to my side.

"Did you have a good dinner?" I asked once inside the truck, smacking my hands together and rubbing them.

"Yes. And thank you for the food. I mean, dinner. Thank you." She closed her eyes and even though it was too dark for me to see, I knew she blushed. "Thank you."

"You're welcome." I grinned. "Thank you for finally agreeing to let me take you out."

She sent me a tentative smile, and a comforting silence fell between us, which was good. My thoughts kept going back to the fact she wasn't doing anything for Thanksgiving. It seemed wrong and lonely and about a hundred other things to spend a holiday alone. An idea formed in my head, one I doubted Avery would go for, but I had to try.

When we got back to University Heights, we stopped

in front of her door and the most awkward moment in any date was about to occur. Part of me couldn't wait to see how she handled this.

Shortcake turned to me, gaze fixed on my chest as she fiddled with the strap on her purse.

"So . . ." I drew the word out, silently praying that she didn't say good-bye.

"Would you like to come in?" she asked, and I did an internal fist bump. "For something to drink? I have coffee or hot chocolate. I don't have any beer or anything more—"

"Hot chocolate would be good." Tap water would be good enough. "Only if you have the kind with those tiny marshmallows."

Shortcake's wide smile did something funny to my chest. "I do."

"Then lead the way, sweetheart."

While she headed into the kitchen, I went into the living room. She joined me on the couch with two cups of hot chocolate. She'd kicked off her boots and tucked her feet under her. I decided there was no one cuter than her. Ever.

"Thank you." I took one, watching the steam billow from the top. "Got a question for you."

"Okay."

Little marshmallows nudged my lips as I took a sip. "So, based on your first-date experience, would you go out on a second?"

She smiled lightly. "Like a second in general?"

"In general."

"Well, this was a very good first date. If second dates were like this, then I guess I would."

"Hmm." I watched her closely. "With just anyone or . . . ?"

Her lashes lowered. "Not with just anyone."

"So it would have to be someone in particular?" I asked.

"I think it would have to be."

"Interesting." When she lifted her gaze to mine, her eyes were soft and endless. "Is this someone in particular going to have to wait another two months if they ask you out?"

Her grin formed around the rim of her mug. "Depends."

"On?"

"My mood."

I laughed. "Get ready."

"Okay."

"I'm going to ask you out again—not dinner, because I like to change things up. It's to the movies."

She tapped a finger off her cheek. "Movies?"

"But it's a drive-in movie, one of the last ones around."

"Outside?" Excitement glimmered in her eyes.

"Yep. Don't worry. I'd keep you warm."

She shook her head, grinning. "Okay."

"Okay to the movies?"

Sucking her bottom lip in between her teeth, she nodded.

Wait. What? It would be that easy? "Seriously, it isn't going to take me another two months?"

She shook her head no.

I laughed under my breath, knowing the hard part waited. "Okay. How about Wednesday?"

"Next Wednesday?" she asked.

"Nope."

She settled against the couch. "The following Wednesday?"

"Yep."

Her brown eyes pinched into a frown. "Wait. That's the Wednesday before Thanksgiving."

"It is."

"Cam, aren't you going home?"

"I am."

"When?" she asked. "After the movies, in the middle of the night, or Thanksgiving morning?"

"See, the drive-in movie theater is just outside of my hometown. About ten miles out."

Avery stared at me, her eyes widening. "I don't understand."

Drinking the rest of the hot chocolate, I set it aside and then scooted over until very little space separated us. "If you go on this date with me, you're going to have to go home with me."

"What?" She burst my eardrum as she sat up straight. "Go home with you?"

To keep from laughing, I pressed my lips together and nodded.

"Are you serious?"

"Serious as my pierced eardrum," I told her. "Come home with me. We'll have fun."

"Go home with you—to your parents' house? Basically for Thanksgiving?" I nodded and she smacked my arm. "Don't be stupid, Cam."

"I'm not being stupid. I'm being serious. My parents won't mind." I thought about what I had told my father. "Actually, they'd probably be happy to see someone other than me. And my mom likes to cook way too much food. The more mouths, the better."

She continued to stare at me, mouth agape.

Not looking good. "We can leave whenever you want, but obviously before Wednesday afternoon. You finishing the rest of your hot chocolate?" I took the mug when she shook her head. "And we can come back whenever."

Avery watched me finish it off. "I can't go with you."

"Why not?"

"Because of a hundred obvious reasons, Cam. Your parents are going to think—"

"They're not going to think anything." That was probably a lie, but she didn't need to know that. I sighed. "Okay. Look at it this way. It's better than you sitting home, by yourself, all week. What are you going to do? Sit around and read? And miss me, because you're going to miss me. And then I'm going to have spend most of my time texting you and feeling bad that you're sitting home, all alone, and can't even eat McDonalds because they're closed on Thanksgiving."

"I don't want you to feel sorry for me. It's not a big deal. I have no problem staying here."

"I don't want you sitting here alone and you're making this into a big deal. I'm a *friend* asking a *friend* to come hang out with me over Thanksgiving break."

"You're a *friend* who just took a *friend* out on a date!" she protested.

I set the mug next to mine. "Ah, that's a good point."

Picking up a pillow, she held it to her chest like a shield. "I can't do that. Visiting family over the holidays? That's way too—"

"Fast?"

"Yes." She nodded furiously. "Way too fast."

"Well, then I guess it's a good thing that we're not seeing each other then, because yes, it would be too fast if that was the case."

Her head cocked to the side. "What the what?"

I tugged the pillow away from her and slid it behind me. "You and I are two friends who went out on one date. Maybe two if you come with me. We're not dating each other. We're just friends who had one date. So we will be going back to my house as friends."

"You make no sense."

"I make perfect sense. We haven't even kissed, Avery. We're just friends."

Her jaw hit the couch.

"Come home with me, Avery. I promise you it won't be uncomfortable. My parents would be happy to have you. You will have a good time and it will be better than what you'd end up doing here. And nothing, absolutely nothing is expected from you. Okay?"

The word no was easily forming on her lips, but she averted her gaze as she turned away, staring at the empty mugs on the coffee table. Several moments passed and then she twisted toward me, her lashes lifting. She swallowed. "Your parents really would be okay with this?"

She wasn't telling me no now. This was good. "I've brought friends home before."

"Girls?" When I shook my head, she clasped her hands together. "And your parents are really going to think we're just friends?"

"Why would I have a reason to tell them we weren't dating if we were? If I say we're friends, that's what they'll think." I met her stare and held my breath.

"Okay. I'll go home with you," she said in a rush. "This is an insane idea."

For a moment I couldn't process anything beyond the fact that she had said yes. "It's a perfect idea." Since she was in such a wonderfully agreeable mood . . . "Let's hug on it."

Her brow knitted. "What?"

"Hug on it. Once you hug on it, you can't go back on it."

Avery rolled her eyes. "Oh my God, are you serious?"

"Very serious."

She grumbled as she rose onto her knees and stretched out her arms. "All right, let's hug to seal our deal before I change—"

My arms went around her waist and I tugged her closer. Her leg tangled between mine as I hugged her. Within seconds, her scent surrounded me. "Deal is sealed, sweetheart. Thanksgiving is at the Hamiltons'."

She murmured something nearly incoherent as she lifted her head. Our mouths lined up and understanding flashed across her face. "You . . ."

I chuckled, and her lips parted. "Smooth move, huh? Got you all the way over here. I would've taken you on your word."

"You're so wrong." Her eyes glimmered, and anticipation rose in a rush.

"I'm wrong in all the right ways. I have to admit something." Lowering my head, I brushed my lips over her smooth, soft cheek, briefly closing my eyes at the sweet sensation that radiated from my lips. "I lied earlier."

"About what?"

Very carefully, so that I didn't send her screaming to the mountains, I slowly slid my hands to her lower back. "When I said you looked great? I wasn't being completely honest."

"You don't think I look great?"

"No." I trailed a hand up her spine, stopping just below her hair as I pressed my temple against hers. "You look beautiful tonight."

Her soft inhale warmed me. "Thank you."

Kissing her was probably pushing my luck, but she was so close and she wasn't pulling away. I had been waiting forever to taste her lips. My heart thundered, rushing heated blood through my veins.

Avery tensed when my lips swept over the hollow of her cheek and then her hands landed on my biceps. As I neared her lips, I could almost taste the hint of chocolate I knew would linger on them. "Avery?"

"What?"

My pulse pounded in several parts of my body. "You've never been kissed before, right?"

"No," she whispered.

"Just so we're clear. This isn't a kiss."

Before she could speak, I swept my lips over hers. It was barely a kiss, more like a brief meet and greet, but the shock that traveled through my system blew the air out of my lungs.

"You kissed me." Avery's fingers clenched my arms.

"That wasn't a kiss." She shuddered as my lips brushed hers. "Remember? If we've kissed, then that means you going home with me could potentially mean something more serious."

"Oh," she sighed. "Okay."

"This is also not a kiss."

I kissed her for real this time, tracing the pattern of her lips, learning the feel of them. They were as soft as I believed they'd be, absolutely perfect against mine. When she leaned into me, making a tiny breathy sound, lust fueled by something far deeper slammed into me.

This was her first—*I* was her first kiss. No one could take that away from us. And no matter what happened a week from now or a month, we would always have this. A primal male pride wrapped itself around me.

Closer—I needed her closer, to feel her body under mine. I shifted her onto her back, keeping only my mouth on hers, and her lips moved against mine. She was kissing me back, tiny little ones that were clumsy and yet entirely sexy in their artlessness.

A sound came from deep within me and my body demanded that I sink into her, but I held myself above her, coaxing her lips open. She shuddered under me, and I shook with a need I'd never quite felt before. Her mouth opened, and I slipped inside, flicking my tongue over hers, deepening the kiss. Her back arched and when her breasts grazed my chest I had to throw the brakes on.

Lifting my head was the hardest thing I'd ever done. It seemed to go against nature, made even more difficult when a whimper escaped her as I nipped at her lower lip.

She was breathing heavily, like me, eyes unfocused. "Still not a kiss?"

Sitting back, I pulled her up. My gaze roamed over her face, searching for any sign that she hadn't enjoyed the kiss. What I found was the exact opposite. Her cheeks were flushed, her eyes fevered, and her chest rose and fell rapidly.

I reached between us, running my thumb over her lower lip as I leaned in. "No, that wasn't a kiss." I brushed my lips over hers, swallowing her sweet sigh. "That was a good night."

Sixteen

"A girl?"

I stared at the ceiling of my bedroom. "Yes, Mom, a girl."

There was a pause on the other end of the phone. "A lady?"

"Yes."

"A real, live female?" she asked.

"Opposed to a fake, dead female?"

Mom shushed me. "You're actually bringing a girl with you home?"

I started to frown. "Why do you sound so shocked?"

"You never bring a girl home, Cameron. You—hold on. Honey!" A rustling sound interrupted her and then, "Honey, Cameron is bringing a real, live girl home for Thanksgiving! Can you believe it? No. I can't—what . . . ?"

"Oh my God," I groaned, squeezing my eyes shut. Maybe this wasn't a good idea.

Her voice was closer to the mouthpiece. "Your father wants to know if her name is Avery?"

I smacked my hand over my eyes. "Yes, it is, but she's just a friend. I mean it, Mom. She's only a friend, so don't act like a freak when you meet her and start planning our wedding."

"That's kind of insulting." She huffed. "I wouldn't start planning your wedding unless you brought her home for Christmas."

I laughed. "I'll keep that in mind."

After an absurd amount of time convincing Mom and then Dad that Avery really was just a friend and to not force me to commit patricide on them, I hung up the phone and tossed it onto the pillow next to me.

A slow smile started across my lips as I pictured Short-cake at home with my parents.

High-pitched giggles radiated from the living room, mixing with the rough, low laughter of Ollie's. I didn't even have to guess what was going on out there.

Groaning, I yanked the pillow out from under my head and smashed it over my face, trying to drown out the sound. It was bad enough that I was in a constant state of hardness. I didn't need an amateur porn flick about to go down in the living room.

I was her first kiss.

Pride swelled in my chest and other parts of my body were also following the same reaction, which wasn't help-ing things. After our date, I'd spent most the night with my hand fisted around my cock. And pretty much every night thereafter. Being around her didn't make it easier, but I couldn't stay away from her. Not kissing her again was driving me mad.

Once it quieted a bit in the living room, I peeked my head out from underneath the pillow. I really hoped that whatever Ollie was doing out there with whoever was not on the couch.

I had to sit on that thing.

Rolling onto my side, I grabbed my phone. I told myself not to, because I would see her tomorrow when we left for my house, but I was a loser, so therefore I couldn't stop myself and I texted her.

Hey.

The response was almost immediate. *Hey you.*

My lips curled up. *What u doing?*

Reading your text. There was a pause and another text came through. *Also reading ahead in history.*

I laughed. *Nerd.*

Jerk.

Easing onto my back, I sent her another text. *Admit it.*

Admit what?

U r excited abt tmrow.

About a minute passed, and I sat up, frowning. Finally a response came through. *I am.*

Took u that long? I sent back. *Fo shame.*

LOL. Sorry. Figured I'd make you sweat.

Shaking my head, I swung my legs off the bed and went to the bedroom door, peeking outside. The living room was dark, but not empty. Two forms were entangled on a makeshift bed made out of pillows and blankets. Grimacing, I crept around them.

I sent her one more text. *Knock. Knock.*

Goosebumps spread across my bare chest as I slipped out into the hallway. My phone dinged and I glanced down. *Sigh. Who's there?*

Grinning like an idiot, I hurried to her door, rapping my knuckles.

About ten seconds later, the door swung open. Avery stood there, her iPhone clutched in her right hand. Her mouth opened, then she snapped it shut and pursed her lips.

I leaned through her doorway, smiling shamelessly as her gaze drifted over my abs and then my chest, getting hung up on the sun tattoo. "Hey, girl, hey . . ."

She burst into laughter as she took a step back. "You are . . . oh my God."

"I'm a sexy beast, I know. Anyway, there's something else I want you to admit."

Pulling her cardigan around her, she stared at me as she pressed her sock-covered feet together. "Aren't you cold?"

"I'm too hot to be cold."

She rolled her eyes. "What do you want me to admit?"

I flashed a quick grin and then shot forward, moving quickly. Her chest rose sharply and her lips parted, as if she anticipated a kiss. As I neared, I saw her lashes flutter closed, and hunger surged through me.

But I didn't kiss her lips. Damn, I wanted to more than anything at that moment, but I knew I had to take things slow with my little Shortcake.

So I kissed the tip of her nose.

Avery jerked back as her eyes flew open and a wide smile broke out across her face. A soft, light giggle erupted from her, and I knew I'd do a ton of terrible things to hear that sound again.

"Admit it," I said, my voice husky. "You enjoyed that."

Eyes dancing and cheeks flushed, she tilted her head to the side. "I did."

It was only after I was back in my own bed that I realized that the bracelet she always wore around her left wrist had been absent.

The giggling girl from last night was nowhere to be found today. For the last hour of our trip, she had been nibbling on her fingernail for so long I wondered how any of it was left.

"Are you sure your parents are okay with this?" she asked for the hundredth time, and I nodded for the hundredth time. "And you did actually call them and ask, right?"

Casting a sideways look at her, I couldn't stop myself from teasing her. "No."

"Cam!" she shrieked.

I laughed. "I'm kidding. Chill out, Avery. I told them the day after you said you'd go. They know you're coming and they're excited to meet you."

She glared at me as she started chewing on her thumbnail again. "That wasn't funny."

"Yes, it was."

"Jerk," she mumbled.

"Nerd."

One side of her lips curved up. "Bitch-ass."

"Oh." I whistled. "Them be fighting words. Keep it up and I'll turn this truck around."

"Sounds like a good idea."

"You'd be distraught and in tears." I reached over, pulling her hand away from her mouth. "Stop doing that."

"Sorry. It's a bad habit."

"It is." I threaded my fingers through hers and brought our joined hands down to my thigh, holding it there.

To distract her, I started talking about the recital my sister was having tonight. Teresa wouldn't be home until early tomorrow morning. The change of subject seemed to work. Truth be told, as we hit the narrow streets of my hometown, I was nervous.

I hadn't brought a girl home since high school, and honestly, those times before really didn't count. Not in this way.

I glanced over at Avery as we came to a red light. She was watching the WVU flag billowing in the wind, her hand still neatly tucked within mine.

"You hanging in there?" I asked, squeezing her hand.

"Yep." She squeezed my hand back.

My throat was dry as I hit the private road leading up to the house. Out of the corner of my eyes, I watched her reaction.

Her eyes widened as she slipped her hand free and leaned forward. Mom had already broken out some of the Christmas decorations. Large green wreaths hung on the front door and on the windows on the second and third floor.

I parked next to the garage and faced Shortcake, smiling slightly. "You ready?"

A brief flash of panic across her face caused me to fear that she'd take off for the woods, but then she nodded and stepped out. When she reached back to grab her bag, I took it.

"I can carry it," she said.

I glanced down at the bag I'd slung over my shoulder. "I'll carry it. Besides I think the pink-and-blue flower print looks amazing on me."

She laughed nervously. "It's very flattering on you."

"Thought so." I waited for Shortcake to make her way over to me and then walked up the slate pathway. We headed under the covered patio, passing the wicker furniture that Dad hadn't stowed away yet. One look at Avery, and I winced. "You look like you're about to have a heart attack."

"That bad?"

"Close." Moving closer to her, I tucked a lonely strand of her hair back as I bent down, catching her stare. "You have no reason to be nervous, okay? I promise."

Her gaze flickered from my eyes to my mouth. "Okay."

The urge to capture her mouth and taste the sweetness that was unique to her was hard to resist, but I did. Turning, I opened the door and was met with the scent of apple. My stomach grumbled. That better be pie I was smelling.

I led a wide-eyed Avery between the pool tables and

the air-hockey table to the stairs. Her gaze darted every-where, not missing a single thing. I found myself hoping that she liked what she saw, which was weird, because none of this was mine.

"This is the man cave," I told her, guiding her to the stairs. "Dad spends a lot of time down here. There's the poker table he kicked my ass on."

A small smile pulled at her lips. "I like it down here."

"So do I." I hesitated at the bottom of the steps. "Mom and Dad are probably upstairs. . . ."

She nodded as she pulled away, silently following me up the stairs and through the living room. Magazines were scattered across the coffee table. Meaning that Teresa had had friends over at some point.

"Living room," I said, going through an archway. "And this is the second living room or some room that no one sits in. Maybe it's a sitting room? Who knows? And this is the formal dining room that we never use but have—"

"We do too use the dining room!" shouted Mom. "Maybe once or twice a year, when we have company."

"And break the 'good dishes' out," I said, glancing down at Avery.

She came to a complete stop at the end of the coffee table, her face paling. I turned, wanting to make this easier for her, but not sure how, and then Mom strolled into the room, smoothing a strand of hair back into her ponytail.

Mom made a beeline for me, catching me in a hug before I could move. "I don't even know where the 'good dishes' are, Cameron."

I laughed. "Wherever they are, they're probably hiding from the paper plates."

Mom laughed as she pulled back, holding on to my shoulders. "Good to have you home. Your father is starting to get on my nerves with all his 'going hunting' talk." Her gaze drifted to Avery and her smile widened. "And this must be Avery?"

"Oh God no," I said. "This is Candy, Mom."

Color spread across her cheeks as she stepped back, dropping her arms. "Uh, I'm . . ."

"I'm Avery," Shortcake said, shooting me a withering look that made me want to kiss her. "You had it right."

Mom spun, smacking me across the arm. My skin stung. "Cameron! Oh my God, I thought . . ." She smacked me again, and I laughed. "You're terrible." Shaking her head, she turned back to Avery. "You must be a patient young lady to have survived a trip here with this idiot."

Shortcake blinked and then a laugh burst from her. Of course, she laughed at that. "It wasn't that bad."

"Oh." Mom looked over her shoulder at me. "And she's well mannered. It's okay. I know my son is a . . . handful. By the way, you can call me Dani. Everyone does."

Mom hugged Shortcake before the poor girl could even see it coming, and I don't know why, but seeing those two together did something weird to my chest. My heart started to pound when Avery seemed to unstiffen, wrapping her arms around my mom.

"Thank you for letting me come up," Shortcake said.

"It's no problem. We love having the company. Come

on, let's go meet the guy who thinks he's my better half. And dear God, I apologize ahead of time if he starts talking to you about how many eight-point bucks he's planning to hunt this weekend."

I watched as Mom took over, guiding Shortcake through the house, and my heart still hadn't stopped pounding like a hammer to a stubborn nail.

Shortcake looked over her shoulder, her gaze finding mine, and she smiled as our eyes met. I winked and . . .

And her smile widened.

Seventeen

Watching Avery with my sister was painful at first. Shortcake was almost unbearably shy and my sister, God love her, had to lead her through almost every conversation, gently pulling her in. But eventually she relaxed, talking to Teresa about dance, and she even volunteered to help my sister get the sides ready for dinner.

The moment Dad and I were alone, he turned to me in the recliner, smiling slightly. "She's a good girl, Cameron."

"I know."

"I mean, she's a really good girl."

I glanced at him, brows raised. "I *know.*"

Dad watched me closely, that strange smile still playing over his lips. "Did she ever go out on a date with you?"

My lips twitched. "What do you think?"

"I think I know the answer." Dad tipped his head back. "Are you two seeing each other?"

"No. I told you and Mom the truth. She's not my girlfriend." I paused, thinking about the conversation I'd over-heard this morning between Mom and Avery. I *would* be bringing her home for Christmas and she *would* be my girlfriend by then. "Yet."

Dad looked like he was about to laugh but didn't. Opening his eyes, he turned his head and looked me dead-on. "Have you told her about what happened?"

Muscles in my stomach clenched. I knew what he was talking about, but didn't answer.

Dad sighed. "Boy, you know how I feel about what happened. Was it necessarily the right thing to do? No. But if you hadn't done it, I would have. But you need to tell her if you're serious about her. Secrets are . . . well, sometimes they are necessary and sometimes they kill things before they have a chance to grow. You get what I'm saying?"

I found myself nodding, but as my gaze drifted to where Avery and my sister had disappeared from, I felt knots of unease twist in my stomach. I knew I wasn't the only one with secrets.

I was ten seconds from grabbing my sister's cell phone and throwing it across the room during Thanksgiving dinner. I dumped another mound of yams on my plate. "Who do you keep texting?"

Teresa smirked. "That's none of your business."

I arched a brow. "I'm your brother, it's my business. Mom . . ." I paused, looking across the table. "You should tell *your* daughter it's rude to text at the table."

Mom sent me a dry look. "It's not hurting anyone."

Well, that was no help. I nudged Shortcake with my knee, and not for the first time. "It's hurting my soul," I murmured to her.

Avery rolled her eyes as she knocked my leg back.

"That's sad." Teresa dropped the phone in her lap. "So, Avery, how did you end up in West Virginia?"

She whipped her spoon through the mashed potatoes. "I wanted to go someplace different. My family is originally from Ohio, so West Virginia seemed like a good place to go."

"I have to be honest, I would've picked New York or Florida or Virginia or Maryland or—" She looked down when her phone chirped and grabbed her cell.

My eyes narrowed as I knocked Avery's knee. Curious as to who my sister could be chatting with, I acted like I was grabbing for turkey, but went for the phone instead.

"Hey!" Teresa shouted. "Give it back!"

Avoiding her grabby hands, I leaned over into Avery as my gaze flicked to the screen. Murphy? What the fuck? "Who's Murphy?"

"It's none of your business! God." Teresa grabbed for the cell. "Give me back my phone."

"I'll give it back when you tell me who Murphy is? A boyfriend?"

The red cheeks were enough of an answer. Granted, I didn't expect my sister to stay single forever, but she hadn't been serious since that dickhead.

She slammed her back into her seat, folding her arms. "Mom."

"Cam, give her back the phone," she ordered, and when

I didn't budge, her smile tightened in the way that was rare for her. "We've met Murphy. He's a really good boy."

I was pretty sure that was what everyone had said about the dickhead.

"He's really nice and I like him," Teresa said quietly.

I snorted. "That's not a ringing—"

"He's not Jeremy," Dad cut in. "Give her back the phone."

Avery had been staring at her plate and when her hand landed on my upper thigh, I suddenly wasn't thinking about Jeremy the Dickhead or Teresa's phone.

Her hand was on my thigh, so close to where I wanted it to be, and in that moment, call me what you want, I didn't give a fuck that it was Thanksgiving dinner. If she just slid her hand up a—

Avery snatched the cell phone from my hands.

Son of a bitch. "Hey, that was so not fair."

She grinned at me as she stretched around me, handing the phone back to Teresa. "Sorry."

"Thank you," she said, smiling at Shortcake like she was the messiah of cell phones.

I shot her a very promising look before I twisted toward Teresa. "I want to meet this Murphy."

My sister sighed but relented. "Okay. Let me know when."

I had no idea what Shortcake thought about this and it wasn't until after the conversation picked back up that I knew this whole situation had to be weird to her. I thought about what Dad said about secrets and there had been plenty of moments today to bring it up, but none of them had seemed right.

How do you explain to a girl that it took months to get out on a date that you beat a teenager into a coma? That wasn't something you brought up over dinner.

But Dad had been right. I needed to tell her.

I had to.

When I left my bedroom that night to go to Avery's, I had every intention of talking to her. I felt like I did when I used to play soccer, right before a game started and my stomach was located somewhere between my knees and ass.

Shutting my bedroom door behind me as quiet as a goddamn mouse on Christmas Eve, I jumped a good foot when I heard my name.

"Cam," Teresa whispered, popping her head out her door several feet down the hall. "You got a second?"

"Sure." I glanced at Shortcake's door and then forced myself away from it. "What's up?"

"I just want to tell you that Murphy's not really my boyfriend." Teresa folded her arms along her stomach. "He's just a good friend and we've gone out on a few dates, but it isn't like that."

Relief flooded me. I wanted Teresa to wait until she was thirty and knew how to handle a loaded gun before she started dating again. "I'm glad to hear that."

She nodded, letting out a little breath. "But if you still want to meet him, I can set that up."

"I'd like that." No reason not to put the fear of God into a "good friend."

She rocked back on her sock-covered heels as she looked up at me. "I really like Avery, by the way. She's *so* sweet and pretty. And smart, which makes me doubt why she's here with you." She flashed a quick grin. "I do like her."

The change of subject warmed me. "She is. I'm glad you like her."

"Well, she's got my seal of approval." Teresa stepped back into her bedroom, pausing. She looked like she wanted to say something and then shook her head. "Good night."

I waited until I was almost 100 percent positive my little sister wouldn't catch me sneaking into Shortcake's room before I knocked on her door as quietly as I could and then opened the door halfway.

All thoughts of having a nighttime confession went out the window.

Resting on her elbows, Avery Morgansten was a fucking sight to behold. Her hair hung down her shoulders and her face tilted to the side. There was an impish quality to the look she sent me, part seductress, part naïve. I knew she had no idea how damn good she looked lying there, which made her so much hotter.

"Hey," I said.

"Hi." Her voice was barely above a whisper.

"I wanted to say good night." That so wasn't the truth, but I couldn't remember why I was seeking her out other than I wanted to see her.

She clenched the bedspread. "You already told me good night."

"I did." I slipped into the room, closing the door behind

me. I was drawn to her like pencil to paper. "But I didn't. Not in the way I want to say good night."

Her soft inhale was my undoing, but as I made my way to the bed and sat beside her, I knew that I was always undone around her. And she had no freaking clue.

My gaze drifted over her upturned face, soaking in the slightly flushed cheeks and parted lips, down to the soft swells under the thin shirt she wore. "I'm glad you decided to come here."

Her eyes were incredibly wide when they met mine. "I am, too."

"Really?" I leaned over her, placing my hand on the other side of her hip. "Did you just admit that?"

The corners of her lips tilted up. "Yeah, I sort of did."

My body followed that barely there smile, drawing me toward her until my upper body hovered over hers. "I wish I had my phone to record this moment."

Her chest rose sharply as she dragged her gaze to mine. "I've . . . had a wonderful time."

"So have I." I took a breath I didn't need. "So what do you think you're going to do for winter break?"

She wetted her bottom lip and a wild bolt of need shot through me. "I don't know. I thought about taking off for D.C. one of the days. I want to see the Smithsonian and the National Mall. I've never been."

"Hmm, that could be fun." My mind was coming up with many different things that could also be fun. "I could be your tour guide."

The grin kicked up a notch. "That . . . that would be fun."

"It would be." Without knowing it, I'd moved close enough that my breath teased her flushed cheek. "Pick a date."

"Now?"

"Now."

"January the second," she said immediately, and for some reason, that blush of hers deepened. "Will you be available then?"

My lips curved up. "I'll be available whenever you want me to be." My heart thudded in my chest when her smile spread, becoming dazzling. I knew that I hadn't come in here for this, but I was going to kiss her. There would be no stopping me. "Guess what, Avery?"

"What?"

"Remember how you just said you were having a good time?" I tilted my head so that my mouth slanted over hers. "It's about to get better."

"Is it?" she whispered.

My nose grazed hers. "Oh, yeah."

"Are you not going to kiss me again?"

"That's exactly what I'm going to do."

Long lashes specked with red swept down as my lips brushed over hers. It was such a gentle kiss, but it was like a clap of thunder in my veins. Dropping my weight onto my other arm, I splayed my fingers along her cheek as I pressed a kiss to the corner of her lips and then the other side.

Sliding my hand along the nape of her neck, I tasted the skin of her jaw, the flesh below her ear. A deep chuckle rumbled through me when she shivered. When I pressed my lips under her ear again, flicking my tongue, she made a sound that blew the thoughts out of my head.

"Good night, Avery."

I kissed her, pressing my lips to hers, working at the seam of her mouth until she opened, allowing me in. The taste of her skin had sparked a fire deep inside me, but the feel of her warm mouth ignited a blazing fire. I couldn't get enough of her lips, of her kisses or the soft, breathy sounds she was making.

I groaned as I slid my hand out from underneath her, guiding her onto her back. Her body immediately stiffened, and I knew I needed to tone it down. The last thing I wanted was to scare her.

God, that was the last thing.

Cupping her cheek, I softly kissed her until her body relaxed under mine and then, shocking the hell out of me, her small hand ended up under my shirt, pressing against the bare skin of my abs.

It was like being branded.

Heat roared through my veins as my body jerked on reflex. Air punched from my lungs. She wanted to touch me? Holy hell, she could touch me. I pulled back, reached down and yanked my shirt over my head.

Avery's mouth parted as her gaze moved over my chest, the tattoo, and then down. It was like a touch, but better. My body was burning to feel hers.

I tugged the comforter down and planted my hands on either side of her head, tangling them in her hair. There was a primal part that took over when her hands flattened over the lower part of my stomach. My entire body tightened.

I dropped my forehead to hers. "You have no idea what you do to me."

She dragged in a deep breath as I lowered my body onto hers. The feel of her softness under me had my pulse pounding like I had run a mile in sand. I clenched my jaw shut as she shifted under me, spreading her thighs and allowing our bodies to meet.

"Fuck," I growled as a tremor shook me to the core.

Claiming her lips in a kiss that scorched my skin, I slowly rolled my hips against her. Fuck-a-dee-fuck, pleasure rolled down my spine. I wanted to sink into her, completely lose myself in her. Her hands gripped my sides as I rocked against her, trailing a path down her neck, to the swell of her breast and lower with my hand. I hooked her thigh around my hip, settling deeper against her. Our bodies rocked and her sweet, soft moan echoed in my thoughts.

"I like that sound." I thrust my hips forward, and she moaned again. "Correction. I love that fucking sound."

I don't know what it was about her, maybe it was everything, but it had never felt this *good* before, this strong and intense with anyone else. Not even my first time when it had felt like I'd jumped over a hundred-story building.

My fingers tangled with hers as her tongue flicked over mine, bringing me to an almost painful point where I thought there'd be a good chance I was going to embarrass myself. Even knowing that, I couldn't stop. I slid my hand up hers, under her sleeve, over delicate skin and—

My hand stilled as my fingers came to a patch of rough, raised skin. Half of my brain was existing at cock level, but the other part took control. I followed the path of skin, dumbly realizing it formed a thin, straight line down the center of her wrist—the wrist she always covered with a bracelet.

No. No fucking way.

My heart literally stopped as I lifted my head, staring down into her unfocused gaze.

"Cam?" she said softly, wiggling under me.

I turned her arm over and I looked. There was no mistaking the deep scar that ran several inches up her vein. My thumb followed it as I realized that this cut—oh God, this cut—had to be severe.

An ache formed in my chest, pouring through my veins. Muscles tightened and lumps formed. I wanted to wipe the scar away, to erase whatever it was that had caused this, because *I knew* she had done this to herself.

"Avery . . . ?" My gaze moved to hers, latching on. I could barely breathe. "Oh, Avery, what is this?"

A moment or two passed when she stared up at me, the blood leaching from her face, and then she tore her arm free. She clambered out from underneath me, yanking her sleeve down with such force I thought she'd tear the arm off her shirt.

"Avery . . ." I twisted toward her, reaching out.

"Please," she whispered, climbing to the end of the bed. "Please leave."

Stomach sinking, I pulled my hand back. "Avery, talk to me."

Her entire body trembled as she shook her head.

"Avery—"

"Leave!" She shot from the bed, taking a step back like a wounded, caged animal. "Just leave."

Every instinct demanded that I not leave, but the wild, horrified glaze to her eyes was more than I could bear. I went to the door and then stopped, trying once more. "Avery, we can talk—"

"Leave." Her voice cracked. "Please."

The muscles along my back tensed at the broken sound of her voice. I did what she asked. Not because I wanted to, but because it was what she wanted.

I left.

— Eighteen —

The moment I realized that Avery was never coming to astronomy class again, I literally couldn't believe it. But it had to be the truth. Since the ride back from my parent's house the Friday after Thanksgiving, I hadn't heard a peep from her. No response to my calls or my texts. The times that I knocked on her door, there was never an answer even though her car was in the parking lot.

She hadn't even answered the door for eggs.

When the weekend came again and the following Monday morning passed without Avery being in astronomy, I knew she had taken an incomplete.

A motherfucking incomplete.

It was *insane* for her to go that far to avoid me, and for what? Because I had seen the scar? I didn't understand and I wasn't stupid. She was obviously embarrassed and had gone to great lengths to hide the scar, but it hadn't been fresh. It was something she had done years ago, so why did she hide from me now?

I talked to Brittany and even Jacob, since Avery didn't show in the Den for lunch. Neither of them knew what the hell was going on with Avery. I hadn't mentioned the scar. I never would, but I had hoped that they had some insight. They had none.

It was driving me crazy—the silence and the confusion. And the longer it went, the more acid that seemed to collect in the pit of my stomach, the worse the knots and the ache in my chest were getting.

Short of camping out in front of her door, there was little I could do, but I was determined to talk to her. And it happened on the last day of finals, at the start of winter break. Like a total stalker, I'd been staring out my front window, waiting for Ollie to return with pizza, when I saw her cross the parking lot with her hands full with groceries.

When I heard the soft footsteps in the hall outside, I threw open the door. Avery was in front of her door, her hair pulled back in a messy ponytail, and the weight of her bags dragging her shoulders down. There was no doubt in my mind that she was trying to ghost through the door before I saw her.

That hurt.

And that fucking pissed me off.

"Avery."

Her back stiffened like she'd been shot full of steel. She didn't turn around or address me, and as my gaze drifted over her, I could see the pink tips of her fingers, strangled from the bags she carried. Some of the steam went out of my anger.

I sighed. "Let me help you."

"I got it."

"Doesn't look that way." I stepped closer. "Your fingers are turning purple."

"It's fine."

She walked into her apartment and I shot forward. Hell to the fucking no. She was not going to disappear on me.

I took a bag from her, and she jerked like she'd been shocked. She dropped a bag. Items spilled forth. "Shit," she muttered, stooping down.

I knelt, picking up items I really didn't see. Her head was bowed as she swiped up a bottle of hair conditioner and then her chin lifted. Our gazes met. Dark shadows had bloomed under eyes, smudges that had not been there before. Was she sleeping? What was she doing during this time? Did she miss me as much as I missed her?

Avery looked away as she snatched a box of tampons from me. "If you laugh, I will punch you in the stomach."

"I wouldn't dare think of laughing."

There was also no way in hell that I would let go of anything else because I was getting in that apartment and she was going to talk to me.

Seeming to sense she wasn't going to get rid of me, she sighed heavily, like the whole world was about to collapse in on her, and marched into her kitchen.

She sat the bags on the counter, ripping items out of them. "You didn't have to help, but thank you. I really need to—"

"Do you really think you're going to get rid of me that easily now that I'm in here?"

"I could only hope." She shut the fridge door.

"Ha. Funny." I watched her head back to the counter. "We need to talk."

She stacked the frozen dinners and headed back to the freezer before she spoke. "We don't need to talk."

"Yes, we do."

"No, we don't." Not once did she look at me. "And I'm busy. As you can see, I have groceries to put away and I—"

"Okay, I can help." I strolled forward, heading to the counter. "And we can talk while I help you."

"I don't need your help."

"Yeah, I think you kind of do."

Leaving the freezer door open, she spun on me. Her eyes narrowed as cold air wafted out. "What is that supposed to mean?"

Where in the hell did that come from? "It doesn't mean what you think it does, Avery. Jesus. All I want to do is talk to you. That's all I've been trying to do."

"Obviously I don't want to talk to you," she snapped, picking up a pack of hamburger meat and tossing it into the freezer. "And you're still here."

Whoa. Anger pricked over my skin and I struggled to keep control of my temper. "Look, I get that you're not happy with me, but you have to fill me in on what I did to piss you off so badly that you won't talk to me or even—"

"You didn't do anything, Cam! I just don't want to talk

to you." She spun around, stalking toward the front door. "Okay?"

"No, it's not okay." I followed her into the living room. "This is not how people act, Avery. They don't just up and drop a person or hide from them. If there's—"

"You want to know how people don't act?" She flinched, and for a moment, she didn't speak. "People also don't constantly call and harass people who obviously don't want to see them! How about that?"

"Harass you? Is that what I've been doing?" I laughed hoarsely, unable to comprehend where this conversation had gone. "Are you fucking kidding me? Me being concerned about you is harassing?"

She took a step back, her eyes wide. "I shouldn't have said that. You're not harassing me. I just . . ." She stopped, smoothing her hands over the top of her head. "I don't know."

My heart rate kicked up as I stared at her. "This is about what I saw, isn't it?" I gestured at her arm. "Avery, you can—"

"No." Her right hand immediately circled the bracelet, as if she could somehow hide what I already knew. "It's not about that. It's not about anything. I just don't want to do this."

My patience stretched thin. "Do what?"

"This!" She squeezed her eyes shut and when they reopened, there was a fine sheen. "I don't want to do *this*."

Air went out of my lungs like I'd been punched. "Good God, woman, all I'm trying to do is talk to you!"

She shook her head slowly. "There's nothing to talk about, Cam."

"Avery, come on . . ." I started to take a step toward her, but stopped when she moved back, *away* from me. The look that shot across her face was part fear and part confusion, but it was the fear that drew me to a stop.

I couldn't believe what I was seeing. There was no way she was afraid of me, but the look on her face was like being shot through the heart with an UZI.

That reaction was killer. Had I hurt her somehow? The question was brief as it flashed through my thoughts and I knew the answer. I hadn't hurt her.

Avery ducked her chin and looked away.

My patience snapped. "Okay, you know what? I'm not going to rake myself over fucking hot coals for this. Fuck it."

The moment those words left my mouth, part of me wanted to take them back. The other part of me wanted to scream them again from the top of my lungs. I headed for the door and then stopped, cursing under my breath. What came out of my mouth made me wonder if I was a glutton for punishment.

"Look, I'm heading home for winter break. I'll be back and forth, so if you need anything . . ." She continued to stare at me like she had been, and I laughed again, realizing that all I was doing was making a complete and utter ass out of myself. "Yeah, you don't need anything."

I stepped out into the hall and then my body seemed to demand that I make an even bigger ass out of myself. I faced her. Avery hadn't moved from her spot.

"You're staying here, all break by yourself, aren't you?" I asked. "Even Christmas?"

Her arms wrapped around her chest and she said nothing.

I worked my jaw, keeping me from saying a whole shitload of things that wouldn't help this situation. But that was it. I realized it then. There was nothing that would help this situation. And it wasn't like I hadn't tried. Avery was there, in my life, at one point, and then gone the next, as if she had never been there. And that was that.

An ache burst through my chest, and with startling clarity, it felt real. Too real. "Whatever," I said, my voice hoarse. "Have a good Christmas, Avery."

I've never in my life wanted to leave home and head back to my apartment as bad as I had over Christmas. Normally I stayed right up until the start of spring semester, but I couldn't do it with all the questions.

Where is Avery?

How is she doing?

Did she go home?

On and on they went, and I wondered those very same questions a hundred times over during break. I had no answers, and every time I picked up my phone to text her, I stopped myself. She had made it as clear as humanly possible that she didn't want anything to do with me.

Whatever we had, as brief as it was, it was over.

My mood was somewhere between shitty and shitastic the day after New Year's. I packed up my stuff early that morning and was out by my truck when Teresa followed me out.

Stopping beside the front of the truck, she pulled her heavy sweater close to her body as wind whipped between the house and the garage. Sleep clouded her blue eyes. "You're leaving without saying good-bye?"

I shrugged as I shut the passenger door. "Didn't want to wake them up."

She stepped back as I rounded the bumper. "That's never stopped you before."

I didn't say anything.

"What's up with you, Cam?" she asked.

"I don't know what you're talking about." I glanced at her. "Shouldn't you be wearing shoes? It's freezing out here."

"Flip-flops are shoes." She hobbled back and forth, squeezing her arms tight against her body. "And you didn't answer my question."

Taking my hat off, I scrubbed my hand through my hair and then pulled the cap back on. I opened my mouth and I had no idea what I was about to say, but there turned out to be no words. The hollowness in my stomach, the empty, achy feeling, had grown and now it throbbed with such intensity, there was no ignoring it.

My sister looked up, squinting in the harsh, cold sun. "It's Avery, isn't it? You haven't talked about her at all. And Mom really thought she'd be coming home with you since—"

"I don't want to talk about this," I cut her off, and her eyes widened. The last thing I wanted to think about was the fact that Avery had spent Christmas—Christmas, for God's sake—alone. I didn't want to feel bad for her. I didn't want to feel *anything*. "Look, I'm sorry. I didn't mean to snap at you. I just need to get back to school."

"For what?" she asked, frowning. "You have days before school starts."

"I know." I stepped forward, hugging my sister. For a moment, she didn't move and then she hugged me back. As I stepped back and opened the door, I looked over my shoulder at her. "Tell Mom and Dad I'll text them or call later."

She didn't immediately respond and then she nodded. "You're going to be okay? Right?"

I climbed in the truck as I barked out a short laugh. Of course I was okay. Wasn't like Avery and I had this extended history and it wasn't like I had that strong of feelings for her. My attraction had to have been an infatuation, because she *was* something new. She *was* something different. That was all.

"Yeah," I said, smiling in a way that made my lips feel weird. "I'm okay."

Teresa watched me with a look that said she didn't believe me at all, and I didn't really believe myself.

I'd just stepped out of the shower and pulled on a pair of sweats when I heard a knock on the front door. Knowing it couldn't be Ollie because he was still back home, I expected to see Jase or someone else when I opened the door.

Brittany stood there, her blonde hair pulled back in a

short ponytail and hands clasped together under her chin. It looked like I interrupted her mid-prayer or something.

"Hey," I said, unable to hide my surprise. I wondered how she knew what apartment was mine and then I remembered that she'd been here once before with Ollie, like half the college female population had been. "What's up?"

She sucked in her bottom lip as she glanced behind her, toward Avery's apartment, and knots twisted in my stomach. I knew Avery was home. Her car had been outside and hadn't left since I returned.

"I hate to bother you and you look . . . um, busy." Her gaze dipped over my bare chest, and I raised my brows. "But I need your help. Well, Avery needs your help."

A sharp set of tingles spread along the back of my neck as I stepped forward. "What do you mean, Avery needs my help?"

"She's really sick. I think she has the flu," she explained in a rush. "She hadn't been returning my calls so I checked in on her and found her passed out in her kitchen and—"

"What?" I brushed past her, heading for Avery's door. "Did you call an ambulance?"

"No." Brittany hurried behind me. "It's just the flu and I need to get her some meds, but I can't get her into her bed. She's too heavy. So I was hoping that you could carry her back and maybe . . ."

I really wasn't listening anymore. My whole focus was on Avery as I entered her apartment. The smell of sickness was strong—too strong—and I could see her denim-clad legs and bare feet.

Darting into the kitchen, I sucked in the sharp breath.

Avery was curled on her side, compressed into a fetal position with one cheek plastered to the floor. Dark, sweat-soaked hair clung to the side of her face. Every few seconds, her body would shake and a tiny, breathy moan would come from her. Concern rose swiftly.

Brittany sighed. "I had her sitting up before I left."

"Are you sure we don't need an ambulance?" I asked, kneeling down. Carefully, I scooped the strands of damp hair off her face. Her lashes twitched, but her eyes did not open.

"I called my mom—she's a nurse. She told me Avery should be fine as long as her fever goes down and she gets fluids in her, but I need to get her some meds."

"I'll stay with her while you go."

Brittany said something else, but I didn't hear it. I was only vaguely aware of Brittany picking up her purse from the back of the couch as I slipped an arm under Avery.

"No," she moaned, twisting toward the floor feebly. "Cool . . . feels good . . ."

"I know, but you can't sleep on the floor." I lifted her up, wincing when her hot cheek landed against my chest. God, she was burning up. I turned, with her in my arms, realizing that Brittany had already left.

Avery mumbled something as she turned her face, but the words were too muffled and too slurred for me to understand.

"It's okay," I told her, because I really had no idea what to say. "You're going to feel better soon."

She didn't respond as I carried her back to her bed. When I laid her down, I sat back and got a good look at the shirt she wore. Areas of the damp material clung to her skin. There were patches that were suspicious and made me think of the stench of sickness.

"Shit," I said.

I looked around the room, finding a pair of pajama bottoms and a sleep shirt folded on her dresser. Taking one look at her, I made up my mind.

Many times over since I'd met Avery, I had imagined undressing her. The very fantasy of doing so had kept me up many nights. I hated to admit that it still did, even though I knew that it would never happen, at least in the way I wanted.

Stripping her of her ruined clothing happened faster than a heart attack and was just as about as fun as one. Especially considering she was mostly unconscious and was nothing more than dead weight.

I didn't peek. Okay. I might've peeked at the pink lacy bra, but it was a brief and totally innocent accident.

Once I had her in fresh clothes, I tucked her legs under the blanket. It was only when I noticed the bracelet did I remember that she didn't sleep with it on. Wanting her to be comfortable, I slipped it off her wrist and placed it on the nightstand.

I grabbed two wet cloths from the bathroom and ran them under cold water. When I returned, she hadn't moved, but she sucked in a sharp breath when I pressed the cloth to her forehead.

I don't know how much time passed, but the first cloth warmed and I replaced it with the second one. Avery turned onto her side, wrapping her arm around mine. It was like she was holding me there, but the girl was in a fevered state and was delusional. She didn't know what she was doing. Several times, she murmured things I couldn't understand. At one point, she smiled, and my chest tightened.

"I miss that," I said hoarsely.

She wiggled closer, and I smoothed the wet towel to her cheek. As the smile faded from her lips, the knots in my chest eased.

Brittany returned, and between the two of us, we coaxed flu meds and water down Avery's throat. It wasn't pretty. A sick Avery made for an extremely disagreeable Avery.

"I'm going to open the windows and air out the funk. Clean up the kitchen and stuff." Brittany hovered by the door. "You don't have to stay, you know, if you don't want to."

I shouldn't stay. I'd done my good deed for the day, and if Avery woke up and saw me here, she'd probably accuse me of being a creeper. Biting the inside of my cheek as yet another soft whimper reached my ears, I turned to her. Under the rapidly warming cloth, her brow was pinched in discomfort. Her body was still curled toward me and that one arm was still wrapped around mine.

Adjusting the cloth, I knew I wasn't going anywhere. "I'll stay."

Nineteen

$\mathcal{I}$ only knew that Avery was feeling better because
she had stopped by the apartment. I wasn't sure why she
had and I wasn't willing to find out. I told Ollie to tell her
I wasn't there. In a moment of rare seriousness, he'd asked
if I was being serious.

I was.

The afternoon I'd spent with her while she'd been sick
hadn't done a damn good thing for me. All it had done was
stir up shit I didn't want to deal with.

Once the semester started, I spotted her all over campus.
I wanted to talk to her, to see how she was doing, but there
would've been no point. At least none I could see, but it was
on Friday when it happened—when I couldn't avoid her.

I was crossing the street, heading toward Knutti, when
I heard my name shouted in a hoarse, barely recognizable
voice. That was why I stopped and turned around.

Avery hurried up the steep hill, coughing so hard her

entire body trembled with the force. Concerned, I shoved my hands into my hoodie to keep myself from acting like some kind of white knight and sweeping her into my arms.

Out of breath, she stopped in front of me. Her face was pale still, but her cheeks were flushed. The shadows were still under her eyes and the sweater she wore enveloped her.

"Sorry." Her voice was horrible sounding. "Need a second."

"You sound terrible."

"Yeah, it's the Black Death and it never goes away." She cleared her throat and then swallowed before she lifted her chin.

Our gazes met, and I thought . . . I thought I saw something in her eyes. A mirror of what *I* felt, but there was a good chance the case of beer I drank the night before was still lingering in my veins.

I looked away, grinding my jaw. "I've got to get to class, so . . . ?"

The look of flight crossed her face, but she remained in front of me. "I just wanted to say thank you for helping Brit out when I was sick."

Shifting my gaze to the diner all the way down the hill and across the street, I drew in air. "It's not a big deal."

"It was to me. So, thank you."

I nodded and dared a glance at her. It was a mistake. The wind had blown a strand of shimmery hair across her cheek and it was hard not to catch it and sneak it back behind her ear. "You're welcome."

"Well . . ." Her brows knitted together.

"I've got to go," I said again, turning to the side entrance. "I'll see you around."

"I'm sorry."

Slowly, I turned around. Those two words were like being punched in the balls, because what exactly was she sorry for? I shook my head. "Me too."

I was probably more sorry than she was.

"I'm beginning to think Ollie is out in the parking lot drinking our beer," Jase said, leaning against the wall.

Beside me, Steph nodded in agreement. "Well, whoever thought it was a good idea to send him to Sheetz is the one at fault."

She had a point, but we could've prepared better for fight night. Our place was packed like it always was for these events.

Steph leaned into my side, pressing her breasts against my arm, and I suspected she wasn't wearing a bra. Wasn't she supposed to have come with Jase? Sliding my cap around backward, I inched forward and glanced over at him.

He shrugged one shoulder and then turned to Henry as one of the preliminary fights picked up. The front door opened, letting in a burst of cold air just as the Canadian on the screen dished out a brutal strike down. The room was a mix of cheers and boos.

"Look who I found!" Ollie shouted.

I ignored him as the two fighters scrambled across the ring, but then Steph whispered, "You have a visitor."

Distracted, I glanced over to my left and almost did

a double take. My brows shot up as my eyes locked with warm, brown ones.

Avery stood beside Ollie, clenching a bottle of beer to her chest. Her hair was pulled up and she was all pink cheeks and wide eyes.

She had never been in my apartment before. Never. And I couldn't believe she was here now and I had no idea why, but seeing her . . . well, it was like seeing the sun after days of rain.

I smiled slightly. "Hey."

"Hey." The hue of her cheeks deepened.

For several moments I was unable to look away from her and I wasn't the only one. Several of the other guys, including Henry, were eyeballing her in a way all guys did when fresh meat was in the building.

I willed my gaze to the TV, but I was aware of Ollie guiding her to the empty recliner. My eyes were on the screen, but my entire body and my thoughts were to the right of me. A thousand questions rolled through my head. Seeing her in my apartment was the last thing I had expected. I was caught completely off guard.

"You want a beer, babe?" Steph asked, curling a hand around my upper arm.

I shook my head, focused on Henry. The fucker had slowly made his way over to where Avery sat. Nothing was wrong with the dude. I kept telling myself that, but when he said something about her socks, I started picturing him as the next serial killer.

Avery was drinking, much to my surprise, and I mean really drinking. Tequila shots and at least two beers for someone who didn't drink was one hell of a way to kick off being a lush.

Her soft giggle hit me straight in the chest. My eyes narrowed as Henry grinned and Avery smiled.

"Seems like your friend likes Henry," Steph commented quietly. "Interesting development."

My heart kicked against my ribs in protest. Was she flirting with him? My hands curled around my knees as Avery laughed again. What the fuck? Jealousy—red-hot, ugly jealousy—hit my veins with the consistency of dunking my head in an acid bath.

I glanced at the screen and then Jase nodded at me, his gaze flickering over to Avery. I sat the beer down on the coffee table as Henry said, "Old enough to know better."

Damn right he was fucking old enough not to even be thinking what I knew he had to be thinking.

"Hey Henry," I called out as my skin stretched tight. "Come here a second."

"Jesus," Steph muttered, crossing her arms as she leaned back against the couch.

Henry leaned down when I motioned him closer. "What up, man?"

"Leave that girl alone," I told him, voice low as I met and held the older guy's gaze. "I'm fucking serious. She's not for you or anyone in this room."

Henry's brows rose and so did the corner of his lips. "Message received, buddy."

I watched him make his way over to Jase, and I felt a little better. Not much, because I couldn't fucking believe that after everything with Avery, she'd show up at my apartment, and start drinking and flirting with Henry the Horn Dog. I was absolutely in a state of fucking shock.

"You totally cock blocked," Steph said, placing her hand on my arm again.

"What?" I twisted to her. "What do you mean?"

She rolled her eyes. "They were getting to know each other and you cock blocked."

Getting to know each other? Fuck no that wasn't happening right in front of me. "Do I look like I give a fuck that I stopped it?"

Steph jerked her hand back, but, honestly, I also didn't give a fuck about her in that moment. Avery was *smiling* at Henry. Her smiles were so fucking rare and she was smiling at *him*. I couldn't even remember the last time I was jealous, but I recognized the bitter taste in my mouth. It mingled well with anger.

Avery glanced at me and her smile started to fade.

"This is not happening," I said.

Steph shot to her feet, and I had no idea what she was pissed about, but I really didn't care. Standing up, I stalked over to where Avery sat. A big, wide and slightly drunk smile broke out across her face.

"Come with me for a sec?" I said, surprised by how even my voice sounded.

Avery shot from the chair like someone lit a fire to her ass. She wobbled way far to the side. "Whoa."

I caught her arm, holding her still. I couldn't believe she was this drunk. "You okay to walk?"

"Yes. Of course." She bumped into me, giggling. "I'm okay."

Wondering exactly how many shots she'd had, I shot a grinning Ollie a death look as I led her into the kitchen. "What are you doing, Avery?"

She held up the bottle. "Drinking. What are you doing?"

"That's not what I'm getting at and you know that. What are you doing?"

She made a face that was sort of cute and a bit weird before she sighed. "I'm not doing anything, Cam."

"You're not?" I arched a brow. "You're drunk."

"Am not!"

"A drunk's famous last words before they fall flat on their face."

"That has not happened . . . yet."

I shook my head as I took ahold of her arm. We needed to talk and the fact that she was here probably meant she wanted to. Or she wanted to hook up with one of the random guys here. I didn't know what, because who the fuck ever knew what was going on in this girl's head, but nothing was happening. She was taking her little drunk ass back to her apartment. Any number of those guys in the living room would love to find themselves between her thighs and I didn't know exactly how far gone she was. I wasn't her babysitter. Fuck, I wasn't anything to her.

"Um . . ." she said, frowning when I led her to the stairwell and closed the door behind us. She looked up at me, confused.

I pointed to her door. "You need to go home, Avery."

Her mouth dropped open as she stared at me. "Are you serious?"

"Yes. I'm fucking serious. You're drunk and that shit is not going down in front of me."

"What shit?" She took a step back. "I'm sorry. Ollie invited me—"

"Yeah, and I'm going to kick his ass later." I took my hat off and ran my hand through my hair. "Just go home, Avery. I'll talk to you later."

Avery swallowed heavily. "You're mad at me—"

"I'm not mad at you, Avery." I was mad at the fucking world right at the moment.

She looked at me and then quickly glanced away, but not quick enough. I saw the sudden sheen in her eyes. Shit. Shit. Shit.

"I don't want to go home. There's no one there and I . . ."

That spot in my chest throbbed. "I'll come over later and we'll talk, okay? But go home. Please, just go home."

Her mouth opened and then snapped shut. "Okay."

The ache grew. "Avery . . ."

"It's totally okay." She smiled, but it wasn't real and it was full of hurt—hurt I knew I put there. She turned and shuffled to her door, and with a low curse, I went back into my apartment.

"Everything okay?" Jase asked as I headed into the kitchen for another beer. Or three.

"No." I screwed off the lid and tossed it in the trash.

His dark brows rose. "Are you not okay because she was here or because she left?"

"I made her leave."

Jase glanced over as Ollie entered the kitchen. I took one look at the pothead. "I should kick you in the balls."

Ollie didn't laugh it off. He stared at me with a level look. "Did you just make that poor girl leave?"

"Poor girl?" I sputtered.

"Yeah, you know, the girl you've been obsessed with since August? She finally came over and you kick her out of the apartment."

I stared at him as I took off my hat, tossing it onto the counter. "Are you high? You have no idea what has been going on between us."

"Ollie," Jase warned.

"You're right. I don't know what's going on, but—"

"Shut up, Ollie." I brushed past him and headed for the living room.

The main fight was about to start. I stopped near the door, realizing I'd left my beer in the kitchen. I started to go back, but I didn't move. I had been serious when I told Avery I would come over and talk to her, but I planned on waiting until tomorrow, when she was sober, for one thing, and I wasn't so fucking pissed off about *everything*. But as I stood there, all I could see were the tears building in her eyes. Tomorrow wasn't too far away, but . . .

"Go," I heard Jase say from behind me.

I was already out the door.

Twenty

Part of me wasn't surprised when I opened her apartment door after banging on it and discovered she wasn't there. Expecting Avery to listen to me just once would obviously be asking too much.

Having no idea where she could've gone, I walked over to the living room window and peered down.

"What the fuck?"

There was a slight form sitting on the curb, hunched over in the cold. What in the hell was Shortcake doing? I hurried outside, wincing as the wind lifted my hair right off my forehead.

"Avery!" I shouted. She started, dropping her beer bottle. It rolled under a nearby car as she twisted toward me. The glassy look, which I couldn't completely blame on the beer, tore up my insides. "What in the fuck are you doing out here?"

She blinked and her damp lashes lifted. "I . . . I'm looking at the stars."

"What?" I knelt down beside her. "Avery, it's like thirty degrees outside. You're going to get sick again."

One shoulder lifted as she looked away. "What are you doing out here?"

"I was looking for you, you little dumbass."

She looked at me sharply. "Excuse me? You're out here, so you're a dumbass, too, you dumbass."

I fought a grin. "I told you I was coming over to talk to you. I checked your apartment first. I knocked and you didn't answer. The door was unlocked and I went inside."

"You went inside my apartment? That's kind of rude."

"Yeah, I saw you sitting down here from your window."

There was a pause and then she asked, "Is the fight over?"

Since it didn't look like she was getting up anytime soon, I sat beside her. The cold of the cement froze my ass in a nanosecond. "No. The main fight just began."

"You're missing it."

Running a hand through my hair, I let out a long breath. "God, Avery . . ." I struggled with what to say. The reaction to seeing her was still too raw, too confusing. "Seeing you tonight? I was fucking surprised."

"Because of Steph?"

"What?" I looked at her. "No. Jase invited her."

"Looks like she was there for you."

"Maybe she was, but I don't give a fuck." Twisting toward her, I dropped my hands onto my knees. "Avery,

I haven't messed around with Steph since I met you. I haven't messed around with *anyone* since I met you."

She inhaled deeply. "Okay."

"Okay?" I almost laughed and then the shit just unloaded. "See, you don't get it. You never fucking got it. You've avoided me since Thanksgiving break. Dropped the goddamn class and I know that was because of me, and every time I tried to talk to you, you fucking ran from me."

"You didn't want to talk to me the day I thanked you for helping me out."

I stared at her. "Gee, I don't know why? Maybe because you made it painfully clear you didn't want anything to do with me. And then you just show up tonight? Out of the fucking blue and get *drunk*? You don't get it."

She wetted her lips. "I'm sorry. I am drunk, a little, and I am sorry, because you're right and . . . I'm rambling."

I let out a short, hoarse laugh. What was I thinking? "All right, it's not the time for that conversation, obviously. Look, I didn't mean to be such a dick inside there, making you leave, but—"

"It's okay. I'm used to people not wanting me at their parties." She rose to her feet unsteadily. "No big deal."

My skin pricked with awareness as I stood. "It's not that I didn't want you there, Avery."

"Um . . . really?" She laughed, but there was no humor to it. "You asked me to leave."

"I—"

"Correction." She held up her hand. "You *told* me to leave."

"I did. It was a dickhead move, but it's the first time you're at my place, you come in there, start drinking and then . . ." I took a deep breath. "Henry was all over you and you're giggling—"

"I'm not interested in him!"

"It didn't look that way, Avery. You're drunk and I didn't want you doing something you'd regret. I don't know what the hell goes on in your head half the time and I had no idea what you were doing here tonight, but I've *never* seen you drink and I didn't know what you were going to do. I didn't want someone taking advantage of you."

"Been there, done that." The moment those words left her mouth, she clamped her lips closed.

A look of horror crossed her face, and everything—oh God—everything about her started to make sense. "What?" I whispered, and she started to walk away. I caught her by the shoulders. "Oh, hell no. What did you just say?"

"I don't know what I said. Okay? I'm drunk, Cam. Duh. Who the fuck knows what's coming out of my mouth? I don't. I really don't know what I'm even doing out here."

"Shit. Avery . . ." My fingers tightened around her shoulders. "What are you not telling me? What *haven't* you told me?"

"Nothing! I swear. I promise you. I'm just running my mouth, okay?" She blinked furiously. "So stop looking at me like there's something wrong with me."

"I'm not staring at you like that, sweetheart." I searched her face for the truth, for the severity of what happened to her, but the only thing I saw in her expression was fear and desperation. She didn't want me to pry any further, and I got that. Of all people, I understood the need to keep some things a secret, but I would find out eventually.

Her eyes welled up, and I thought she mouthed the word *please*. There was a lot of shit between us. Things that we needed to clear up, but all of that needed to wait.

I hauled her against me, wrapping my arms around her tightly. She stiffened for a second and then placed her hands on my sides as she pressed her face against my chest. The feel of her went straight through me.

"I've missed you," she whispered.

In that moment, whatever happened between us after I had seen her scar didn't matter. I buried my hand in her hair, pressing her closer. "I've missed you, sweetheart." I held onto her, lifting her up in the air and then back down, thrilled to be just holding *her* again. I cupped her cheeks, laughing at the feel of her. "You feel like a little ice cube."

"I feel hot." Our gazes met and she smiled. "Your eyes are really beautiful, you know that?"

"I think that's the shots of tequila talking. Come on, let's get you inside before you freeze."

Reaching down, I threaded my fingers through hers. The last thing I wanted was for her to fall and break her neck. Once inside her warm apartment, her fingers spasmed around mine.

"You're missing the fight," she said.

"So I am." I led her around the couch and tugged her down. "How are you feeling?"

"Okay." She ran her hands over her thighs. "Your friends are probably wondering where you are."

I leaned back, getting comfortable. "I don't care."

"You don't?"

"Nope."

A brief smile crossed her lips as she sat forward and then glanced back at me. I wasn't planning on going anywhere. The fight and the friends weren't as important as the one sitting next to me. Besides, I was a little concerned about her alcohol intake, especially when she jumped up and almost ate the coffee table.

"Maybe you should sit down, Avery."

"I'm okay." She stumbled around the coffee table. "So . . . what did you want to do? I can, um, turn on the TV or put a movie in, but I don't have any movies. I guess I can order one from—"

"Avery, just sit down for a little while."

She picked up a pillow and placed it on the couch. I guess she was going to start cleaning the house? But then she went to the moon chair. "You don't think it's hot in here?"

"How much did you drink?"

"Um . . ." Her face screwed up. "Not much—maybe like two or three shots of tequila and two beers? I think."

"Oh wow." I grinned as I scooted forward. "When's the last time you've really drank?"

"Halloween night."

I cocked my head to the side. "I didn't see you drink Halloween night."

"Not this past Halloween night." Back on her feet, she started tugging on the sleeves of her sweater. "It was . . . five years ago."

"Whoa. That's a long time." Oh, this wasn't going to end well. I stood. "You got water in here? Bottled?"

"In the kitchen."

I headed to the fridge, grabbed a bottle and then returned. "You should drink this." When she took the bottle, I sat on the edge of the couch. "So that made you, what? Fourteen? Fifteen?"

"Fourteen," she whispered, ducking her chin.

"That's really young to be drinking."

Sitting the bottle down, she fixed her ponytail. "Yeah, you didn't drink when you were fourteen?"

"I snuck a beer or two at fourteen, but I thought your parents were strict?"

She snickered as she dropped into the moon chair. "I don't want to talk about them or drinking or Halloween."

Didn't take a rocket scientist to figure out those three things were connected. And it also didn't take a vivid imagination to picture a young Avery getting too drunk at a party and doing something she came to regret later. At least, I hoped it was that. "Okay."

Shortcake watched me a second and then went about trying to take her sweater off. A laugh built up in my throat, but got stuck when she dropped her sweater. She wore a tank top underneath, but the material was thin and exposed a lot of flushed skin. Her nervousness seemed to run deeper than a beer buzz or even because I was here after all the crap between us.

She stood again and started pacing. When she stopped, in between the kitchen and the hall, she curled her fingers under the hem of her tank top.

"What are you doing?" I asked.

She didn't respond as her slightly unfocused gaze met mine. I had no idea what she was thinking. I never really did, but she sucked her bottom lip between her teeth. Wariness settled in my bones. She was definitely up to—

Avery pulled her tank top off.

Holy. Shit.

I inhaled sharply. *"Avery."*

Holy. Shit. Shit. Shit. That's about all I could think as I stared at her in her black bra. I'd seen her when she was sick, but I had not seriously really seen her. Not like now. Her breasts were full, straining against the lacy cups as she dragged in one deep breath after another.

When she leaned against the wall and let her arms fall to her sides, I clamped my jaws together as I breathed deeply. My gaze dipped from her face again, to her breasts and then down the smooth line of her stomach. Her jeans hung low and her belly concaved around her navel. The sweet curve of her waist begged to be touched.

She was obviously drunk and if I was a good guy I wouldn't be staring at her like I wanted to eat her up, but I couldn't look away. I didn't remember standing, but I was and somehow I had moved around the couch. Heat built between my legs, thickening and potent.

"Cam?" she said breathlessly.

My body demanded that I go to her and I almost did, but I stopped, clenching my hands. "Don't."

"Don't what?"

I closed my eyes, but the sight of her was branded into my mind. "This—don't do this, sweetheart."

"Isn't this what you want?" she asked, voice ringing with uncertainty.

My eyes flew open. What? "I don't expect that, Avery."

She sucked in a breath. "You don't want me."

Don't want her? I could barely remember a time when I hadn't wanted her, for fuck's sake. My cock was pushing against the zipper of my jeans, swelling to the point of almost bursting. That's how badly I *wanted* her.

But the look of self-deprecation had crept onto her pretty face.

I shot forward, slamming my hands onto the wall on either side of her head. I bent down so that we were eye level. "Fuck, Avery. You think I don't want you? There's not a single part of you that I *don't* want, you understand? I want to be on you and *inside* of you. I want you against the wall, on the couch, in your bed, in *my* bed, and every fucking place I can possibly think of, and trust me, I have a vast imagination when it comes to these kinds of things. Don't ever doubt that I want you. That is not what this is about."

Confusion poured into her wide eyes.

I pressed my forehead against hers. "But not like this—never like this. You're drunk, Avery, and when we get together—because we *will* get together, you're going to be fully aware of everything that I do to you."

She held my gaze and then closed her eyes, turning her head to the side, causing our skin to glide together. "You're a good guy, Cam."

"No, I'm not." I breathed her in, making a silent promise that I would always be whatever she needed me to be. "I'm only good with you."

Twenty-One

It was about an hour after I got Avery to cover up with a blanket that everything she drank decided to make a reappearance.

Throwing aside the quilt I had wrapped her in like it was covered in snakes, she tore through the living room, making a beeline for the bathroom. I followed quickly, expecting this, considering she didn't normally drink.

It was terrible.

Unable to do anything more than hold her hair and rub her back while she prayed to the porcelain gods, I'd never felt more helpless. When it was finally over, I propped her against the bathtub and grabbed a damp cloth. It was just like when she had been sick, except this time around, she was actually conscious.

"Feel better?" I asked.

"Kinda." She squeezed her eyes shut. "Oh God, this is so embarrassing."

I laughed under my breath. "It's nothing, sweetheart."

"This is why you stayed, right?" She moaned pitifully. "You knew I was going to be sick and here I was, taking off my clothes."

"Shh." I brushed the loose strands of hair back from her face. "As charming as it was to watch you vomit up your guts, that's not why I stayed and you know it."

Her eyes drifted shut again. "Because you want me, but not when I'm drunk and puking all over the place?"

I let out a loud laugh. Intoxicated Avery was a funny Avery. "Yeah, you know, that sounds about right."

"Just making sure we're on the same page."

"We're not."

One eye opened. "Ha."

"Thought you'd like that." I moved the cloth under her chin.

She smiled slightly. "You're very . . . good at this."

"Had a lot of practice." Tossing the towel aside, I grabbed a new one and started all over. "Been where you are quite a few times." I brought the towel down her neck and over her arms, willing my gaze to stay on her face and not stray to the swells of her breasts so beautifully on display. "Want to get ready for bed?"

She stared at me with sudden wide eyes.

I grinned.

"Get your mind out of the gutter."

"Oh," she murmured, looking chagrined.

"Yeah, oh." I turned and grabbed a toothbrush. Loading it with paste, I faced her. "Thought you'd want to get the taste out of your mouth."

"You are wonderful," she said, reaching for it.

"I know." When she was all done, I knelt again and unzipped my hoodie. Taking it off, I grabbed the hem of my shirt to slip it over my head. "I've been trying to get you to say I'm wonderful from the first time you plowed into me. If I'd known that all it would take was handing you a toothbrush, I would have done that a long time ago. My loss."

"No. It was my . . ." She managed to sit up straighter. "My loss—what are you doing?"

"I don't know where your clothes are." Which was a lie. I'd found her clothes before.

"Uh-huh."

I grinned as I watched her gaze move over my chest, fixing on my tattoo. "And I figured you'd want to get out of your clothes."

"Yeah," she murmured.

"So the easiest thing would be to let you borrow my shirt."

She took a shallow breath. "Okay."

"Then you'd be more comfortable."

I had the suspicion she wasn't listening to a word that was coming out of my mouth. Not when her eyes were traveling south, causing my body to react.

"Sure," she murmured.

"You haven't been listening to a single thing I've said."

"Nuh-uh."

I grinned as I took ahold of her hips, lifting her onto the edge of the tub.

"Don't lift your arms yet, okay." I told her. She held

still as I pulled my shirt on over her. "Keep your arms down." I let go of the shirt and reached around her, deftly unclasping her bra.

"What are you doing?" Her voice pitched high.

I laughed as I slid the straps down her arms, but it died off when she shivered. I think I was into punishing myself, because I wanted to drop her bra and pull her into my arms. "Like I said before, get your mind out of the gutter. Your virtue is safe with me."

"My virtue?"

I looked at her through my lashes. "For now."

"For now?" she whispered.

I nodded. "Put your arms through."

She obeyed, and I rolled up the sleeves. Sitting back, a surge of possession nearly knocked me off my feet. I liked her in my clothes. Really liked it. Sliding my hand down her arm, I stopped above the bracelet.

"Don't—" Panic filled her voice as I unhooked the tiny clasps.

I tightened my grip, refusing to let her pull her arm away. "I've already seen it, Avery."

"Please, don't." Her gaze lowered. "It's embarrassing and I can't take back that you saw this. I wish I could, but I can't."

My earlier suspicions were finally confirmed. I wrapped my hands around the bracelet and her wrist. "It's because of this, isn't it? Why you freaked out on me? Wouldn't talk to me? Dropped the class?"

When she didn't speak, I closed my eyes briefly. "Oh, sweetheart. We've all done stuff we aren't proud of. If you knew . . ." Now wasn't the time for *that*. "The point is, I don't know why you did this. I just hope that whatever the reason was, it's something that you've come to terms with. I don't think any less of you because of it. I never did."

"But you looked so . . ." She couldn't finish.

I took the bracelet off with my other hand and placed it on the sink. "I was just surprised and I was concerned. I didn't know when you got this and I'm not going to ask. Not right now, okay? Just know that you don't have to hide it around me. All right?"

She nodded, but doubt and distrust poured into her brown eyes. Wanting to prove what I said was true, I bent my head as I turned her arm over and pressed my lips to the scar. A shudder rocked Avery.

"I'd just turned sixteen." Her voice was quiet and terribly young. "That's when I did it. I don't know if I really meant to do it or if I just wanted someone to . . ." She shook her head. "It's something I regret every day."

"Sixteen?"

"I would never do anything like that again. I swear. I'm not the same person I was then."

"I know." I placed my arm on her leg, wanting to take away the distant, painful look that darkened her eyes. "Now it's time to take your pants off."

She blinked and then laughed. "Nice."

I helped her stand. My shirt reached her knees and I think it looked better on her than me. When I reached for the button on her jeans, she smacked my hands away. "I think I can do that," she said.

"Are you sure?" I teased. "Because I'm here at your

service and taking your jeans off is something I feel I'd be exceptionally wonderful at."

Her lips twitched. "I'm sure you would be. Put your hoodie back on."

I leaned against the sink, stretching out my back. "I like when you look."

"I remember." She turned and wiggled her ass in the most enticing way, shedding her jeans.

Looking away, I snatched my hoodie off the floor. "You think you'll be good out of the bathroom?"

"I hope so."

Once I had her back in the living room, I found aspirin and grabbed another bottle of water. After she drank up, I sat on the couch and tugged gently on her arm. "Sit with me." When she started to climb over my legs, I stopped her. "No. Sit with me."

Confused, she shook her head. I leaned back and pulled her down. She was stiff as a dollar bill for about a second and then her body caved into my lap. I grabbed the quilt, tossing it over her bare legs.

"You should try to go to sleep." I wrapped my arms around her waist as the TV cast flickering shadows across the room. "It'll help in the morning."

Shortcake let out a little sigh as she snuggled against my chest. "You're not leaving?"

"Nope."

"At all?"

Lowering my chin, I brushed my lips across her forehead. "I'm not going anywhere. I'll be right here when you wake up, sweetheart. I promise."

I woke the following morning the same way I had fallen asleep. Avery was still curled up in my lap, but she was awake now and she kept wiggling around. I groaned, tightening my arms around her as her hip pressed against my erection.

"Sorry," I said. "It's morning and you're sitting on me. That's a combination meant to bring any man down."

I opened my eyes in time to see a flush sweep over Shortcake's cheeks. I moved a hand to her hip, watching her sleepy expression through heavily hooded eyes.

"Do you want me to get off you?" she asked.

"Hell no." I slid my other hand up her spine, threading my fingers through her soft hair. "Absolutely fucking not."

She grinned. "Okay."

"Finally, I think we're actually agreeing on something."

Tilting her head to the side, she studied me for a long moment. "Did last night really happen?"

I grinned. "Depends on what you think happened."

"I took my shirt off for you?"

At the mention of that, my gaze dipped. The hardened tips of her breasts were nicely visible. "Yes. Lovely moment."

"And you turned me down?"

My hand drifted to the side of her thigh. "Only because our first time together isn't going to be when you're drunk."

"Our first time together?"

I grinned lazily. "Uh-huh."

She turned a pretty shade of pink. "You're really confident about there being a first time between us."

"I am." I leaned back against the cushion, watching her as I smoothed my hand up and down, from hip to thigh.

"We talked, right?" She glanced at her bare wrist. "I told you when I did this?"

"Yes."

Her lashes lifted. "And you don't think I'm a raving bitch?"

"Well . . ."

She pinned me with a dry-as-sand look.

I grinned as I moved my other hand up to the nape of her neck. "You want to know what I think?"

"Depends."

I led her head down so that our lips almost touched. "I think we need to talk."

"We do," she whispered.

But the longer she sat in my lap, the less likely we were to talk. I gripped her hips and lifted her up, dropping her on the cushion beside me.

"I thought we needed to talk," she asked as I stood.

"We do. I'll be right back."

Confusion poured into her expression.

"Just stay there, okay?" I started for the door. "Don't move from that spot. Don't think about anything. Just sit there and I'll be right back."

She rested her chin on the back of the couch. "Okay."

"I mean it, don't think about anything." I opened the door. "Not the last couple of minutes or last night. Not the last month. Or what's coming next. Just sit there."

"All right," she whispered. "I promise."

I held her gaze for a moment and once I was sure she wasn't going to lock herself in her bedroom, I hurried to my apartment. It was quiet inside, but there was a pair of heels next to the couch. Smiling, I quickly brushed my teeth and then grabbed the required items from the kitchen. Took me all of five minutes and when I returned to her apartment, she was where I left her.

Her gaze dropped to what I held in my hands and she smiled. "Eggs—you brought eggs."

"And my skillet." Using my hip, I nudged the door closed. "And I brushed my teeth."

"You didn't put a shirt on."

I cast her a long look. "I know it would break your heart not to be able to see me shirtless."

As I put the eggs on the counter, I heard a muffled squeak and turned toward the door. "Avery, what in the hell are you doing?"

"Nothing," was the response.

I smiled to myself as I turned back to the counter. "Then get your ass in here." When I heard her feet hit the floor, I frowned. "And don't you dare change." I paused. "Because I really like seeing you in my clothes."

"Well, when you put it like that . . ." She appeared in the doorway.

"What?" I looked over my shoulder at her. "You missed my eggs that badly?"

She blinked slowly. "I didn't think I'd have you in my kitchen making eggs again."

Those words affected me more than she knew. I adjusted the controls on the stove. "You missed me *that* much?"

"Yes."

I turned to her, running a hand through my hair. "I've missed you."

Shortcake inhaled deeply. "I want to say I'm sorry for how I acted when you . . . well, when you saw my scar. I've never let anyone see it." She inched forward, worrying her lower lip. "I know that's not an excuse, because I was a terrible bitch, but . . ."

"I'll accept your apology on one condition." I folded my arms.

"Anything," she said passionately.

"You trust me."

"I trust you, Cam."

"No, you don't." I walked to the table and slid out a chair. "Have a seat."

Once she sat and adjusted the borrowed shirt, I went back to the stove and cracked an egg. "If you trusted me, you wouldn't have reacted the way you did. And that's not me judging you or any of that kind of shit. You got to trust me that I'm not going to be an ass or freak out over that kind of stuff. You have to trust that I care enough about you."

At the sound of her soft inhale, I turned to her. "There's a lot I don't know about you and I hope we fix that. I'm not going to push you, but you can't shut me out. Okay. You have to trust me."

Her gaze met mine. "I trust you. I will trust you."

"I accept your apology."

I finished up the eggs and returned to the table with OJ before I broached the issue at hand. "So where do we go from here? Tell me what you want."

She stopped with a fork full of fluffy eggs. "What I want?"

"From me." I popped a whole egg in my mouth. "What do you want from me?"

Shortcake sat back, placing her fork down on the plate. She opened her mouth and then squared up her shoulders. "You."

My chest spasmed and for a moment I couldn't speak. "Me?"

"I want you," she said, flushing. "Obviously, I've never been in a relationship and I don't even know if that's what you want. Maybe it's not—"

"It is."

"It is?" she asked.

I chuckled, feeling lighter than I had in weeks as I picked up another egg. "You sound so surprised, like you can't believe it. It's really kind of adorable. Please continue."

"Please continue . . . ?" She shook her head. "I want to be with you."

I chewed the egg slowly. "That's the second thing we're in agreement on this morning."

"You want to be with me?"

My lips curved up. "I've wanted to be with you since the first time you turned me down. I've just been waiting for you to come around. So, if we're going to do this, there are some ground rules."

"Rules?"

Nodding, I peeled the third egg. "There's not that many. No shutting me out. It's just you and me and no one else. And finally, you keep looking damn sexy in my shirts."

Her laugh burst from her, deep and real. "I think all of them are doable."

"Good." I wondered if she saw how my hands shook as I peeled the final egg.

"I've never done of any of this before, Cam. And I'm not easy to get along with all the time. I know that. I can't promise this will be easy for you."

"Nothing fun in life is easy." As I finished off the milk, I was done talking for now. I needed to tell her about what happened three years ago and what I had to do every Friday night, but it had to wait. I needed to do what I'd wanted to do since the night of Thanksgiving.

I stood and went to her side. Taking her hands, I tugged her onto her feet and wrapped my arms around her waist. I lowered my head, brushing my lips across her cheek. "I'm serious about you, Avery. If you want me for real, you have me."

Shortcake pressed her palms to my chest. "I want you for real."

"Good to know." I slanted my lips over hers. "Because, if not, this would get a whole lot awkward."

She laughed, but the sound was lost when I pressed my mouth to hers. The contact felt right, as necessary as breathing. The kiss was soft and slow, but as she slid her hands into my hair, I deepened the kiss, giving her what she quietly asked for. My lips slid over hers, back and forth, nudging and pushing, and then coaxing them open with my tongue.

Her moan set a fire to my blood and she tasted like juice and something far sweeter. My hands dropped to her hips and I hauled her against me, lifting her up. Surprise shuttled through me as her legs wrapped around my waist. I pressed her back against the wall, fitting our bodies together.

Kissing her was all that I'd planned, but the feel of her breasts flattened against my chest and her core hot against me was my undoing. I was lost in her. Shortcake was timid and she was innocent of a lot of things, but she was also very passionate and her response was natural and so very seductive.

I groaned as she tilted her hips, pressing against me in that wonderful artless way of hers. Her fingers tightened in my hair as she held my mouth to hers. I was so hard and swollen and the scrap of clothing covering her between her thighs wasn't enough of a barrier. I wanted nothing more than to take her right here, against the wall, and I doubted she'd protest, but it wasn't right.

With effort, I lifted my mouth. "I need to go."

Her hands slid back down to my cheeks. "You're leaving now?"

"I'm not a saint, sweetheart." My voice was deep, rough with desire. "So if I don't leave now, I won't be leaving for some time."

She shuddered, and my body tightened. "What if I don't want you to leave?"

"Fuck." I gripped her thighs, briefly squeezing my eyes

closed. "You're making this very hard to be the good guy you said I was last night."

Her lips grazed my cheek. "I'm not drunk."

Laughing softly, I pressed my forehead to hers. "Yeah, I can see that and while the idea of taking you right now, against the wall, is enough to make me lose control, I want you to know that I'm serious. You're not a hookup. You're not a friend with benefits. You're more than that to me."

Her eyes drifted shut as her chest rose against mine. "Well, that was . . . really sort of perfect."

"I'm really sort of perfect," I teased, untangling her legs and setting her on her feet. "Everyone else knows that. You're just a little slow on the uptake."

She laughed, warming her eyes. "What are you going to do?"

"Take a cold shower."

"Seriously?"

"Yep."

Another laugh bubbled up from her. "You coming back over?"

"Always." I kissed her tenderly, pouring what I felt into the quick, all too brief kiss.

"Okay." Her smile spread across her face and it was the most divine thing I'd ever seen. "I'll wait for you."

Twenty-Two

"You're not coming over tonight, are you?" Jase asked, his voice barely audible over the thumping music.

Slipping my feet into my shoes, I held my cell between my cheek and shoulder. "Nah. I'm taking Avery out to dinner. I guess if we get back—"

"No explanation needed. I don't blame you." He sounded bored, not with me, but with the whole scene. There was a pause. "Your girl doesn't seem like the type who's into the party scene."

I got hung up on the phrase "your girl" and the rush of pride it sent through me for what was probably a second too long. "Yeah, I don't think so."

Jase chuckled softly. "She's turned you into a changed man, hasn't she?"

I smiled as I grabbed my keys. Jase might be right. Since I'd met Avery in August, a lot of my habits had changed, even more so during the weeks following fight night. "Something like that."

"Well, have fun. Don't impregnate her."

A laugh burst from me. "Jase, man, come on . . ."

He chuckled again. "I'm kidding."

Rolling my eyes, I said my good-byes and headed over to Avery's.

We had a quick dinner in Martinsburg and then headed back to her apartment. I made a pit stop and picked up Raphael, letting him roam around Avery's kitchen for a bit. The little guy needed his exercise after all. And Shortcake seemed to enjoy picking him up and turning him around in the other direction, so that he shuffled his way back and forth between us. This wasn't something I ever thought I'd be doing on a Saturday night, but I wasn't bored or wanting to be anywhere else. Truth be told, I was having more fun doing this than I ever had at one of the frat parties.

"It's a terrarium," I corrected her when she called his habitat an aquarium. "And he has a rocking terrarium. Got him a new one for his birthday."

"You know when his birthday is?" She grinned.

"Yep. July twenty-sixth." Speaking of such . . . "When is your birthday?"

"Uh, you have a while until you have to worry about that." She crossed her ankles. "When's yours?"

"June fifteenth." I would not be deterred. "When is yours, Avery?"

She sighed. "It was January second."

"I missed your birthday?" My brows rose as I leaned forward.

"It's not a big deal." She shrugged. "I went to the Smithsonian and then I got sick, so it's probably a good thing you weren't around."

Went to the Smithsonian . . . ? It struck me then and I felt like an ass. "Aw, man, that's why you said you wanted to go there on the second. You were alone? Shit. I feel so —"

"Don't," she said, raising her hand. "You don't need to feel terrible. You didn't do anything wrong."

I knew I hadn't done anything wrong. I would've taken her if she had let me, but it still didn't set well in my chest. "Well, there's always next year."

Her lips split into a wide smile that caused my heart to stutter. Needing a moment to myself before I did something incredibly stupid like get all vagina-emotional, I scooped up Raphael and took him back home, promising to come right back. I planned to talk to her when I did, about what I had done, but when I did return, I discovered Shortcake standing in the hall that led back to her bedrooms with a look on her face that did funny, twisty things to my insides.

The look on her face was part anticipation, part uncertainty, and the driving force behind it was an innocent curiosity that literally blew my thoughts out of my head. I had no idea why exactly it was important to talk about serious shit right now. Since the Sunday we cleared everything up, I'd been taking things slow, so slow I wondered if I could go any slower. Every night I ended up going one on one with myself to the point that my hand was starting to get numb while I took notes in class.

It was worth it though. The last thing I wanted to do was rush her, but right now . . .

Avery wetted her lower lip as I pulled my sweater off, draping it along the back of her couch. Her gaze dipped to the width of skin exposed between my shirt and jeans and a flush spread across her cheeks.

Yeah, Shortcake looked like she wanted to be *rushed*.

I sat on the couch while she remained by the hall, fiddling with the edge of her sweater dress in the soft glow of the TV. When she had pulled off her tights earlier, after returning from dinner, I'd spent an ungodly amount of time staring at her bare legs like a teen who'd never seen so much skin before.

"You going to come over here or stare at me the rest of the evening?" I asked, grinning as she took a deep breath and approached the couch slowly. I lifted a hand to pull her down next to me, but little Shortcake had something else entirely planned.

My grin faded as she put her knees on either side of my thighs and sat in my lap. My body's response was ridiculously immediate. I hardened as I curled my fingers around her hips. "Hey there, sweetheart."

"Hey," she whispered.

"Did you miss me this much? I was only gone a few minutes."

She laid her hands on my shoulders as she pressed down, bringing our bodies together in all the right places. "Maybe."

Moving my hands up her sides, I cupped her cheeks.

She had to feel me between her thighs. There was no hiding that. "What are you doing?"

Her tongue darted out, wetting her lips, and I bit back a groan. "What does it look like?"

"I can think of a few things." I smoothed my thumbs over her cheeks, waiting to see what she was up to. Truth was, wherever she was taking this, I'd willing to plunge headfirst. "All of them have me extremely interested."

"Interested? That's good."

Her eyes met mine for the briefest moment and then her lashes swept down, shielding her eyes as she closed the distance between us. She brushed her lips across mine, making slow and sweet passes. Then she increased the pressure. I let her lead, taking her cues as the kiss deepened. My hands splayed across her cheeks as her mouth opened. I flicked my tongue over hers and she returned the gesture tentatively. Something about that drove me insane. Perhaps it was the knowledge that she was learning all of this with *me*.

I trailed my hands down her back and she arched into the caress. My hands tightened on her waist as she rocked her hips. Good God, the way she moved in my lap was going to kill me. I shuddered as I balled my right hand into her dress, sliding it up her thighs. I had to touch her.

Sweeping my other hand around her front, I followed the path of her ribs and cupped one breast in my hand. Learning the curves of her body, I smoothed my hand over the tip. Avery broke the kiss, moaning as I circled my thumb over her peak.

"You liked that?"

"Yes," she breathed.

Ah, that's what I wanted to hear. I teased her as I trailed tiny kisses down her neck, guiding her head back. She pressed her breast into my hand as her hips shifted again. Intense pleasure rolled up my spine. Making a sound low in my throat, I pulled back, watching the flush of arousal spread over her.

Damn, she was beautiful.

"Tell me what you want, sweetheart." I covered her other breast, feeling the nipple through her clothes. Wouldn't want it to get lonely. "Anything. And I'll do it."

Her chest rose sharply. "Touch me."

My body tensed up and then shook. When I spoke, I barely recognized my own voice. "May I?"

I slid both hands under the scoop neckline of her dress after she nodded, slipping the material down her shoulders, exposing her. I pulled it down, freeing her arms and letting the dress gather at her waist.

"Beautiful." I traced the edge of the lace on her bra. "Look at that blush. So fucking beautiful."

Lowering my head, I closed my mouth over the tip of her breast, kissing her through the thin satin. A strangled cry escaped her as I gripped her hips, sucking deep. My heart thumped against my ribs as her fingers dug deep into my hair, holding me close as I moved to the other breast. I nipped gently and was rewarded with another breathy cry.

Her body already trembled against mine, but I was nowhere near done with her. I slid my hands under the hem of her skirt, moving them up her smooth thighs as I blazed a trail of kisses to her sweetly swollen lips.

"Tell me something, sweetheart." I made tiny circles along her inner thigh, coming close to her center. "Have you come before?"

She stiffened in embarrassment and when she didn't answer, I made those little circles *down* her thigh. "Yes," she said. "I have."

"By yourself?" I moved my hand back up her thigh.

She squirmed closer, pressing down on my erection as she rested her forehead against mine. "Yes."

I was relieved to hear that, even though I shouldn't have been surprised. I skimmed a finger across the center of her damp panties. Her body jerked in a tempting way. I kept moving my finger, back and forth softly.

I could touch her forever.

Maybe I would. We could stay right here, one hand deep between her thighs and the other cradling her breast. I could deal with that.

But then Avery moved.

She slid her hand down my chest, over my abs, stopping above the band of my jeans. My cock swelled at how close she was. Part of me wanted to take her hand and finish it off, but the other part worried that I would lose control the moment she touched me. She rocked her hips as I made another pass between her legs, circling the bundle of nerves.

I was totally willing to risk losing control.

Nipping at her lower lip, I stilled under her. "What do you want, Avery?"

"I want to . . . I want to touch you." A look of surprise scuttled across her face. "But I don't know what you like."

Oh God, I groaned at her words and pleasure bubbled up to my tip. I placed my hand over hers. "Sweetheart, anything you do is something I'm going to like."

"Really?"

"Hell yeah." I pressed back against the couch, creating space between us. "Whatever you want to do to me, I'm going to love it. You don't have to worry about that."

Happiness and heat flared in her gaze and then her lashes swept down as she flicked the button of my jeans open and then pulled down the zipper. I chuckled as she gasped.

"Easy access." I reached down between us, easing myself out.

Avery's eyes remained fixed, and there was nothing hotter than that. My entire body was taut as a bowstring. I couldn't help myself. I moved my hand up to my tip and then back down to my base as my heart rate kicked up.

"I've thought about you," she whispered.

Every muscle in my body froze. "How?"

She hesitated. "When I . . . touched myself, I thought of you."

"Holy fuck," I growled and then clamped my jaw down. I almost came right then and there. She thought about me while she touched herself? Good God almighty and the devil down below . . . "That is the hottest thing I've ever heard."

Her lips tipped up, and I kissed her, harder and rougher than I probably should've, but she didn't shy away. I brought her hand down to me, coaxing her fingers around my thickness. At first contact, my entire body jerked and then she moved her hand up and down.

What she lacked in skill, she sure as hell made up in eagerness. The innocence in the way she stroked me was almost too much.

"You're perfect," I murmured against her lips as I slid my hand back between her thighs.

Our breaths mingled, fast and hard as I cupped her through her panties, pressing my palm against her clit as I pushed my finger into her warmth, separated only by a flimsy barrier. I kept my mouth on hers, taking her tongue into mine as she rode my hand and I thrust into hers.

I felt her body tense and then she cried out in a harsh expulsion. "Cam!"

Her body spasmed against my hand, wave after wave as I eased her down. Tremors rocked my body as my release barreled through me. I came harder than I ever had and I was amazed by that. She held on, her head dropped against my shoulder as I clamped one arm around her waist.

Only when I became too sensitive, I gently removed her hand. She was boneless in my embrace as I tucked her against my chest. I knew I needed to let her go. I'd made a mess of her and me, but I loathed to part with her body just yet.

Reaching up, I tilted her head back and kissed the lids of her eyes and then her parted lips. The silence stretched out between us, comforting until I felt her tense in my arms. Concern flooded me. I knew I hadn't hurt her, but maybe it was too much?

"Hey," I said, smoothing my thumb along her cheek. A troubled look filled her gaze. "You okay? I didn't—"

"It was perfect." She kissed my jaw, closing her eyes. "This is perfect."

Avery was right. Oh God, this was the most perfect moment, but a ball of unease formed in my gut. A cloud had passed over her. It was gone now, but it had been there and I couldn't help but fear that it would come back.

Twenty-Three

Ollie stood on the edge of the bench across from us,
Avery's left-over Chinese food in a carton. The fact that
he'd brought that to campus with him was weird. And that
food had been in the fridge for a couple of days.

"All I'm saying is that Presidents' Day is more interesting than Valentine's Day," he said, digging his chopsticks
into the noodles. "After all, Hallmark created V-Day. It's
not a real day."

Sitting next to where he stood, Brittany shook her head.
"Presidents' Day is boring. What happens on Presidents'
Day?"

Avery sat in my lap, curled up against my chest. It was
a brutally cold day in February and I had unzipped my
hoodie, gathering the ends around her. "Did those two
hook up at some point?" she asked quietly.

I laughed under my breath. "I honestly don't know for
sure."

"There're car sales and furniture sales on Presidents'

Day," Ollie said, grinning as if he was proud of what he came up with. "And banks are closed."

"Wow." Brittany exchanged a look with Shortcake and then turned her gaze up at Ollie. "You don't get laid on Presidents' Day. You do on Valentine's Day."

Ollie paused, a noodle blowing softly in the wind as he looked down at her. "You offering?"

"Wow," I murmured. "Smooth."

Shortcake giggled.

Throwing out her arm, Brittany knocked Ollie off the bench. "No. I am not offering."

Ollie landed nimbly on his feet. "That's a shame." He bent down so close to Brittany that his blond hair tangled with hers. "I'd change your life, baby."

Unable to control herself, Avery laughed out loud, and I dropped my head on her shoulder, hiding my face as secondhand embarrassment washed over me.

Brittany looked unimpressed. "You're probably right. I imagine that after one night with you, I'd be paying a visit to the health clinic for the rest of my life."

"Ouch." He slammed his free hand against his chest. "You wound me."

She laughed then. "I doubt that."

Ollie plopped down next to her and held up his chopsticks. "Noodle?"

Smiling slightly, she shook her head. "No. Thank you."

Avery sat up, and cold air sifted in between us. I reached for her, dragging her back against my chest. "Don't go," I said, wrapping my arms around her. "You're like my heated blanket."

She twisted toward me, pressing a kiss to the corner of my lips. "I have to go to class."

"Skip," I murmured, seeking out her lips. "Come home with me." I chased down her mouth, slipping my tongue between her cool lips. "I'll warm you up."

Her body shivered, and I doubted it had anything to do with the cold. "That's about as classy as Ollie changing Brittany's life."

"Hey!" Ollie shouted. "Don't bring me into your little love nest."

Shortcake's cheek flushed, and I wondered if she'd forgotten that we weren't alone. She wiggled her way free, like she had done that night before in my bedroom, on my bed, and I swallowed a groan.

I really did not need to be thinking about that right now.

"I'll see you in a little while?" she said to Brittany, giving her a quick hug.

Brittany nodded. "You got it."

Saying good-bye, I dropped my arm over her slim shoulders, intent on walking her to Whitehall. She smiled up at me, squinting. "You're supposed to be on the other side of campus, right?"

"Maybe." I pulled off my cap and slipped it on her head, shielding the sun. "What are you and Brittany doing later?"

"Going to the mall." She pushed the brim of the cap up a little as she stepped to the side, reaching out with her hand. "We have some special shopping to do."

"Hmm." I threaded my fingers through hers. "What kind of special shopping?"

"It's a secret."

I grinned and then inhaled deeply. There was dampness in the air. "Does it have something to do with a day that's not Presidents' Day?"

She laughed, and my grin spread. Shortcake had been laughing a lot lately. "I'm not going to tell you."

"I see how it is." We stopped near the covered entrance of the social-sciences building, and I pulled her toward me. She came willingly, stretching up on the tips of her toes. Sliding the cap around so it was backward on her head, I rested my forehead against hers. "Can you smell it?"

She laughed as she placed a hand on my chest. "My breath?"

Rolling my eyes, I wrapped an arm around her waist. "No, you little dork. There's snow in the air."

"Oh." She giggled.

I kissed her softly. "Well, be careful on your special, secret shopping trip."

"I will." She reached up, taking off the cap and then fitting it on me. "You coming by tonight?"

"That's a stupid question." I didn't want to let her go.

She made a face at me. "Thought there were no such things as stupid questions."

"That's a lie." Dipping my head, I kissed her once more and then let go. When she turned to leave, I tapped her ass, causing her to jump and shoot me a dirty look. I laughed. "You liked it."

Her flushed cheeks told me I was right.

The snow fell outside, coming down pretty fast. I was glad I was able to convince Shortcake to skip with me tomorrow. Classes would still be happening, but the campus would be an ice-pit death trap.

I glanced down at her and smiled. After eating pizza and hanging out with Ollie, she was tuckered out. Deeply asleep, she was curled on her side, her head resting on my leg. I scooped a strand of her hair off her cheek, tucking it back.

"She's cute, you know?" Ollie bent forward and picked up the last slice of pizza and stood. "Only she could pass out in the presence of our awesomeness."

I laughed softly. "It was too much for her. She was overwhelmed."

He grinned as he stepped over my legs. "I'll let myself out."

In the following silence, I traced the elegant curves of her face with my gaze, committing the sweeps and angles to memory. Earlier in the day, as I'd walked over to West Campus with Ollie, he'd made some kind of comment about me being whipped. Funny thing was, it hadn't ticked me off. I'd laughed. Maybe I was a little whipped. Maybe I was a little obsessed. Maybe I was—

On the coffee table, Avery's phone beeped and the screen lit up, and I looked before I realized what I was doing.

You're a lying whore. How can you live with yourself?

I leaned forward, reading the message three times before the light faded from the screen and the text disappeared.

Shock made me stupid. I had to have read it wrong. Three times? Not likely. Muscles in my back and neck locked up. I don't know how long I sat there in stunned silence, but beyond the shock, anger simmered in my veins like a slow-burning brushfire. Who in the fuck would've sent that to her? Lying whore? I wanted to find the person responsible and rip their spine right out.

But why would someone send that to her? If Avery was a whore, so was a nun, but why? A muscle began to thrum in my jaw and didn't stop when Avery stirred.

Yawning, she sat up and pushed long strands of hair out of her face. A sleepy smile formed on her lush lips. "Sorry. I didn't mean to fall asleep on you."

I looked at her, unsure if I should say something.

She straightened as her gaze flickered over my face. "Is everything okay?"

Fuck it. There was no way I could let this pass. I glanced at the table. "You got a message while you were sleeping."

Her brows knitted as she followed my gaze and then she lurched forward, snapping up her cell. She inhaled sharply when she tapped on the screen.

I watched the blood seep out of her face and felt the knots of unease grow. "It flashed across your screen when it came through."

Slowly, she sat the phone down with trembling hands. She didn't look at me, but kept staring at it. "You looked at the text?"

"It's not like I did it on purpose." Tense, I leaned forward. "It was right there, sitting on your screen."

"But you didn't have to look!" She stood, hands curling at her sides.

Whoa. Hold up. "Avery, I wasn't sneaking through your stuff. The damn text came through. I looked before I could stop myself. Maybe that was wrong."

"It was wrong!"

I took a deep breath. "Okay. It was wrong. I'm sorry, but that doesn't change the fact that I saw that text."

She stopped in the middle of the room and there was no mistaking the look of panic darkening her eyes.

"Avery," I said carefully. Her gaze darted to me. "Why would you get a text like that?"

She crossed her arms over her chest. "I don't know."

I didn't believe her.

"I don't know," she said again, and then rushed on. "Every so often I get a text like this, but I don't know why. I think it's a wrong-number kind of thing."

I still didn't believe her. "You don't know who that's from?"

"No. It says unknown caller. You saw that." She continued on before I could speak. "I'm sorry for freaking out on you. It just surprised me. I was asleep and I wake up and I could tell something was wrong. Then I thought . . . I don't know what I thought, but I'm sorry."

"Stop apologizing, Avery." I hated it when she did that. "I don't need to hear that you're sorry. I want you to be honest with me, sweetheart. That's all I want. If you're getting messages like that, I need to know about that."

She took a step back. "Why?"

Sometimes I wondered if we spoke the same language.

"Because I'm your boyfriend and I care if someone is calling you a whore!"

Avery flinched.

Taking another deep breath, I looked away. "Honestly? It pisses me off, even if it's an accidental text. No one should be sending you shit like that." I paused, finding her gaze and holding it. "You know you can tell me anything, right? I'm not going to judge you or get mad."

The moment those words left my mouth, I realized how absolutely fucking fake I was. Here I was telling Avery she could tell me anything, getting pissed off because I *knew* she wasn't, and I was keeping secrets.

"I know," she whispered, and then louder, "I know."

My heart kicked in my chest as I stared into her eyes. "And you trust me, right?"

"Yes. Of course I do."

"Shit," I growled, and my muscles tensed even further. A ball of ice formed in my chest. Telling her was a risk. She could think I was a violent person and walk away, but I needed to be honest, especially if I expected her to be.

I was scared shitless.

Closing my eyes, I said, "I haven't been entirely honest with you."

"What?"

I scrubbed my hand along my jaw. In for a penny, in for a pound or some shit, right? "I tell you that you should trust me and that you can tell me anything, but I'm not doing the same thing. And eventually you're going to find out."

Avery hurried around the coffee table and sat on the edge of the couch.

"What are you talking about, Cam?"

I could lose her, I realized, but I had to tell her the truth. "You know how I told you we all have done shit in our past we aren't proud of?"

She nodded. "Yes."

"I can say that from firsthand experience. Only a few people know about this." I paused. "And it's the last thing I want to tell you."

"You can tell me," she said, scooting closer. "Seriously, you can talk to me. Please."

I didn't know where to start. It took me a few moments. "I should be graduating this year, along with Ollie, but I'm not."

"I remember you telling me you had to take some time off."

"It was sophomore year. I hadn't been home a lot during the summer because I was helping coach a soccer camp in Maryland, but whenever I did go home, my sister . . . . she was acting different. I couldn't put my finger on it, but she was super jumpy and when she was home, she spent all her time in her bedroom. And apparently she was rarely home, according to my parents. My sister, she's always been this bleeding heart, you know. Picking up stray animals and people, especially stray guys. Even when she was a tiny thing, she always buddied up with the most unpopular kid in the class." I smiled at the memory. "She met this guy. He was a year or two older than her and I guess their relationship was serious—as serious as they can be when you're sixteen. Met the kid once. Didn't like him. And it had nothing to do with the fact he was trying to get with my little sister. There was just something about him that rubbed me the wrong way."

I dropped my hands to my knees as I felt the familiar anger building inside me. "I was home over Thanksgiving break and I was in the kitchen. Teresa was in there and we were messing around. She pushed me and I pushed her back, on her arm. Not even hard and she cried out like I'd seriously hurt her. At first I thought she was just being dumb, but there were tears in her eyes. She played it off and I forgot about it for that night, but on Thanksgiving morning, Mom walked in on her in a towel and she saw it."

Avery took a deep breath, and I shook my head. "My sister . . . she was covered in bruises. Up and down her arms, on her legs." I closed my hands into helpless fists. "She said it was from dancing, but we all knew you couldn't get bruises like that from dancing. It took almost all morning to get the truth out of her."

"It was her boyfriend?" she asked quietly.

I swallowed hard. "The little fuck had been hitting her. He was smart about it, doing it in places that weren't so easily noticeable. She stayed with him. I didn't know why at first. Come to find out that she was too scared of him to break up." Unable to sit still, I stood and prowled toward the window. "Who knows how long it would've continued if Mom hadn't walked in when she did. Would Teresa have finally told someone? Or would that bastard have just kept hitting her one night and killed her?"

My head hung forward. All of this felt like yesterday—the anger and helplessness. "God, I was so pissed, Avery. I wanted to kill the fuck. He was beating up my sister and my dad wanted to call the police, but what were they really going to do? Both of them were minors. He'd get his hands slapped and get counseling, whatever. And that's bullshit. I wasn't okay with that. I left Thanksgiving night and I found him. Didn't take much, fucking small town and all. I knocked on his door and he came right out. I told him he couldn't come around my sister anymore and you know what that little punk did?"

"What?" she whispered.

"He got all up in my face, puffing his fucking chest at me. Told me he would do whatever the fuck he wanted." I laughed, but there was no humor in it. "I lost it. Angry isn't even the word to use. I was *enraged*. I hit him and I didn't stop." Pulse pounding, I faced her. "I didn't stop hitting him. Not when his parents came out or when his mom starting screaming. It took two police officers to get me off him."

Avery didn't say anything as she stared at me.

I rubbed my palms over my cheeks. "I ended up in jail and he ended up in a coma."

Her mouth opened in shock, and there it was. Ducking my chin, I looked away as I sat in the moon chair. "I'd been in fights before—normal shit. But nothing like that. My knuckles were busted wide open and I didn't even feel it. My dad . . ." I shook my head. "He worked his magic. I should've gone away for a long time for that, but I didn't. Guess it helped that the kid woke up a few days later.

"I got off easy—not even a night in jail." I smiled wryly. "But I couldn't leave home for several months while it got worked out. I ended up with a year's worth of community service at the local boys' club and then another year's worth of anger management. That's what I do every Friday. My last session is in the fall. My family had to pay restitution and you don't even want to know how much that cost. I had to stop playing soccer because of the community-service gig, but . . . like I said, I got off easy."

Avery looked away, brows pressing together. Her face was pale and the longer she was silent, the sicker I felt. What had I—

"I understand," she said quietly. I stared at her, not sure I was hearing her correctly.

"What?" I said hoarsely.

"I understand why you did it."

Did she hear anything I had done? I stood. "Avery—"

"I don't know what it says about me, but you were defending your sister and beating the crap out of someone isn't the answer, but she's your sister and . . ." She paused, seeming to search for the right words. "There are some people who deserve an ass kicking."

I stared at her.

She unfolded her legs. "And there are probably some people who don't even deserve to breathe. It's a sick and sad thing to say, but it's true. The guy could've killed your sister. Hell, he could have beaten some other girl to death."

"I deserve to be in jail, Avery. I almost killed him."

"But you didn't."

I opened my mouth, but there were no words. How could she be so understanding?

"Let me ask you a question. Would you do it again?"

The million-dollar question. "I still would've driven to

his house and I would've hit him. Maybe not as badly, but honestly, I don't think it would've changed anything. The bastard beat my sister."

She inhaled deeply. "I don't blame you."

I continued to stare at her, feeling as if I should drop to my knees. "You're . . ."

One slim shoulder rose. "Twisted?"

"No." I smiled, absolutely dumbfounded. "You're remarkable."

"I wouldn't go that far," she said, grinning slightly.

"Seriously." I sat down beside her on the couch. "I thought you would be disgusted or angry if you knew."

Avery shook her head, sending strands of coppery hair everywhere.

My God, she was . . . there were no words. Dropping my forehead to hers, I cupped her cheeks. It felt like a gorilla had been lifted off my shoulders. "It feels good getting that off my chest. I don't want there to be secrets between us."

Her lips curved up and I kissed their corners. Overcome with relief, I sat back, cradling her to my chest. This girl was . . . she was perfect in all the ways that mattered.

I kissed the top of her head, and her chest rose sharply. The relief I felt was staggering, and I honestly hadn't prepared myself for Shortcake to be so accepting. Sighing, I closed my eyes and gathered her as close as I could.

Avery had accepted my secret. Now if only I could get her to see that I would do the same for her.

Twenty-Four

"You don't think that's enough roses for today?" Ollie asked, nodding at the single-stem rose I held in my hand. And then he glanced at the newest addition in the corner of the living room. "Plus that? You're making the rest of us guys look bad."

Jase laughed from his position on the couch, bottle of beer in his hand. "I really don't think you could appear any badder, Ollie."

He huffed as he kicked up his legs onto the coffee table. "At least I know 'badder' isn't a word."

Jase smirked. "That's about all you know."

I rolled Shortcake's present into the outside hallway and then turned back to them, brows raised. "Are you guys going to be here all night getting drunk?"

"Yep," they replied in unison.

"Well, have fun with that." Saluting them, I slipped outside and placed her present beside her door, against the wall. I knocked, fighting an idiotic grin as I heard the soft thuds coming from her gift.

Avery opened the door, her gaze dropping to the rose. "For me?"

"Of course," I said, handing it over as I stepped inside. "I am really sorry about not being able to take you out tonight, but—"

"It's cool. I know you have those meetings." She carried the rose to the vase on her kitchen counter, where the rest of the roses I'd been giving her were. Looking over her shoulder at me, she cocked her head to the side. "What are you doing?"

I grinned. "Stay right where you are and close your eyes."

"I have to close my eyes?"

"Yep."

Excitement flashed across her face, but she was desperate to play it cool. "So it's a surprise?"

"Of course it is. So close your eyes."

Her lips twitched. "Your surprises are just as scary as your ideas."

I scoffed. "My ideas *and* my surprises are brilliant."

"Remember when you thought it would be a good idea to—"

"Close your eyes, Avery."

Her grin spread into a wide smile as she obeyed. Spinning around, I hurried out to the hall and rolled the gift inside. I kicked the door shut. "Don't peek."

Her brows rose. "Cam . . ."

"A couple more seconds." I wrapped my hand around

hers, leading her from the kitchen into the living room. "Keep your eyes closed, okay?"

"They're closed."

I squeezed her hand and then let go. Stepping up from behind her, I slid an arm around her waist and leaned over her, kissing her temple. Her fingers curled around my arm as she sighed.

"You can open your eyes now." I kissed her cheek. "Or you can stand there with your eyes closed. I like that, too."

She laughed, and I knew the moment she opened her eyes. "Oh my God, Cam . . ."

I'd decked out a fifty-gallon terrarium, complete with sand and rock bedding and foliage. Peeking out from a hidey-hole was a small tortoise, craning its neck, checking out its new home.

She made a tiny, squeal-like noise.

I chuckled. "You like?"

"Like?" Shortcake pulled free and placed her hands on the glass. "I . . . I love it."

"Good." I moved to stand beside her. "I thought Raphael could use a playdate."

She laughed as she squeezed her eyes tight and re-opened them. "You shouldn't have done all of this, Cam. This is . . . too much."

"It's not that much and everyone needs a pet turtle." I swooped down, kissing her cheek once more. "Happy Valentine's Day."

Avery spun around and threw her arms around me. She kissed me, stealing my breath. "Thank you."

I brushed my lips over hers. "You're welcome.

She slid her arms around my waist and leaned in. "Is it a boy or a girl?"

"You know, I really don't know. Supposedly you can tell by the shape of their shell, but hell if I know."

"Well, boy or girl, I'm going to name him Michelangelo."

I threw my head back and laughed. "Perfect."

"We just need two more."

This girl was fucking perfect. "So true."

She wiggled free, smiling. "Be right back."

Before I could say a word, she pivoted around and took off down the hall. While she was gone, I pushed the terrarium against the wall and turned the heat lamp on. Hearing her approach, I turned around.

"Happy Valentine's Day. It's not as cool as your gift, but I hope you like it."

A card was shoved at my chest. Smiling, I took it and peered down at her. "I'm sure I will." Carefully, I opened the card. There was a message written inside.

You mean everything to me.

I stared at the message for probably what was too long. My heart was pounding and warmth flooded my veins. I smiled—I smiled like I'd just been handed a million dollars. And that was before I even saw the tickets.

I held them between my fingers. "This is an absolutely amazing gift, sweetheart."

"Really?" She clasped her hands together under her chest. "I hoped you'd like it. I mean, I know not playing soccer sucks and I hope this doesn't make you sad going to the game and you don't have to take me—"

I caught the rest of her words with my lips and my tongue. I liked the tickets. The gift was great, but I'd never tell her that it was those five words that I loved. "Of course I'm taking you. The gift is perfect." I nipped at her lower lip, and she gasped. "You're perfect."

Those words replayed over and over in my hand as I clasped her hips and pulled her against me. I was fully aroused, which seemed like a constant state of being around her.

My stomach dipped as she looped her arms around my neck. I didn't have to say anything as I lifted her. Short-cake wrapped those legs right around my waist as I kissed her deeply, drinking her in and refusing to let her go. She moaned, and a painfully intense lust slammed into me.

I was on a mindless autopilot as I carried her back to her room and my stomach was still dipping as I laid her on her back. I stared down at her for a few seconds and then I leaned back, tugging my sweater off and tossing it aside. I leaned over, planting my hands on either side of her head. My chest was rising and falling in uneven breaths. I needed her as badly as I needed the rush of taking a ball down the field, of scoring. Maybe even more so than that.

She traced a delicate, slender finger over the flames surrounding the sun on my chest. "I love this tattoo. Why did you get it?"

"You really want to know?"

Her thick lashes lifted. "Yes."

"It's pretty lame."

She continued to follow the design, sending a bolt of electricity through my body. "I'll be the judge of that."

"I got it after the fight with Teresa's ex." I slid my hands under her shirt, smiling at the feel of her soft skin and when she lifted up so I could remove it. "I was kind of messed up for a while. Couldn't go back to school, was stuck in my home, and I'd done that to myself. I was worried that there had been something wrong with me to lose it like I did."

She lowered her hands to her sides as I placed mine on her bare stomach, mere centimeters under the fragile clasp of her bra. My hair fell into my face as I leaned over, placing my other hand beside her head. "I was depressed. I was pissed off at myself and the world and all that bullshit." I smoothed my hand down her belly, smiling when her hips lifted just a little bit. "I think I drank just about every liquor my dad had in his bar over the course of a couple of weeks. I knew my parents were worried, but . . ."

The hollow between her raised breasts looked absolutely lonely and distracted me. Lowering my head, I pressed a kiss between them and did it again when she sucked in a soft breath. "Jase came to visit me often. So did Ollie. I probably would've lost my fucking mind without them." Placing my fingers on the clasp, I looked up, my eyes locking with hers. "May I?"

She nodded.

"Thank you." I lowered my gaze as I unhooked the clasp, leaving the rest in place. I'd never seen her bare there before. I wanted to take my sweet-ass time. "It was something Jase had said to me while I was drunk off my ass. Don't know why, but it stuck with me."

Her chest rose as I dragged a finger up the center of her chest. "What did . . . what did he say?"

"He said something like things can't be that bad if the sun is out and shining. Like I said, that stuck with me. Maybe because it's the truth. As long as the sun's shining, shit can't be that bad. So that's why I got a tattoo of the sun. Sort of a reminder."

"That's not lame." She smiled.

"Hmm . . ." It was pretty lame, but it had worked. I hooked my finger under the edge of her bra and pushed it aside, doing the same to the other cup.

I devoured her with my gaze. The dusky pink tips of her full breasts immediately puckered, begging me. Staring down at them, I felt like I'd never seen breasts before. I wanted to touch them, lick them, and suck them. All at once.

"God, you're beautiful, Avery."

"Thank you," she murmured.

I gently ran my hand over her breasts, marveling in the feel of them. Her back arched and my gaze flicked up to her face. "So perfect," I said, the words a rushed, low growl as I captured a hardened nipple between my thumb and finger.

I wanted to see more of her.

Meeting her gaze, I lowered my hand to the button on her jeans. When she nodded again, it was like winning the fucking World Cup. I slid her jeans down, stopping at the skull-and-bones socks. "Nice socks. Very goth."

When her jeans and socks were gone, I slid the bra

down her arms. Within seconds, she was in panties. Rocking back, I admired my handiwork. The length of her legs and the curve of her waist were only separated by a scrap of lace. I almost went to remove it, but instinct told me no.

It didn't matter what had happened in her past. Either way, I knew beyond a doubt she had no experience in *any* of this. All of these things—the kissing, the touching through clothes, being naked—all of it was a first for her. And I wanted to experience all of those things right along with her.

I kissed her slowly as I skimmed my hand over her chest, following the swell with my fingers. She moaned softly when I left her lips, trailing a path of tiny kisses down her throat. I hesitated for only a second and then closed my mouth over the tip of her breast.

Lust pounded like rain from a summer storm as her back arched and her hips moved. The taste of her went straight to my cock, blew a hole through my chest, and scattered all my thoughts. I twirled my tongue around the tightened tip as I slid my hand under the lace covering her.

Her legs tensed beside mine as my finger brushed her clit and her head fell back as I moved to her other breast and then worked my way down her stomach. I raised my head, my gaze locking with hers as I slowly slid a finger into her slick wetness. God, she was so tight, so wet.

"Is this okay?" I asked.

She nodded. "Yes."

A smile played over my lips as I pushed with my finger. Her entire body reacted, trembling and flushing. *I* was shaking. As I held her gaze, I started a slow pace, thrusting my finger in and out.

"You're so tight," I said.

Lowering my mouth to hers, I kissed her as her hips moved against my hand. The feel of her chest against mine was a sensation I'd long remember. It wasn't long when she cried out against my mouth and I felt her clenching around my finger. I almost lost it right then and there.

I burrowed my head on her throat as she shook. "I love how you say my name."

Reluctantly, I forced myself to ease my finger out of her and to pull away, but before I could get very far, she surprised me. Sitting up, she placed her hands on my chest, rolling me onto my back. A second later, she had straddled me.

Hellooo.

Drawing in a sharp breath, I almost lost it right there at the sight of her, almost nude as she rose up. Totally unaware of how she appeared made it all the more seductive. I reached for her, but damn, Shortcake was quick when she wanted to be. She slid down, her fingers trembling as she fumbled with the button on my jeans. I started to help her, but then she got them unbuttoned and was sliding them down my legs.

I clenched the comforter when her hand wrapped around me and her warm breath teased the head of my cock. My heart jumped. "Oh shit."

Her smile was pure woman. Then her head lowered and her hair slipped forward. I came off the bed, back bowing and hips jerking as her warm, wet mouth closed over me. Fire flooded my blood and I swelled as she gripped me and laved her tongue over the sensitive tip.

I cupped her hand with mine and wrapped my other around the back of her head, holding her hair back. But as she took me deeper into her mouth, I couldn't stop myself from pushing her down.

My moans echoed through the room and it was mere minutes before my release was on me. I pulled her away before I came, hauling her up against my chest and kissing her as I pressed against her belly.

Weak and totally spent, I collapsed onto my back and Avery did the same. Both of us were breathing raggedly. "This was the best fucking Valentine's Day ever."

She laughed. "I have to agree."

I slapped around between us until I found her hand and squeezed. Several moments passed and while I wondered what to say, the stupidest thing came out of my mouth. "You hungry?"

"No." She yawned. "Are you?"

I was an idiot. "Not yet."

Another stretch of silence fell between us and then she asked, "Stay with me? The night?"

Rolling onto my side, I trailed a hand over her shoulder. "You don't have to ask twice."

Twenty-Five

Winter hadn't wanted to loosen its hold on West "by God" Virginia. The sun came out most of February and March, but the temps were brutal. Even over spring break. While most everyone headed south, Avery and I headed west. We spent most of the break at my parents' house. Needless to say, Mom was happy that I'd brought a real live girl home again.

As spring recess, or whatever the hell they were calling the four-day weekend in April, came into sweet, sweet view, it seemed like yesterday when Avery sat outside on the curb with a beer bottle and we'd made our way inside. I couldn't believe how much time had passed.

I couldn't believe Shortcake was also skipping the rest of the day with me and had allowed me to make up for her birthday. On the eve of our mini-break from school, we'd spent the day in D.C. and had returned late.

"Guess what?" I slid my hands up her sides until they rested under her rib cage. "Got another idea."

"Does it involve eggs?"

I laughed as I tugged her hips against mine. "It doesn't involve eggs."

Her eyes took on the glazed, unfocused quality that I had become familiar with over the last months. "It doesn't?"

"But it does involve something equally tasty." I pressed my mouth to her temple, tracing her cheekbone with my lips. "And it involves you, me, a bed, and very little, if any, clothing."

"Does it now?"

"Yes." I moved my hands to her lower back, my fingers brushing the pockets of her jeans. I kissed her brow. "What do you think?"

She tipped her head back, luring me in. The kiss started off slow, but then, like always, it turned into something different. Something hungry. Something that always wanted more.

My hands found their way under her shirt and I pulled away long enough to tug her shirt off. Our mouths crashed back together—lips, tongues, teeth. We bumped into the couch and I lost my balance. I fell backward, half on the couch, half off.

Avery's laughter reached deep inside me and I captured her cheeks in my hands. Staring into her dancing eyes, the words formed in my thoughts.

I loved her.

That feeling had been there for a while, probably longer

than I dared acknowledge. Maybe even from the first time she'd turned me down, I'd begun to fall *in* love with her.

I was *in* love with her this very second.

The realization shook me to the core. I stared into those warm, whiskey-colored eyes and I wanted to see my future there—*our* future there. Never in my life had I ever wanted to see that when I stared into a chick's eyes, but with Avery Morgansten, I wanted nothing more.

My brain turned off and everything I did from that point on was fueled by those three words. I loved her. My hands shook and I was surprised by how fast I got her jeans off.

I cupped her breasts, running my thumbs over her nipples. Her muffled moan reverberated through me. I wanted—no, I needed to hear her call out my name. Dammit, I needed to hear her say those three words or at least feel them.

Thrusting my hand under her panties, I palmed her, rubbing my thumb over the spot that always made her cry out and it did. She undid my jeans and slipped her hand inside, wrapping her fingers around me.

The desire was almost too much. I thrust against her palm. "Avery."

She came apart at the sound of her name, throwing her head back, and it was fucking beautiful.

I don't remember standing, but she wrapped herself around me as I carried her back to the bed. After I placed her in the center, she watched me strip bare. Her lips parted, and I groaned.

Crawling onto the bed, blood pounded in my ears as I

hooked my fingers under her panties and waited for her to give me a sign that it was okay.

She lifted her hips.

I praised God and baby Jesus.

Finally, after so long, there was nothing between us. Not true, whispered a voice in the back of my head, but it fell to the side as my gaze swept over her. I said she was beautiful a million times and I'd say she was beautiful a million more. From the dusky tips of her breasts to the sweet curve of her hips and the shadowy area between her thighs, she was fucking beautiful.

I tasted my way down her body and back up, too far gone to *really* taste her. I hovered over her, letting her feel me between her thighs. Avery shuddered and I squeezed my eyes shut as she placed her hands against my chest.

My body strained to be inside hers. "Do you want this?"

"Yes," she said, and it was like angels harking in my head.

Our gazes met as I bent my head, kissing her as I lowered my body onto hers. Getting a condom was a distant thought but I couldn't stop. The tip of my erection slid through and then into her wetness, causing my muscles to tense. The feeling was overwhelming. My kiss turned deeper and I eased my hips—

Avery twisted her head to the side. "No. Stop." She pushed against my chest with surprising strength. "Please stop."

Those words cut through the haze and I froze. "Avery? What the—?"

"Get off." Her voice pitched high, full of panic. "Get off. *Please*. Get off me."

I had no idea what was going on, but within an instant, I was off her and she was moving. Crawling across the bed, she grabbed the comforter and held it to her chest as she stood. She backed up until she hit the dresser, rattling the bottles and knocking some over. The skin around her lips was pale and her eyes were wide and dark.

"Oh God," she whispered hoarsely.

Concern and horror warred inside me as I stared at her. "Did I hurt you? I didn't—"

"No. No!" She squeezed her eyes shut. "You didn't hurt me. You didn't even . . . I don't know. I'm sorry . . ."

I rested my hands on the bed. "Talk to me, Avery. What just happened?"

"Nothing," she said hoarsely. "Nothing happened. I just thought—"

"You thought what?"

She shook her head "I don't know. It's not a big deal—"

"Not a big deal?" My brows shot up. Was she serious? "Avery, you just scared the shit out of me. You started panicking like I was hurting you or—" The next words tasted like ash and vomit as I spoke them. "Or like I was forcing you to do this."

"You weren't forcing me, Cam. I liked what you were doing."

I didn't understand what just happened. "You know I would never hurt you, right?"

"Yes." Tears filled her eyes.

"And I would never force you to do anything you didn't

want to do." I held her gaze. "You understand that, right? If you're not ready, I'm okay with that, but you have to talk to me. You have to let me know before it gets to that point."

She nodded, but I didn't feel any better. All I could hear was the terrified note in her voice when she had begged me to stop. Air caught in my lungs and what I knew about Avery flashed through my thoughts, all building to what I had already assumed, what I prayed wasn't what had happened to her.

"What are you not telling me?" I asked. When she didn't say anything, a muscle jumped along my jaw. "What happened to you?"

"Nothing!" she shouted. "There's nothing to talk about, dammit. Just fucking drop it."

"You're lying." I took a breath. It was time. No more secrets. "You're lying to me. Something happened, because that?" I gestured at the bed behind me. "That wasn't about not being ready. That was about something else, because you know—*you know*—I would wait for you, Avery. I swear, but you have to tell me what's going on in your head."

She still said nothing, and my chest began to ache as a terrible realization occurred. Didn't she trust me? Didn't she realize how I felt? But did that matter if she didn't trust me? The answer was an icy wind down my spine.

"I'm begging you, Avery." I leaned forward, clenching the sheet. "You've got to be up-front and honest with me. You said that you trusted me. You've got to prove it, because I know there is more to this. I'm not stupid and I'm not blind. I remember how you acted when we first met and I sure as hell remember what you said that night you were drunk. And that text message you got? Are you telling me that has nothing to do with this? If you trust me, you will finally tell me what the hell is going on."

"I do trust you," she whispered.

I waited for her to say more, to say anything that would prove her words, but she said nothing and there was this horrible cracking feeling in my chest. I threw off the sheets and stood. Grabbing my jeans, I pulled them on as my heart pounded in a way that made me feel sick.

Facing her, I smoothed my hands through my hair. "I don't know what else to do with you, Avery. I've told you shit that I'm not proud of. Stuff that hardly anyone in this world knows and yet you keep shit from me. You keep *everything* from me. You don't trust me."

"No—I do." She started toward me but stopped "I trust you with my life."

Anger whipped through me like a barb-tipped chain. "But not with the truth? That's such bullshit, Avery." I stalked out of the bedroom. "You don't trust me."

She followed me, trailing the thick comforter behind her. "Cam—"

"Stop it." I grabbed my sweater off the floor and turned to her. "I don't know what else to do and I know I don't know everything in the world, but I do know that relationships don't work this way."

"What are you saying?" Her voice shook, and I steeled myself against it.

"What do you think I'm saying, Avery? There are some obvious issues with you, and no, don't fucking look at me like I kicked your puppy. Do you think I'd break up with you because of whatever the hell went on with you? Just like you thought I'd think differently of you when I saw the scar on your wrist? I know you think that and that's bullshit." I sucked in a breath as raw pain hit me in the chest. The next words *hurt*. "How can there be any future for us if you can't be honest with me? If you can't really trust that how I feel about you is strong enough, then we have nothing. This is the shit that ends relationships. Not the past, Avery, but the *present*."

"Cam, please—"

"No more, Avery. I told you before. All I asked from you was to trust me and not shut me out." I forced myself to walk to the door. "And you don't trust me and you shut me out again."

I closed the door behind me, ignoring the burn building up my throat. The one thing I'd asked from Avery was the one thing she couldn't give me. Nothing, not even love, would work without trust.

It was over.

Twenty-Six

"*A*h, it's good to see that you've showered finally and have left your bedroom."

I stopped halfway between the living room and the bathroom. Spying Jase on the couch, I ignored the statement as I pulled a shirt on over my head. "Did I get a new roommate or are you in the habit of just letting yourself into my house now?"

His lips curved up in a smirk. "Actually, while you were scrubbing two days' worth of funk off your crusty ass, Ollie let me in."

I dropped onto the other end of the couch, picked up my cap and pulled it down low. "And where is my esteemed roommate?"

"He's over at the house." Jase rested his legs on the coffee table, crossing his ankles. "There's a mean game of Call of Duty going on."

"And why aren't you there?"

He pinned me with a look as dry as my throat. "Really? Ollie hasn't seen you in two days. You finally just stepped out of your bedroom. He's concerned."

I rolled my eyes. "I doubt that."

Jase watched me, and I knew that look. I groaned, and he grinned shamelessly. "What the hell is going on, Cam?"

How could I answer that question? And where could I even start? I leaned my head against the back of the couch and sighed. The familiar burning sensation was building in my chest. Thinking about her, knowing that she was so close and completely out of my reach just killed me.

"Cam?"

I shook my head, laughing dryly. "She doesn't trust me."

There was a pause. "Care to explain that further?"

"Not really." I raised my hands, scrubbing my palms down my cheeks. "She's not telling me the truth about . . . well, about something I know that's really important."

"Does it have to do with what you thought that night of the party?" he asked.

I nodded without saying anything.

"I see." Jase sighed. "That's got to be some hard shit to talk about, man."

"I know. Fuck. I know, but you don't understand . . ." I trailed off, swallowing hard. "There is shit I'm not going to talk about, Jase. I wouldn't do that to her."

"I get that. I understand." Jase dropped his feet onto the floor and hunched forward. He let out another heavy breath. "But what happened? I'm assuming you guys had a fight."

"A fight?" I laughed again, but it sounded so wrong. "I left her."

"Whoa." Jase pursed his lips. "Shit."

I raised my hands helplessly. "I asked her—I begged her to tell me the truth and she didn't."

"And you left her?"

"I know how it sounds." I shot him a look. "I feel like a big enough fucking ass without you thinking it."

His brows rose. "Didn't say a thing."

"You're thinking it." My eyes narrowed. "But you don't get it. There's nothing if we don't trust one another—there's nothing if she doesn't trust me."

Jase nodded. "I agree. It's just that it's obvious you really care for her . . ."

"I do, but . . ."

But I wanted what my parents have. I wanted something that could last with Avery, and how could we build a relationship when she didn't trust me with the truth of her past? When I trusted her? We couldn't. And I couldn't go through what happened with her Wednesday night again. I never wanted to see that horror in her face. I never wanted to think that I had been the cause of it. Thinking about it now still made me sick. Not because of what might have happened to her, but because what I was doing had, in one way or another, terrified her.

And that would never change until she was honest with me.

Jase left shortly after that, but not before trying to get me to go with him. I wasn't in the mood to be around other people, especially a bunch of drunk people. When a knock came about an hour later, I figured it was him again, but when I opened the door, I was caught off guard.

Avery stood there, arms huddled around her waist. Her eyes were red and swollen. Fresh tears tracked down her cheeks. I opened my mouth, but closed it.

"Can we talk?" Her voice cracked in a way that made my chest splinter. "Please, Cam. I won't take up much of your time. I just—"

"Are you okay, Avery?" Concern for her overshadowed everything else.

"Yes. No. I don't know." She gave a little shake of her head. "I just need to talk to you."

Drawing in a deep breath, I stepped aside. "Ollie's not here."

A little bit of tension seeped out of her shoulders. I led her into the living room and sat on the couch. I had no idea what was going on, but I doubted she was about to unload a confession. "What's going on, Avery?"

She sat on the edge of the tattered recliner that had belonged to Ollie's dad. "Everything."

Tensing, I scooted forward, twisting my cap backward. "Avery, what's going on?"

"I haven't been honest with you and I'm sorry." Her lip started to tremble and the urge to gather her in my arms was hard to resist. "I'm so sorry, and you probably don't have time for—"

"I have time for you, Avery. You want to talk to me, I'm here. I've been here. And I'm listening."

I held her gaze until she let out a deep breath and then she began to talk—to really talk. "When I was fourteen,

I went to this party on Halloween. I was there with my friends. We were all dressed up and there was this guy there. It was his house and . . . and he was three years older than me and friends with my cousin."

Avery's gaze drifted to her hands. They opened and closed every few seconds. "He was really popular. So was I." She laughed dryly. "That might not seem important, but it was. I never thought someone like him could do—could be like he was. And maybe that was stupid of me, like a fatal flaw or something. I don't know." Her lashes lifted, piercing me with watery eyes. "I was talking to him and I was drinking, but I wasn't drunk. I swear to you, I wasn't drunk."

"I believe you, Avery." God, I knew where this was heading and I already hurt for her. "What happened?"

"We were flirting and it was fun. You know, I didn't think anything of it. He was a good guy and he was a good-looking guy. At one point, he pulled me into his lap and someone took our picture. We were having fun." The second laugh was just as harsh. "When he got up and pulled me into one of the empty guest rooms that was on the ground floor, I didn't think anything of it. We sat on the couch and talked for a little while. Then he put his arms around me."

Avery stopped, rubbing her hands together, and I prepared myself. I truly tried to. "At first I didn't mind, but he started doing things I didn't want him to. I told him to stop and he laughed it off. I started crying and I tried to get away from him, but he was stronger than me, and once he got me on my stomach, I couldn't do anything really, but to tell him to stop."

I stopped breathing. "Did he stop?"

Please tell me he stopped. Please. Please. Please.

"He didn't," she said quietly. "He never stopped no matter what I did."

It was like being shot in the spine. I started to stand, because I *had* to move, but I couldn't make my legs work. "He raped you?"

She closed her eyes and then . . . then she nodded and opened her eyes, and I wanted nothing more than to change that yes into a no. But I couldn't. "I am still a virgin. He didn't touch me there. That's not how he . . . raped me."

At first I didn't get it. Maybe it was brain overload, because I couldn't figure out how she could've been raped and was still a virgin, but then it hit me. Horror gripped me. He . . . the sick motherfucker had sodomized her. My hands closed into fists. "Son of a bitch, you were *fourteen* and he did *that* to you?"

"Yeah."

I dragged my hands through my hair, wanting to pull it out. "Shit. Avery. I suspected something. I thought that something like that might have happened to you."

"You did?"

I nodded. "It was the way you acted sometimes. How jumpy you could be, but I'd just hoped it didn't go that far. And when you told me you were still a virgin, I thought that was the case. Avery, I'm so, so sorry. You should have never had to go through something like that, especially at that age . . ." Anger for her clogged my throat. "Please tell me that motherfucker is in jail for this."

"He is now." She turned her gaze to the TV. "It's a long story."

"I have time." I gave her a moment, not wanting her to shut down on me, not after we came so far, not when I wanted to commit murder. "What else, Avery? Please talk to me, because I'm seconds away from booking a flight to Texas and killing a motherfucker."

She leaned back, tucking her knees against her chest. "After he stopped, I really don't think he had a clue that he'd done anything wrong. He just left me there on his couch and when I could get up, I knew I needed to tell someone. I knew I needed to go to the hospital. I was in so much . . ." *Pain.* She didn't finish the sentence, but I could see it in her eyes. "I couldn't find my friends, but I found my purse, and I ended up walking out of the house and I kept walking until I remembered I had my phone with me. I called 911."

She stood suddenly. "I ended up at the hospital and they did an exam. The police showed up and I told them what happened and it was the truth."

"Of course it was the truth." I watched her pace, her steps quick and agitated.

"By the time the police left the hospital, the party was over, but Blaine was at his house," she continued as if she hadn't heard me. "They arrested him and took him in. I went home and I stayed out of school for the next two days, but everyone found out that he'd been arrested for what he'd done. And then his parents showed up."

"What do you mean?"

"His parents and mine were—*are*—country-club buddies. All they ever cared about was image. My mom and dad have more money than they could ever want, but . . ." Her voice turned thick and hoarse. "The Fitzgeralds offered my parents a deal. That if I dropped the charges and remained quiet about what happened, they would pay me and them an ungodly sum of money."

I gaped at her. "And your parents told them to go fuck themselves, right?"

She laughed, but it sounded broken. "They showed my parents the picture that was taken of Blaine and me at the party and they said that if this went to court, no one would believe the girl in the 'slutty costume sitting in his lap.' And my parents, they didn't want to deal with the scandal. They'd rather it all go away, so they agreed."

"Holy shit," I whispered hoarsely.

"It happened so fast. I couldn't believe what my parents were telling me to do. They hadn't really talked to me about it before, but they . . . they had been so worried about what everyone would think if the whole thing went public—the pictures and the fact that I *had* been drinking. I was just so scared and confused and you know, I'm not even sure they believed me." She tugged her hair back, squeezing her eyes shut. "So I signed the papers."

Not only did I want to kill the fucker who did this, I wanted to add her parents to the list.

"I agreed to take the money, half of which went into my account so that when I turned eighteen, I had access to it, and I agreed to pull the charges and to not speak about it again." She lowered her hands as she looked at me. "That makes me a terrible person, doesn't it?"

"What?" Oh no . . . "You're not a terrible person, Avery. Jesus Christ, you were fourteen and your parents should've told them to fuck off. If anyone is to blame, besides the fucker who did that to you, it's them. You don't have any fault in this."

Relief flashed in her eyes, but as she dropped into the recliner, I knew there was more. Fuck. There was more. "Within days, everyone at school turned on me. Apparently, there was nothing in the agreement about Blaine keeping his mouth shut. He told people that I had lied. That I had done all those things with him willingly and then falsely accused him. Everyone believed him. Why wouldn't they? I dropped the charges. I wouldn't talk about it. School was . . . it was terrible after that. I lost all my friends."

Things started making sense. "This is why you stopped dancing?"

"Yes. I couldn't stand people looking at me and whispering about what they'd heard or talking openly about it in front of my face. And I did this . . ." She raised her left arm. "My mom was so pissed."

I couldn't believe what she had just said. "She was mad because you . . ." I shook my head. "No wonder you don't go home to see them."

"It's why I picked here, you know. It was far enough to just get away from all of it. I thought that was all I needed to do—to distance myself."

"That message I saw? It was someone who knew about what happened?

"Whoever came up with the saying you can't escape your past really knew what they were talking about."

I could feel the muscle in my jaw thrumming like crazy. "What else has been going on, Avery? You said this *Blaine* was in jail? But who's been messaging you?"

She hunched over, pressing her head into her hands. Her face was shielded with a veil of shimmery hair. "I've been getting these messages since August. I just thought it was some asshole and ignored it. And my cousin had been trying to reach me, but I ignored him, too, because . . . well, for obvious reasons. I finally talked to my cousin over winter break, the night before I came over to your apartment."

"The night of the fight?"

"Yeah . . . he was trying to get in touch with me to tell me that Blaine had been arrested for doing the same thing to another girl at the start of summer. He actually apologized. That meant a lot to me, but . . . I didn't know that this girl had been the one who has been contacting me this entire time." Taking a deep breath, she lifted her head. "Blaine had done it to another girl. And she apparently had tried contacting me, because she didn't know about the money. She contacted the police and held her ground. She put him in jail and I . . . All she thought when I didn't respond was that either I lied about Blaine or whatever. And the longer I didn't respond to her, the madder she got. If I hadn't signed those papers, he would've never been able to hurt her."

I shook my head. "What happened to her is fucking terrible and I'm glad that bastard's ass is going to jail. Better yet, he should be fucking castrated, but what happened to her isn't your fault, sweetheart. You didn't make him do that to you or her."

Her eyes filled. "But me not telling anyone allowed him to do it again."

"No." I stood. "Don't fucking tell yourself that. No one knows what would've happened if you didn't drop the charges. You were fourteen, Avery. You did the best you could in the situation. You *survived*."

"But that's it, you know? All I've been doing is surviving. I haven't been living. Look at what I've done to us. And yes, I've done this! I pushed you away *again*."

"But you're telling me now."

"I've let what happened to me five years ago still affect me! When we almost had sex? I wasn't afraid of you or if there'd be pain. It wasn't that. I was afraid that once we started, that what Blaine had done would ruin it for me or that I would ruin it for myself. I am a coward—I *was* a coward." She shot to her feet, face flushed with tears. "But it's too late, isn't it? I should've been honest with you months ago so you knew what you were getting into and I'm so sorry that I wasn't."

I reached out for her. "Avery . . ."

"I'm so sorry, Cam. I know telling you now doesn't change anything, but I needed to tell you that you didn't do anything wrong. You were perfect—*perfect* for me—and I love you. And I know you can't look at me the same now. I understand."

What? My arms fell to my sides as I stared at her. And then I was in front of her, cupping her cheeks. "What did you say?"

"That you can't look at me the same?"

"Not that. Before that."

"I love you?" she whispered.

"You love me?"

"Yes, but—"

"Stop," I told her. "Do you think I look at you differently? I told you I always suspected that something happened—"

"But you had hope that it wasn't that!" She tried to pull away, but I wasn't letting her run away again. No more. "You looked at me before with *hope* and you don't have that anymore."

"Is that what you really think? Has that been what has been stopping you this whole time from telling me?"

She lowered her gaze. "Everyone looks at me differently once they know."

"I'm not everyone, Avery! Not to you, not with you. Do you think I still don't have hope? Hope that you will eventually get past this? That it won't haunt you five more years from now?"

Avery looked too afraid to speak as I guided her hands to my chest, above my heart. "I have hope." I held her gaze. "I have hope because I love you—I've been *in* love with you, Avery. Probably before I even realized that I was."

Her eyes widened. "You loved me?"

I pressed my forehead to hers. "I love you."

"You *love* me?"

I smiled slightly. "Yes, sweetheart."

Avery held my gaze for a few moments, and I saw the very second she cracked. When the walls she had built around herself to just get by every day finally crumbled. Tears poured out of her eyes, so many I honestly believed it was possible for someone to drown in them. With everything in the open, she was laid bare, for the first time in years.

Emotion crawled up my throat as I circled my arms around her tightly. She came willingly, clutching my shirt. And she kept sobbing, and I knew I couldn't stop her. That she had to get this out.

I lifted her into my arms and carried her back into my bedroom. I laid her down on the bed. I crawled in beside her, cradling her against my chest, and she held on to me as she continued to cry, like she was afraid I would leave her.

And leaving her was something that would never happen again.

Twenty-Seven

It was after midnight when my phone vibrated off my nightstand. Half asleep, I rolled over and smacked around until my hand landed on my cell. The soft white glow lit up the one word text from Shortcake.

Incoming.

Things were definitely different in the weeks following the day she had opened up to me.

I grinned as I threw the sheets off me and hurried through the living room and opened the front door. Avery stood there, barefoot and wearing a pair of tiny sleep shorts and a thin shirt. In the still cool night of early May, the shirt left very little to the imagination.

She smiled as I took her hand and pulled her inside, quietly shutting the door behind us.

"What the . . . ?" she whispered, staring at the floor between the coffee table and the couch.

Ollie lay facedown, cheek propped on the pillow I'd

shoved under his face before I'd gone to bed. His soft snores would soon turn into chainsaws.

"Don't ask," I whispered back.

Giggling quietly, she squeezed my hand. We quickly made our way back to the bedroom and once inside, I spun her into my arms. "What are you doing?" I asked. "You have a nine-A.M. exam tomorrow."

"I know." She walked backward, guiding me to the bed. When she sat, I remained on my feet. "But it's my last exam and I've already studied so much I think my brain is broke."

I laughed. Over the last week, the time we spent together we spent studying for our own exams. "But shouldn't you be sleeping?"

"I was lonely." Her lips curved up as she tugged on my hands. "And I missed you. And I miss . . ."

She didn't have to finish her sentence. I knew what she was thinking, what she wanted. Knowing the truth about what had happened was a blessing, but I wasn't sure how to . . . well, how to really initiate things. The last thing I wanted to do was push her into something she wasn't ready for. So I hadn't pushed at all.

"Miss me?" I quickly changed the subject. "I know. Going even a few hours without my presence can cause heart palpitations, abnormal sweating, the occasional—"

"I think your arrogance is actually a disease."

I gave her a cocky grin. "I like to think it's a character strength."

"Keep telling yourself that." Sliding her hands free, she rose onto her knees in front of me. My mouth dried as

I looked down at her upturned face. "Actually, keep telling yourself that quietly. Right now, try not talking."

My brows shot up. "Well . . ."

She grinned, but I could see the deepening color spreading across her cheeks as she reached forward, placing her hands on my bare chest, and then she stretched up, sliding her fingers to my cheeks. She guided my head down to hers.

"I've missed you, Cam." The tip of her nose brushed mine. "Haven't you missed me?"

I closed my eyes as I wrapped my fingers along her slender wrists. "I have."

"Good," she murmured.

Her lips grazed mine once and then she kissed me softly. There was nothing like her kisses, especially when our positions were flopped. She pushed, working at the seam of my lips until I opened. The taste of her clouded my thoughts. I didn't realize she had let go of my face until I felt the tips of her fingers slipping under the band of my nylon shirts.

My grip tightened around her wrists as I lifted my head. "Avery, maybe we——"

"Maybe you should let me do this." Her chest rose sharply as her gaze dipped. There was no hiding that I wanted her to do this. The corners of her lips spread into a winsome smile. "I think you *really* want me to do this."

"I do. God, I do, but——"

She silenced me with a kiss that told me that I needed to let her do whatever she wanted to do. Removing my fingers one at a time, I dropped my hands to the sides.

This was all her.

Avery broke away and then placed a kiss on my chest, above my heart. I tensed as she tugged my shorts down. Loosened, the shorts pooled on the floor in a second. I stiffened, aching, as she placed her hands on my hips and kissed her way down my abs. When the edges of her hair brushed me, my hands curled into fists. And she kept going, sliding one hand around my front, causing my body to jerk as she wrapped her fingers around me. I pulsed—my entire body pulsed. Then her breath danced over my hardness.

I cupped her cheek, stopping her. "Avery, you don't have to do this."

She lifted her head. "But I want to."

My mouth opened, but the words—whatever the hell they were—died on my tongue as she took me into her mouth. Sensation exploded in several points. I kicked my head back, groaning as her hand moved, steady and strong in rhythm with her mouth.

I didn't want to last. My back bowed as she worked me. Fuck. I couldn't last. There was no way. Release powered through me as my hips jerked. I tried to pull her away, but she was latched on. She wasn't going anywhere. I came, shouting her name.

After what felt like forever, she pulled away. As my chest rose and fell raggedly as I dropped a damn near out-of-breath kiss on her forehead. "Avery . . ."

"You liked?"

I coughed out a laugh. "I *loved*."

"I'm a quick learner."

Damn straight she was. Placing my hands on her shoulders, I guided her onto her back. "Avery?"

She let her hands fall beside her head. "Yeah?"

"Get ready."

A puzzled look crossed her face. "Get ready for what?"

I captured her mouth, letting my lips and my tongue tell her exactly what to get ready for and it was a hell of a long time before I used those two things for anything other than loving her.

"Cookies! I got cookies!"

"Oh! What kind?" Shortcake's voice floated from the bedroom.

She'd left the door unlocked for me, something that I was going to have to talk to her about later, but right now I had a warm plate of special delivery. I headed back to the bedroom, finding her lying on her bed, hands folded across her stomach.

"Peanut-butter cookies," I told her. "But special."

She grinned as she stretched her bare feet. "How are they special?"

"Well, besides the fact that I just baked them in honor of you finishing your last exam, they're not just any kind of peanut-butter cookies." I sat the plate on the nightstand. "But Reese's peanut-butter cookies."

Her brows rose. "And that makes them different?"

"Hell's yeah." I jumped on the bed, grinning as Short-cake bounced. "What are you doing in here?"

"Being lazy."

I studied her closer. "You okay?"

"Yes." When she smiled and it reached her eyes, I relaxed. "Cookie?"

"Cookie . . ." I reached over, eyeing the plate for one that appeared moist. Once I settled on one, I handed it over.

Holding one hand under her chin, she bit and immediately moaned. "Oh my God, these are . . ." She took another bite. "So damn good."

"I know, right?" I picked up one, popping the whole thing in my mouth.

Shortcake reached for another and I grabbed the plate, holding it away from her. She punched me in the stomach. I gave her a cookie.

After eating our weight in peanut-butter goodness, I stretched out beside her and picked up a strand of her hair, twirling it around my fingers. I smacked the ends across her nose as her eyes drifted shut. "So what does it feel like to finally be a sophomore in college?"

She retrieved her hair from me. "I'm not officially a sophomore. Not until school starts again in the fall."

"I deem you a sophomore now." Undeterred, I caught another strand and trailed it across her cheek. "What I say goes."

"Then how does it feel finally being a senior? Next year *is* your last."

"Amazing." I traced her lower lip. "It feels amazing."

Shortcake rolled onto her side, wrapping her fingers around the collar of my shirt. "It feels pretty damn good to be a sophomore."

"Would be better if you didn't sign up for summer classes."

"True," she agreed.

But it would work out. I was doing the summer soccer camp with the kiddos, so I'd be here anyway.

She wiggled closer, resting her head on my shoulder as she threw a leg over me.

"Close enough?" I asked.

"No."

I laughed as I ran my fingers up and down her spine in a slow, idle line as I turned my head, kissing her forehead. These quiet moments were the best. I'd almost dozed off when she rolled suddenly, straddling my hips.

"Hey," she said.

I liked where this was heading. I skimmed my hands over her waist. "Hey there."

"So I've been doing some thinking."

"Oh God."

"Shut up." She bent down, kissing me softly. "Actually, I've been doing a lot of thinking. There's something I want to do."

"What?" I slid my hands down over her shorts, resting them on her thighs.

She sucked her bottom lip between her teeth. "I want to go home."

Was not expecting that, nor did I like that. "Like back to Texas?"

"Yes."

"For how long?"

She placed her hands on my stomach and rocked back, pressing down on me. I tensed, eyes narrowing on her. I had a feeling that was totally on purpose.

"You're not getting rid of me that easy," she said. "For just a day or two."

"Damn. There goes my master plan of spending the summer like a sex-crazed bachelor."

Shortcake rolled her eyes.

"What do you want to do if you go back there?"

"I want to see my parents. I need to talk to them."

I patted her thighs. "About what happened?"

"I've never talked to them about what happened, not since that night." She matched my movements with her fingers along my chest. "I need to talk to them. I know this sounds like a bitch fest, but I need to tell them that what they did was wrong."

"It doesn't sound like a bitch fest, but do you think it's wise?" I placed my hands over hers. "I mean, do you think it's going to help you and not . . ."

"Hurt me?" She smiled. "There's really nothing more my parents can do that will hurt me, but I feel like I need to confront them. Does that make me a bad person?"

"No." I didn't like the sound of this. They could still hurt her.

"I need to do this. I also need to talk to Molly."

Okay. I really didn't like the sound of this. "What?"

"I need to talk to her and try to explain why I did what I did. I know it's risky and if it comes back and bites me in the ass with the nondisclosure, then it does, but if I can get her to understand just a little bit, then maybe it will help her and she'll stop contacting me."

"I don't know about that. The girl seems like she's not the most stable person out there."

"She's not crazy," she said. "She's just mad and she has a reason to be."

"And you're not the reason why it happened to her." I brought her hands to my lips, kissing the knuckles. "You know that, right? You're not responsible."

She was quiet for a few moments. "I need to do this for myself and for Molly. I don't want to run anymore, Cam. And I know I can never really put this behind me. What happened . . . well, it will always be a part of me, but it won't be me. Not anymore."

This wasn't what I wanted her to do and I didn't think she truly needed to. What she didn't realize was that she'd already begun to make peace with everything, but I wouldn't stop her. "You know what I think?"

"I'm awesome?" Her grin was cheeky.

"Besides that."

"What?"

"I think you've already made it that far, Avery. I think you have accepted it will be part of you, but it's not you. You just haven't realized that, but if you want to do this, then you'll do this and I'll be there with you."

"You want to go with—"

She squealed as I shifted, rolling her onto her back. I hovered over her. "You're not doing this by yourself. Hell to the motherfucking no. I'm going with you. And you're not talking me out of it. When do you want to do this?"

Staring at me for a long moment, she smiled. "Got any plans this weekend?"

"Jesus."

Shortcake placed the tips of her fingers against my cheek. "I need to do this."

I dropped a kiss to the tip of her nose. "I don't think you do, sweetheart, but if you think you do, then that's what matters."

"You really want to come with me?" she whispered.

"That's a stupid question, Avery. And yes, there is such a thing as stupid questions. That was one of them. Of course I'm going to be there with you."

Her lips spread into a wide, beautiful smile. "I love you."

"I know."

"Cocky."

"Confident." I kissed her softly. "I love you, sweetheart."

She started to wrap her arms around me, but I moved away, climbing over the side of the bed. "Hey!" She frowned. "Get back here."

"Nope. We got stuff to do." I took her hands, hauling her off the bed. "And if you start feeling me up, we aren't going to get anything done."

The look on her face was bemused. "What are we doing?"

I bent, picking her up over my shoulder, and then pivoted toward the door. "We got some tickets to book."

Twenty-Eight

$\mathcal{T}$exas was ungodly hot. Like the circles of hell kind of hot. Even in the shaded interior of the rental car with cool air blasting from the vents, the heat seeped in from every tiny crack.

I couldn't believe that I was actually in Texas.

My gaze drifted from the marble fountain to the monstrous-sized house. Avery hadn't been joking when she said her parents were rich. They were like the 1 percent. Hell, maybe even the half of a percent.

Leaning back in the driver's seat, I blew out a long breath. "Fuck."

Shortcake was inside that place, with a mom that made Anthony Bates mommy look stable and loving. And I was out here, waiting in the car, half tempted to dive into the fountain.

She'd been in there for at least ten minutes and she hadn't wanted me to go inside with her. Probably because she knew I'd lose my shit with a quickness. When she had opened up to me that day, she really hadn't gone into a lot about her parents with the exception of how they had responded to what had happened to her, but over the last couple of weeks she'd told me about them.

And what I did know, I didn't like.

At the fifteen-minute mark, I couldn't sit any longer. I climbed out of the car and stepped into the sweltering heat. Sliding my cap around, I pulled the brim down to shield the sun.

I walked around the rented sedan, eyeing the entrance to the house. The marble columns were a nice touch. As I turned, gazing out over the manicured landscape that went as far as I could see, there wasn't a single person moving about.

The place was empty, and in spite of the body-breaking temps, it was cold. I couldn't picture Shortcake growing up in this kind of atmosphere or figure out how she'd come out as warm and loving as she was.

My shirt was already beginning to stick to my shoulders as I returned to the fountain. Closing my eyes, I willed my legs not to turn around and bust up into that house. I knew Shortcake needed to do this on her own, but I hated that she was facing them without me by her side.

I stuck out my hand, letting the warm water trickle across my open palm. What would her parents think if I took a dip? I was half tempted. I was also five seconds away from barging into the house when I heard a door shut behind me. Turning, I saw Avery heading down the wide stone stairs.

She was *smiling* broadly.

I hadn't been expecting that.

Tension seeped out of my shoulders as I jogged around the car, catching her in the middle of the circular driveway. "How'd it go?"

"Ah . . ." She rose onto the tips of her sandaled feet, slanted her head and kissed me. "It went as expected."

I held on to her hips, my fingers tightening as a surge of lust and love and a thousand other complicated emotions roared through me. "Want to tell me about it?"

"Over dinner?" She started to move away, but I captured her hand, holding her in place. "I'm going to take you to Chuy's—"

"Avery?"

Steel poured down my spine at the sound of her name and I tightened my hold on her hand. She turned as my gaze narrowed on the tall man walking down the front stairs.

This was her father.

I knew it immediately.

His dark brown hair was gray at the temples and he didn't look a day over fifty. He was dressed as if he were heading out to the golf club, pants pressed and polo shirt tucked in.

"If he says something ignorant, I cannot promise I will not lay him out right here, right now," I warned her.

She squeezed my hand. "Hopefully that won't become an issue."

"Just saying."

Her father stopped in front of us, his eyes—identical

to Shortcake's—looked from his daughter to where our hands were joined together. I *dared* him to say one thing.

"This is Cameron Hamilton," she said, clearing her throat. "Cam, this is my father."

Since it would be rude to give him the middle finger or punch him in the face, I extended my free hand. "Hi."

He shook my hand. "Nice to meet you."

"What's up, Dad?" she asked when I didn't return the polite greeting.

Mr. Morgansten dragged his eyes from me, and his gaze landed on his daughter for maybe a fraction of a second before flicking away. I could see the age on him now, settling in the creases around his eyes and mouth.

His chest rose with a deep breath and then said, "You know what I've missed most of all? I miss watching you dance."

Shortcake was handling everything better than I thought she would, which meant I hadn't given her enough credit. The girl was stronger than any of us realized.

Over dinner she told me how everything had gone down, and I was angry and disappointed for her when it came to how she was received by her so-called mother, but Avery had done what she had come here to do.

And it seemed her father expressed at least some amount of remorse or distress. The dancing comment . . . I got what it meant. There were so many things that Avery lost out on, and due to their own ignorance, so had her parents.

She still wanted to see Molly tomorrow, and no matter

what I tried over dinner to change her mind, she was determined and I was going to support her the best I could. But to be honest, I wanted nothing more than to get her back home and away from all of this.

When we returned to the hotel room that evening, Shortcake immediately disappeared into the bathroom to take a quick shower. I watched her retreating form with an arched brow. She had been acting weird since the end of the dinner, in a hurry to get back here. I had no idea what she was up to, but I forced myself to lie down instead of joining her in the shower, which was something I wanted to do really, really badly.

I discovered the remote control and was still trying to figure out what channel was what when steam rolled out from the opened bathroom door about twenty minutes later. I looked up and the air halted in my lungs.

She stood in the doorway, her hair a dark red, clinging to her shoulders. She wore only a white towel.

Holy shit.

I sat up, speechless as my gaze swept over her, starting at the tips of her painted toes and ending at her flushed cheeks. My skin tightened as she walked to where I sat, her fingers curling around the knotted towel between her breasts.

I closed my eyes. "Avery."

She placed a hand on my shoulder and climbed up, like she had done the evening on the couch, straddling me. "Cam?"

A small grin split my lips; it was all I could manage as I clutched her hips.

"What are you up to?"

"Nothing." She paused. "Everything."

My gaze dipped to the knot. "Those are two opposite things."

"I know." She pressed down on my erection, sending a bolt of red-hot pleasure through me. "Kiss me?"

She didn't give me a chance to respond, which was fine by me. Her lips brushed over mine, a sweet sweeping of her lips. My hold on her hips tightened when she parted my lips with her tongue. The kiss went on until I was aching for her.

Hell, I was *always* aching for her.

"Touch me," she whispered. "Please."

Who in the hell was I to deny her? I ran my hands under the hem of the towel, gliding them over her thighs, coming close to the center of her heat.

"Now," she demanded.

I laughed at her bold demand, but I wouldn't be rushed. I brushed the back of my hand over her dampness, smiling when she moaned. "What do you want?"

She made a sound of frustration. "I want you to touch me."

Bringing my fingers close to where she wanted me, I retreated quickly. "I am touching you, sweetheart."

Her eyes flashed. "You know what I mean."

"I don't."

"Please." She pressed her forehead to mine. "Please touch me, Cam."

I leaned back, brushing our lips together. "Well, when you say it like that, I think I get what you mean."

"Finally," she groaned.

I laughed again and then nipped at her chin. Her body jerked when I cupped her between the thighs. "Like this?"

"Yes."

As I kissed the center of her throat, I slipped a finger into her wetness. "And this?" My voice was gruff, heavy.

Her back arched. "Uh-huh."

Wrapping an arm around her so she didn't tumble backward, I pressed down on her clit. Her body tensed in the most amazing way. "What about this?"

Her hips tipped forward. "Oh, yeah. Definitely that."

"Definitely that?" I pumped my finger in and out of her slowly.

Avery moaned, and I could listen to a chorus of them all day, but then she reached between us and unraveled the knot. The towel slipped away from her, fluttering to the floor.

My hand stilled.

My heart jumped.

My cock hardened and throbbed.

Rosy breasts thrust up, cheeks flushed, and legs spread wide over mine. . . . Dammit, she was . . . she was stunning.

I ran my other hand over her breast, fixated when the tip puckered. "Fuck, Avery . . ."

She placed her hand over mine. "Don't stop."

"I wasn't planning on it."

"Not what I meant." Reaching with her other hand, she found the zipper on my jeans. "I want you, Cam."

"You have me." I moved to her other breast. "You so fucking have me."

Avery smiled as she wrapped her hand around my wrist, pulling my hand away from her heat. "I really want you." She unzipped my pants, her fingers brushing me, and I shuddered. "Don't you want me?"

"More than you know." I groaned as she palmed me. "Avery . . ."

Her hand disappeared, and I didn't know if I should be grateful or if I should start cussing. But then she tugged my shirt up, over my head. "I want this, Cam."

When her words sunk in through the red haze fogging my thoughts, I inhaled deeply. "Are you sure, Avery? Because if you're not, we don't have—"

She kissed me, sliding her hands down my chest. "I'm sure."

I froze, hands on her hips, and then rolled her onto her back. Over her, I caught her lips, kissing her with everything that I had in me. Maybe another guy would've asked her again or done something else, but those two words. *I'm sure*. They broke the tiny hold I had on my self-control.

Breaking the kiss, I stood and all but ripped off my jeans. When her gaze dropped and eyes widened, I couldn't help but smile.

Avery looked almost untouchable as she lay there, staring up at me with those beautiful brown eyes. "I could stare at you for a lifetime. It would never grow old."

"Even when I'm old?"

"Even then."

Unable to wait any longer, I came to her. I wanted this moment to be perfect for her. I wanted everything to be beautiful and I wanted her to *feel* how much I loved her.

So I started at those tiny toes, working my way up her legs and over her soft stomach with kisses. I took my time, sucking and nipping until the peaks of her breasts were tight and she was panting. Every part of me felt hard, heavy, and swollen, but I wanted her ready, even if raw, intense desire rode me to drive deep inside of her.

Her body arched against mine as I reached her lips once more. Shifting my weight to one arm, I matched the thrusts of my tongue with my finger and then two, stretching her slowly.

She clutched my arms, my sides as she moved restlessly and when I put my mouth to her down there, she came apart in a way that almost undid me right then.

I was shaking like a weed in the middle of a storm as I rose, positioning myself between her thighs. Wrapping my hand around myself, I lined up our bodies. The first contact with her wetness sent shards of pleasure through me.

There was a point when you couldn't stop and I was at that part, my body trembling with need, but I waited for her. I gave her time.

"I love you," I told her, resting my hand to her cheek. "I love you so very much."

Her arms wrapped around me, holding me tight, urging me forward. "I love you."

Dropping my hand to her hip, I deepened the kiss as I rolled my hips into hers. She stiffened under me, and her soft gasp of surprise went straight to my soul.

I stilled. "Are you okay?"

She nodded. "Yes."

I didn't want to hurt her and I knew that had to hurt. I remained still, deep inside her. My heart hammered out of control as I kissed the corner of her lip and then the other. Her mouth opened, and I slipped inside, slowly tasting her, giving her body time to adjust.

I groaned as she tilted her hips tentatively, creating startling friction between us. "Av . . ."

She did it again, and I rocked back. A cry of pleasure ripped from her as she gripped me in her tightness, wrapping her legs around my waist. Between that and the way she moved her hips, I lost myself in her in the most glorious way possible.

God . . . nothing felt like her and nothing compared to the feeling of her, of how she invaded every cell of my being. There was no me. There was no her. As we moved together, our mouths clinging to one another, our hands exploring and our hips sealing together, there was only *us*.

Avery broke under me, throwing her head out and crying my name when I slid a hand between us, touching her as I ground against her. Feeling the tight spasms, the way she held on to me was too much.

"Avery," I grunted, burying my head in her shoulder as my release blew through me, shocking in its intensity.

The release felt like it kept coming in tight waves. I rested above her, my body jerking every couple of moments. Forever went by before I trusted myself to move. A deep sound came from my chest as I eased out of her.

I kissed her and fuck if I didn't feel a burning sensation

in the back of my throat. I shook my head, dumbfounded by the force of what I felt. "That was . . . there are no words. You okay?"

She placed her hands on my cheeks and they trembled slightly. In her steady gaze, I saw the mirror of what I was feeling. "Perfect. You were perfect."

The truth was, if I was perfect, it was only because of her. It would only ever be because of her.

Twenty-Nine

That's where I need to be.

Those were Avery's words as she'd spoken to the other girl. Molly. I had struggled not be angry when I'd seen the red mark on her cheek. The only thing that helped was hearing those words.

Shortcake finally got it.

The healing she needed did rest in the truth, in speaking out to her parents and to talking to Molly, but she had begun to heal all the way back in February, then again in April. Going to Texas was something she felt she needed to do and she had done it.

So I brought her home and here we were, back in the somewhat cooler state of West Virginia, the night before Avery would start her summer classes and I'd start working with the kids during camp.

Shortcake sat on the kitchen floor across from me, bare legs tucked under her. She wore one of my shirts and that was all. I had a hard time thinking about anything other than that.

Between us, Michelangelo and Raphael were currently head-bobbing each other.

"It's like a tortoise version of smack talk," she said, brows pinched. "I'm not sure they like each other."

I grinned as I leaned back against the fridge, running my hand over the bare skin of my abs. "They still need some time. And Mikey-Mike is territorial."

"Oh, blame it on my tortoise." She rolled her eyes. "Yours started the head-bobbing crap first."

The timer dinged, and I climbed to my feet, heading over to the stove. "He was just showing yours who's boss."

"Michelangelo is boss." Shortcake picked up her little guy, setting him back several feet.

Eyeing the chocolate cookies and finding them done, I quickly washed my hands, then retrieved an oven mitt I was sure Shortcake had never used. The tag was still on it. Grinning, I tore it off and then removed the tray from the oven. The cookies were super-sized, golden and oh-so gooey-looking.

"Are they ready?" She looked up, eyes gleaming.

"You'll burn your tongue." I tossed the mitt aside. "Again."

She grinned. "But it is so worth it."

"Uh-huh." I sauntered up to her, enjoying the way her cheeks still flushed when her eyes dipped below my navel. Swooping down, I kissed her upturned lips. "Give them—"

My cell went off from the living room. "Be right back."

She nodded as I carefully avoided stepping on a poor

tortoise and traumatizing myself and Shortcake. I swiped my cell off the coffee table. A sigh of relief exited me as I saw that it was from my sister.

Out of surgery. Doing ok. Will call u later.

Closing my eyes, I said a little prayer. It hadn't been a major surgery, but it was still a surgery and fucked-up things happened in hospitals. She was home. That was good, but . . .

"Was that Teresa?"

Putting my phone down, I turned. Avery stood in the door, holding two squirming tortoises. Combining that with the shirt that read I WANNA BE YOUR MAN-WICH, it was a pretty adorable sight.

"Yes."

She walked the two tortoises over to their habitat and gently placed them inside. While she closed the lid, the two green guys immediately eyed each other from their respective corners. "Is she okay? How did the surgery go?"

"She says she's fine. It was just a text." I paused. "She said she'd call me later."

Facing me, her brows were pinched in worry. If anyone knew what Teresa was facing right now, it would be Short-cake, with all her years of dancing. "She didn't say any-thing about dancing?"

I shook my head as I pressed my lips together. Teresa had torn her ACL a week ago during a recital. For athletes and dancers, it could be an injury fatal to their careers. All my sister had ever wanted to do was become a professional dancer. Only time would tell if that would be possible at all.

But from what Mom had said, it wasn't looking good.

Shortcake disappeared into the kitchen, washed her hands and returned. Coming up to me, she wrapped her arms around my waist and pressed her cheek against my chest. Her skin was warm.

"I'm sorry," she said.

"Why are you apologizing?" I folded my arms around her, holding her close.

"Because I know you're worried," she said, rubbing her cheek along my skin. "And I know this injury is serious. I just hope it's not as serious as it can be."

I dropped a kiss to the top of her head as I slid my hand up her spine, cradling the back of her neck. "Me too."

She was quiet for a few moments. "Thank you."

Laughing softly, I leaned back so I could see her face. "Now what are you thanking me for, sweetheart?"

"Thank you for going to Texas with me."

I cupped her cheek with one hand. "You've already thanked me for that."

"And you told me that I didn't need to thank you." She placed her hand over mine. "But I need to thank you again, because I wouldn't have done it without you."

"Yes, you would've."

She shook her head. "Maybe I would've, but I don't really know. I needed you there and you were there, no questions asked. I can't thank you enough for that—for everything."

"Oh, Shortcake, you still don't have to thank me."

"But I . . ." She stopped, frowning. "Shortcake?"

I opened my mouth and then realized my slip. Dropping my hands, I stepped back and laughed. "Did I say that out loud?"

"Yeah. You kind of did." She tugged on the hem of the borrowed shirt. Curiosity filled her face. "What's up with that?"

Fuck me, but I felt my cheeks start to burn.

Her eyes widened as she smiled. "You're blushing! Oh my God, you're actually blushing!" She pinched my cheek. "I need to know now why you're so *flushed*."

"What do I get if I tell you?"

She pinned me with an arched look that said what I *wouldn't* get if I *didn't* tell her. That pissy look turned me on. Then again, when she breathed, it made me hot.

"It's really kind of stupid." Catching her hand, I pulled her back to me. Once she was close enough, I dipped low and slid an arm under her legs.

"Hey!" She smacked my back. "Stop trying to distract—" She squealed as her feet went off the floor. "Cam!"

Picking her up, I held her close to my chest as I turned toward the hallway. "I'm not distracting you. I'm helping you back to the bedroom."

She narrowed her eyes. "Besides the fact that I don't need help going back to the bedroom, why are you carrying me back to the bedroom?"

"You don't walk fast enough," I told her as I carried her to her bed. "Hey."

Her look grew exasperated. "What?"

I winked a second before I dropped her over the middle of the bed. Her squeal ended in a grunt as she bounced. Her mouth opened, and I knew she was about to cuss me every way but straight. I was on her before she could start what she was about to say, sliding my hands up under the hem of the shirt. In a second I had it off her and she was beautifully, magnificently bare. I shucked off my pants.

Her breath leaked out of her as I climbed onto the bed, admiring my handiwork. "So," she said, her voice soft. "What about this Shortcake business?"

"Well, it's a nickname." I kissed the space between her breasts. "For you."

"That much I figured."

I placed another kiss along the underside of one breast and then below her rib cage. "I came out with it the first time I met you."

"The first—*oh*!" She jerked as I tongued her navel, clenching the covers on her bed. When she spoke again, her voice was husky as I moved down. "The first time we met?"

"Yep." I kissed the inside of her left thigh and then the right. "It was the day you ran into me outside of astronomy class—a class you need to retake."

Shortcake groaned. "Don't remind me."

I didn't know if she was talking about the class or the running into me part. "When I first saw you and your hair . . ." I paused, kissing her between her legs. Her soft gasp brought a smile to my face. "All I could think was that Strawberry Shortcake . . ." I paused once more, running my tongue the length of her. "That Strawberry Shortcake had run me off."

She laughed as I lifted my head, prowling back up so

that we were eye level. "Wow. I don't understand how your brain works."

"You love it."

"I do." She slid her foot along my calf. "So you've been calling me Shortcake in your head all this time?"

I nodded as I settled between her legs. "I might have . . . a few times."

"And you never slipped until now. Wow. That's kind of amazing." Her eyes danced with humor. "And it's kind of cute."

"It's definitely cute. It's—" I groaned as she rolled her hips up, joining us together. "Well then . . ."

She giggled and then neither of us were laughing or talking. I let out a ragged moan at the tight fit. I lost sense of everything except her body and I wanted to be deeper, closer. We moved together, our bodies flushed and straining. It was crazy, but I couldn't get enough of her. It appeared the same for her. My mouth closed around her breast as I thrust into her. She matched me move for move until she arched her back, crying out.

Her release slammed into me. Gathering her close, I sat up, keeping her in my lap. The new position had lust zinging through me. I couldn't last. Not when her little teeth scraped over my neck.

Minutes went by where all that could be heard was the sound of our ragged breathing. I was still inside her. There was a peace in this completion. And I held everything in my arms.

Later, much later, we sat on the bed with the plate of

chocolate cookies between us. A tiny smudge of chocolate ended up on her lips and I leaned over the plate, kissing it away.

And well, I kissed her for real.

I kissed her, and it was like kissing her for the very first time. The initial zap, the shock of our lips together hadn't faded. Dumbly I realized that love made it that way, making sure that a simple kiss never dulled, never lost its luster.

My chest swelled as I pulled back and stared into her warm eyes and my heart did that crazy, stupid jumping thing. Something I also knew would never truly go away.

Shortcake placed her small hand on my cheek. "What?"

At first I didn't know what to say. I . . . I had waited for Avery—I had waited for her for months. Hell, I would've waited for her for years, but she . . .

Turning my cheek, I pressed a kiss to the inside of her palm. "Thank you for trusting in me."

Ready for more?
Read on for a sneak peek at the next
fabulous story from J. Lynn

BE
with me

Ready for more?

One

Sweet tea was apparently going to be the death of me. Not because it contained enough sugar that it could send you into a diabetic coma after one slurp. Or because my brother had nearly caused a triple-car pileup by winging the truck around in a sharp U-turn after receiving a text message that contained two words only.

Sweet. Tea.

Nope. The request for sweet tea was bringing me face-to-face with Jase Winstead, the physical embodiment of every girly-girl fantasy and then some, outside of campus, and in front of my brother.

Oh sweet Mary mother of all the babies in the world, this was going to be awkward.

Why, oh why did my brother have to text Jase and mention that we were at his end of town and ask if he needed anything? He was supposed to be taking me around so I could get familiar with the scenery. Although the scenery

I was about to witness was sure to be better than what I'd been seeing of this county.

If I saw another strip club, I was going to hurt someone.

Cam glanced over at me as he sped down the back road. We'd left Route 9 years ago. His gaze dropped from my face to the tea I clutched in my hands. He raised a brow. "You know, Teresa, you could put that in a cup holder."

I shook my head. "It's okay. I'll hold it."

"Okay." Cam drew the word out, focusing on the road.

I was acting like a spaz and I needed to play it cool. The last thing anyone in this world needed was Cam finding out why I had reason to act like a dweeb on crack. "So, um, I thought Jase lived up by the college?"

That sounded casual, right? Oh God, I was pretty sure my voice had cracked at some point during that not-so-innocent question.

"He does, but he spends most of his time at his father's farm." Cam slowed his truck down and hung a sharp right. Tea almost went out the window, but I had a death grip on it. Tea was going nowhere. "You remember Jack, right?"

Of course I did. Jase had a five-year-old brother named Jack, and I knew the little boy meant the world to him. I obsessively remembered everything I'd ever learned about Jase in a way I imagined Justin Bieber fans did about him. Embarrassing as that sounded, it was true. Jase, unbeknownst to him and the entire world, had come to mean a lot of things to me in the last three years.

A friend.

My brother's saving grace.

And the source of my crush.

But then a year ago, right at the start of my senior year in high school, when Jase had tagged along with Cam and visited home, he'd become something very complicated. Something that a part of me wanted nothing more than to forget about—but the other part of me refused to let go of the memories of his lips against mine or how his hands had felt skimming over my body or the way he had groaned my name like it had caused him exquisite pain.

Oh goodness . . .

My cheeks heated behind my sunglasses at the vivid memory and I turned my face to the window, half tempted to roll the window down and stick my head out. I so needed to pull it together. If Cam ever discovered that Jase had kissed me, he would murder him and hide his body on a rural road like this one.

And that would be a damn shame.

My brain emptied of anything to say and I so needed a distraction right now. The perspiration from the tea and my own trembling hands were making it hard to hold on to the cup. I could've asked Cam about Avery and that would've worked, because Cam *loved* talking about Avery. I could've asked about his classes or started talking about mine, but all I could do was think about the fact that I was finally going to see Jase in a situation where he couldn't run away from me.

The thick trees on either side of the road started to thin out and through them, green pastures became visible. Cam turned onto a narrow road. The truck bounced on the potholes, making my stomach queasy.

My brows lowered as we passed between two brown poles. A chain link lay on the ground and off to the left was a small wooden sign that read WINSTEAD: PRIVATE PROPERTY. A large cornfield greeted us, but the stalks were dry and yellow, looking as if they were days away from withering up and dying. Beyond them, several large horses grazed behind a wooden fence that was missing many of its middle panels. Cows roamed over most of the property to the left, fat and happy looking.

As we drew closer, an old barn came into view. A scary old barn, like the one in *The Texas Chain Saw Massacre,* complete with the creepy rooster compass thing swiveling on the roof, and several yards beyond the barn was a two-story home. The once-white walls were gray, and even from the truck I could tell there was more paint peeling off than there was on the house. Blue tarp covered several sections of the roof and a chimney looked like it was half crumbling. Red dusty bricks were stacked along the side of the house, as if someone had started to repair the chimney but grew bored and gave up. There was also a cemetery of broken-down cars behind the barn, a sea of rusted-out trucks and sedans.

Shock rippled through me as I sat up a bit straighter. This was Jase's farm? For some reason, I pictured something a little more . . . up-to-date?

Cam parked the truck a few feet back from the barn and killed the engine. He glanced over at me, following my stare to the house. Unlocking his seat belt, he sighed. "His parents have had a really hard time. Jase tries to help with the farm and stuff, but as you can see . . ."

The farm needed more help than Jase could provide.

I blinked. "It's . . . charming."

Cam laughed. "It's nice of you to say that."

My fingers tightened around the cup in defense. "It is."

"Uh-huh." He flipped his baseball cap around, shielding his eyes. Tufts of brown hair poked out from the back rim.

I started to speak, but movement out of the corner of my eyes caught my attention.

Racing out from the side of the barn, a little boy seated in a miniature John Deere tractor hooted and hollered, his chubby arms bone straight, his hands gripping the steering wheel, and a mop of curly brown hair shining under the bright August sun. Pushing the tractor from behind was Jase, and even though I could barely hear him, I was sure that he was making engine noises. They bounced along the uneven gravel and ground; Jase laughed as his little brother shouted, "Faster! Go faster!"

Jase appeased his brother, pushing the tractor so it zigged and zagged to a stop in front of the truck as Jack squealed, still clenching the steering wheel. Plumes of dust flew into the air.

And then Jase straightened.

Oh man, my mouth dropped open. Nothing in this world could've made me look away from the splendor before me.

Jase was shirtless and his skin glistened with sweat. I wasn't sure what ethnicity he had in his family background. There had to be something Spanish or Mediterranean, because he had a naturally tan skin tone that remained that way all year round.

As he walked around the tractor, his muscles did fascinating things. His pecs were perfectly formed and his shoulders were broad. He had the kind of muscles one got from lifting bales of hay and tossing them places. Boy was ripped. His stomach muscles tensed with each step. He had a very distinctive six-pack. Totally touchable. His jeans hung indecently low—low enough that I wondered if he had on anything underneath the faded denim.

It was the first time I saw the full extent of his tattoo. Ever since I'd known him, I'd caught glimpses of it peeking out from his collar on his left shoulder and from under a shirtsleeve. I never knew what it was until now.

The tat was massive—an endless knot shaded in deep black, starting at the base of his neck, looping and twisting over his left shoulder and halfway down his arm. At the bottom, two loops opposite one another reminded me of snakes.

It was a perfect fit for him.

A flush spread across my cheeks and traveled down my throat as I dragged my gaze back up, mouth dry as the desert.

Sinewy muscles in his arms flexed as he pulled Jack out of the driver's seat, lifting him into the air above his head. He spun around in a circle, laughing deeply as Jack shrieked and flailed.

Ovaries go boom.

He sat Jack down on the ground as Cam opened the driver's-side door, yelling something at his friend, but I had no idea what he said. Jase straightened again, dropping his hands to his hips. He squinted as he stared into the truck.

Jase was absolutely gorgeous. You couldn't say that about a lot of people in real life. Maybe celebrities or rock stars, but it was rare to see someone as stunning as he was.

His hair was a mess of rich russet waves falling into his face. His cheekbones were broad and well defined. Lips were full and could be quite expressive. A hint of stubble shaded the strong curve of his jaw. He didn't have dimples like Cam or me, but when he did smile, he had one of the biggest, most beautiful smiles I'd ever seen on a guy.

He wasn't smiling right now.

Oh no, he was staring into the truck with a searing intensity.

Parched as I was, I took a sip of the sweet tea as I stared through the windshield, absolutely enthralled by all the baby-making potential on display before me. Not that I was in a hurry to make babies, but I could totally get behind some practice runs. At least in my fantasies.

Cam eyed me and made a face like I'd lost my damn mind. I might have. "Dude, that's his drink."

"Sorry." I flushed, lowering the cup. Not that it mattered. Wasn't like Jase and I hadn't swapped spit before.

On the other side of the windshield, Jase mouthed the word *shit* and spun around. Was he going to run away? How dare he? I had his sweet tea!

In a hurry, I unhooked my seat belt and pushed open the door. My foot slipped out of my flip-flop and because Cam just had to have a redneck truck, one that was feet off the ground, there was a huge difference between where I was and where the ground was.

I used to be graceful. Hell, I *was* a dancer—a trained,

damn good dancer—and I had the kind of balance that would make gymnasts go green with envy. But that was before the torn ACL, before my hopes of dancing professionally ended when I came down from a jump wrong. Everything—my dreams, my goals, and my future—had been over in an instant.

And I was about to eat dirt in less than a second. There was no stopping it.

I reached out to catch the door, but came up short. The foot that was going to touch the ground first was connected to my bum leg and it wouldn't hold my weight. I was going to crash and burn in front of Jase and end up with tea all over my head.

As I started to fall, I hoped I would land on my face, because then at least I wouldn't have to see his expression.

Out of nowhere, two arms shot out and hands landed on my shoulders. One second I was horizontal, halfway fallen out of the truck, and the next I was vertical, both feet dangling in the air for a second. And then I was standing, the cup of tea clutched to my chest.

"Good God, you're going to break your neck," a deep voice rumbled. "Are you okay?"

I was up close and personal with the most perfect chest I'd ever seen and I watched a bead of sweat trickle down the center of it and then over the cut abs, disappearing among the fine hairs trailing up from the center of his stomach, forming a line that continued under the band of his jeans.

Cam hurried around the front of the truck. "Did you hurt your leg, Teresa?"

No. I was fine. More than fine. I hadn't been this close to Jase for a year and he smelled wonderful—like man and a faint trace of cologne. I lifted my gaze, realizing that my sunglasses had fallen off.

Thick lashes framed eyes that were a startling shade of gray. The first time I'd seen them, I had asked if they were real. Jase had laughed and offered to let me poke around in his eyes to find out.

He wasn't laughing right now.

I swallowed, willing my brain to start working. "I have your sweet tea."

Jase's brows rose.

"Did you hit your head?" Cam asked, stopping beside us.

Heat flooded my cheeks. "No. Maybe. I don't know." Holding out the tea, I forced a smile, hoping it didn't come across as creepy. "Here."

Jase let go of my arms and took the tea, and I wished I hadn't been so eager to shove it in his face, because maybe then he'd still be holding me. "Thanks. You sure you're okay?"

"Yes," I muttered, glancing down. My sunglasses were by the tire. Sighing, I picked them up and cleaned them off before slipping them back on. "Thanks for . . . um, catching me."

He stared at me a moment and then turned as Jack ran up to him, holding out a shirt. "I got it!" the little boy said, waving the shirt like a flag.

"Thanks." Jase took the shirt and handed over the tea. He ruffled the boy's hair and then, much to my disappointment, pulled the shirt on over his head, covering up that body of his. "I didn't know Teresa was with you."

A chill skated over my skin in spite of the heat.

"I was out showing her the town so she knows her way around," Cam explained, grinning at the little tyke, who was slowly creeping toward me. "She's never been down here before."

Jase nodded and then took back the tea. There was a good chance that Jack had drunk half of it in that short amount of time. Jase started to walk toward the barn. I was dismissed. Just like that. The back of my throat started to burn, but I ignored it, wishing I had kept the tea.

"You and Avery are coming to the party tonight, right?" Jase asked Cam, taking a sip of the tea.

"It's the luau. We're not missing that." Cam grinned, revealing the dimple in his left cheek. "You guys need help setting it up?"

Jase shook his head. "The newbies are in charge of that." He glanced over at me, and I thought for a second that he'd ask if I was coming. "I've got a few things to take care of here first and then I'm heading back home."

A small hand tugged on the hem of my shorts, causing me to look down and into gray eyes that were both young and soulful.

"Hi," Jack said.

I grinned. "Hi to you."

"You're pretty," he said, blinking.

"Thank you." It was official. I liked this kid. "You're very cute."

Jack beamed. "I know."

I laughed. This boy was definitely Jase's little brother.

"Alright, that's enough, Casanova." Jase finished off the tea and tossed the cup into a nearby garbage can. "Stop hitting on the girl."

He ignored Jase, sticking out his hand. "I'm Jack."

I took the little hand in mine. "I'm Teresa. Cam's my brother."

Jack motioned me down with his little finger and whispered, "Cam doesn't know how to saddle a horse."

I glanced over at the boys. They were talking about the party, but Jase was watching us. Our gazes collided, and like he'd been doing since I'd started at Shepherd University this past week, he broke eye contact with distressing speed.

A pang of disappointment lit up my chest as I returned my attention to Jack. "Want to know a secret?"

"Yeah!" His smile grew big and broad.

"I don't know how to saddle a horse either. And I've never even ridden one before."

His eyes grew as wide as the moon. "Jase!" he bellowed, spinning toward his brother. "She's never ridden a horse before!"

Well, there went my secret.

Jase glanced at me, and I shrugged. "It's true. They scare the crap out of me."

"They shouldn't. They're pretty chill animals. You'd probably like it."

"You should show her!" Jack rushed up to Jase, practically latching himself to his brother's legs. "You could teach her like you teached me!"

My heart lurched in my chest, partially at the proposition of Jase teaching me anything and partially due to my fear of those dinosaurs.

"It's 'taught,' not 'teached,' and I'm sure Tess has got better things to do than ride around on a horse."

Tess. I sucked in a breath. It was his nickname—he was the only person who ever called me that. I don't even know why he called me that, but I didn't mind it. Not at all. While Jack demanded to know why I had told him my name was Teresa and Jase explained that Tess was a nickname, I was sucked back into the memory of the last time he'd called me by it.

"You have no idea what you make me want," he said, his lips brushing my cheek, sending shivers down my spine. "You have no fucking clue, Tess."

"Mind if I use the john before we get out of here? I've gotta get back," Cam said, drawing my attention. "I promised Avery dinner before the party."

"I'll show you," announced Jack, grabbing Cam's hand.

Jase arched a dark brow. "I'm sure he knows where the bathroom is."

"It's okay." Cam waved him off. "Come on, little bud, lead the way."

The two of them headed off toward the farmhouse, and we were officially alone. A hummingbird took flight in my stomach, bouncing around like it was going to peck its way out of me as a warm breeze picked up, stirring the hairs that had escaped my ponytail.

Jase watched Cam and Jack jog over the patchy green grass like a man watching the last life preserver being oc-

cupied as the Titanic started to sink. Well, that was sort
of offensive, as if being alone with me was equivalent
to drowning while being nom-nommed by cookie-cutter
sharks.

I folded my arms across my chest, pursing my lips.
Irritation pricked at my skin, but his obvious discomfort
stung like a bitch. It hadn't always been like this. And it
definitely had been better between us, at least up until the
night he'd kissed me.

"How's the leg?"

The fact that he'd spoken startled me and I stuttered.
"Uh, it's not too bad. Barely hurts anymore."

"Cam told me about it when it happened. Sorry to hear
that." He paused. "When can you get back to dancing?"

I shifted my weight. "I don't think I will." The real
answer was that I didn't know. Neither did the doctors or
the physical therapist or my dance instructor, but I'd rather
prepare myself for never than believe that I could dance
once again. I didn't think I'd survive that heartbreak a
second time. "So, yeah, that's that."

Jase's brows knitted. "God, that sucks. I'm really sorry,
Tess. I know how much dancing means to you."

"Meant," I murmured, affected more than I should've
been by the genuine sympathy in his voice.

His gray eyes finally made their way back to mine,
and I sucked in a breath. His eyes . . . they never failed
to stun me into stupidity or make me want to do crazy-
insane things. Right now his eyes were a deep gray, like
thunderclouds.

Jase wasn't happy.

Thrusting a hand through his damp hair, he exhaled deeply and a muscle in his jaw ticked. The irritation inside me turned into something messy, causing the burn in the back of my throat to move up to my eyes. I had to keep telling myself that he didn't know—that there was no way he could've known, and that the way I was feeling, the hurt and the brutal wound of rejection, wasn't his fault. I was just Cam's little sister; the reason why Cam had gotten into so much trouble almost four years ago and why Jase had started making the trip to our home every weekend. I was just a stolen kiss. That was all.

I started to turn, to go wait in the truck for Cam before I did something embarrassing, like crying all over myself. My emotions had been all over the place since I injured my leg, and seeing Jase wasn't helping.

"Tess. Wait," Jase said, crossing the distance between us in one step with his long legs. Stopping close enough that his worn sneakers almost brushed my toes, he reached out toward me, his hand lingering by my cheek. He didn't touch me, but the heat of his hand branded my skin. "We need to talk."

About the Author

#1 *New York Times* and *USA Today* bestselling author J. LYNN lives in Martinsburg, West Virginia. When she's not hard at work writing, she spends her time reading, working out, watching really bad zombie movies, pretending to write, and hanging out with her husband and her Jack Russell terrier, Loki.

Visit www.AuthorTracker.com for exclusive information on your favorite HarperCollins authors.